BECAUSE YOU LOVED ME

Trickle Creek

Book 4

ELENA AITKEN

Chapter One

ASHER

CONTROLLED CHAOS.

There was no other way to describe the steady stream of people coming in and out of the lodge. Some guests were checking in, while others were already headed out to the ski hill for a day on the slopes. The bellboys in their red and black flannels were shuttling carts full of bags to rooms, while in the lounge the servers were loaded down with trays of drinks. Children hopped up on the complimentary s'more station in the courtyard darted around, only narrowly avoiding crashing into the giant Christmas trees that were set up throughout the lobby.

Forget controlled. It was straight-up chaos.

But I loved every minute of it. As the CEO of the Carlson Corporation, there were many aspects of the business I had to oversee, but the main lodge at the base of the ski hill was always my home base. Especially during the busy winter ski season.

My siblings would all tell me I worked too much, but they didn't understand that I thrived on the busyness of it all. Just like my father and founder of the business, Michael, had, I preferred a hands-on approach, and I was tired of trying to explain it to them.

"Penny." I pulled out the barstool next to me as my general manager, Penny Daniels, walked into the Black Diamond Lounge, where I'd been working from the far end of the bar. "Sit."

She glanced up from her ever-present clipboard and met my gaze with glazed-over eyes. The worry lines on her forehead were deeper than normal, and I knew, without looking, that her fingernails would be broken and bitten way too short. She thought she was so sneaky, hiding her nervous tic from me, but I didn't miss a thing.

"You look far too stressed out," I said as soon as she sat and Brian, the bartender on duty, slid her a cup of black coffee.

Penny glanced at the coffee. "Is it too early for tequila?" She shook her head and sipped at the hot liquid. "Did you know we're completely booked?" It was a rhetorical question. Of course I knew. "The restaurant is already taking two sittings for dinner every night, and don't even mention the room service orders." She shook her head and took another gulp of coffee. "And now, the banquet staff…" She stared into space for a moment before turning to face me. "Whose idea was it to host a wedding over Christmas?"

I lifted my eyebrows and tilted my head. It took a gargantuan effort on my part to keep my mouth closed, because pointing out the obvious to my number-one employee wouldn't help the situation.

A moment later, Penny groaned and dropped her head onto her clipboard. "I know, I know. I thought it was a good idea at the time, and really, it's going to be fine. I'm just—"

"You just need to breathe." I reached over and rubbed

Penny's shoulder. "You are ridiculously tense. You should see if Claude has any openings for a massage." Judging by the look she shot me, there were no bookings available in the spa either. "You know I'd volunteer for the job," I added with a chuckle. "But we probably shouldn't go there." Again.

Penny laughed and slapped my hand away. "Don't tempt me, Asher. I just might take you up on that offer one day."

We both knew she wouldn't. A few years earlier, before I'd taken over as CEO and she'd been promoted to the general manager position, we'd hooked up a few times. It hadn't been serious. None of my *relationships* ever were.

That hadn't changed, only now I kept my hookups far away from anything to do with Carlson Corp, which was not always easy in a small town like Trickle Creek. Still, complicated was the last thing I needed.

Fortunately, there had never been any weirdness between me and Penny. We worked well together, which definitely wouldn't have been the case with all the women I'd dated over the years. I'd always been upfront with what I wanted, and more specifically, what I did not want. Still, it never failed that, every once in a while, a woman would be convinced that she could change me and make me fall in love with her.

She couldn't. I wouldn't. End of story.

"What can I do to help, Penny?" I refocused on the problem at hand. "Where are you at with the wedding? I couldn't help but notice the sign." I used my head to gesture toward the lobby where a massive red and gold sign announcing "Alessandra & Ryan Forever" had been positioned next to the huge river rock fireplace.

"They really have taken over," Penny said with a laugh. "But I kind of love it. It's cute to see how excited the mother of the bride and the mother of the groom are."

I didn't bother mentioning that it should be the bride and groom who were excited because truthfully, I had no idea. I'd never paid much attention to weddings beyond the ones that were hosted at either the Trickle Creek Lodge in the winter, or the club house in the summer, and even then, I had Penny to handle the details.

"As long as everyone's happy, that's all that matters." I gestured to Brian for a refill on Penny's coffee, but she shook her head.

"If I have any more, I'm afraid I'll start to vibrate. It's not a good look."

"You always look good, Penny." I winked and turned in my stool to see my big sister Charli walk into the lounge, my brand-new niece in her arms.

I swallowed down a lump in my throat. Poppy was only a few weeks old. There was only one reason my sister would make the effort to visit me at work.

"You know how to find me if you need anything," I said to Penny as I excused myself and made my way through the busy lounge to Charli, who had already been surrounded by staff and visitors, all clamoring to get a peek at the newborn.

"Hey, sis." I squeezed through the small crowd and led her gently to a quiet corner of the busy lobby and a free seat. "It's always good to see you." I looked down at the sleeping bundle. "Both of you. She's sweet."

"Do you want to hold her?"

Instinctively, I took a step back. "Hold her?" I looked in horror from my big sister to my baby niece. "Char, she's *brand new.*"

She laughed. "I'm well aware of how old she is. I was there for it, remember?"

I remembered. I'd been on a date and had just gotten back to my suite in the lodge when our little sister Kat called me to let me know that Charli and Symon were rushing to the hospital. Poppy Angela Scott was born only three hours later.

"She won't break, Asher."

I wasn't convinced. "Next time." I jammed my hands into my pockets. "I haven't washed my hands."

Charli shook her head but thankfully didn't push. "It looks amazing in here, Asher. You've done a great job."

"I have a great staff." I brushed off the compliment, but it always meant a lot more than I let on when one of my siblings praised my work for the family company. "To what do I owe the pleasure of this visit? Not that it's not great to see you both, but…"

I already knew what Charli was going to say. I'd been expecting it ever since Poppy was born. William Evans, the family's lawyer, had given us all a reprieve while we were waiting for the baby to be born, but I wasn't surprised that our little break was now over.

"It's time, Asher," Charli confirmed. "The family meeting was called for tonight."

"Tonight?"

She nodded.

"That's kind of fast."

"Is it?"

It wasn't. It had already been almost two years since our father had passed away and left us all with our very own tasks to carry out as stipulations to his last will and testament. My older half-brother and sister had taken their turns first, and in a twist, Craig, my younger brother, had recently had his turn. It was only myself and my baby sister Kat left.

"I suppose I'll finally find out my fate." To my surprise, I didn't feel any particular way about it. Not that it would matter if I did, because there was nothing to be done about it except doing whatever my father had dreamed up for me. It was either that or my family lost everything. And that would never be an option.

"You don't know it's your turn."

I raised my eyebrow, and Charli shrugged. We both knew

that Michael Carlson would keep his baby girl for last. Kat was the youngest and although we'd all had our own special relationships with our father, the connection between him and his youngest child had been extra special.

"Seven?"

Charli nodded. "At the big house. We'll have dinner first if you can make it."

"I'll do my best." I kissed my sister on the cheek and gazed down at the still-sleeping bundle in her arms. "She really is beautiful, sis."

NOA

Torture. That's what it was. Torture.

There was no other word to describe being twisted and turned around and around while cousins and family members I didn't even know existed wrapped me up in toilet paper, of all things.

As far as traditions went, I was pretty sure this was the stupidest one there was.

"Turn!"

I turned.

"Not that way." My cousin Sarah's hand reached out and spun me around. "This way. Hurry," she hollered. "They're beating us."

I forced myself to feign interest in the activity. "I didn't realize it was a race."

Sarah froze, a roll in her hands, and stared at me. "Noa. *Everything* is a race."

I laughed, but quickly swallowed it when I realized she was completely serious. My elder cousin had always been hypercompetitive when it came to games growing up. Still. It was a ridiculous bridal shower game.

I tipped my head back and gazed up at the ceiling of the meeting room that all the female wedding guests had been stuffed into for the last few hours for the traditionally themed bridal shower. I was very quickly hitting my limit with the festivities.

"Five more minutes!" Jeannie, the mother of the groom, yelled out from somewhere across the room. "Make your brides beautiful."

With the time ticking down, Sarah kicked things into over-drive and soon, I was not only wrapped in something that was supposed to resemble a gown made of toilet paper, but also had an elaborate headpiece attached to my head and woven through my blonde strands.

"Okay, time!" Jeannie called.

"No!" Sarah immediately began to protest, but I saw my chance to escape.

I shimmied away from my cousin with the roll of toilet paper trailing after me.

"Noa!" Sarah called after me. "Where are you going?"

"I have to pee." I clenched my teeth together and shrugged apologetically.

"Now? We still have the judging and I know—"

"When you have to go, you have to go." I twirled dramati-cally. "But great job, cuz! Best dress here." I blew Sarah a kiss and slipped out the door into the hallway.

I leaned against the door and huffed out a breath.

"Don't tell me you're a runaway bride?"

Jolted, my eyes flew open to stare directly at my grandma. "What? I…"

"It's a very pretty dress." She winked, and I shook my head.

"Sarah is…"

"Say no more." Grandma Rose squeezed my arm. "Your cousin always did love everything to do with weddings. She used to beg me to wear my veil around the house when she came to visit."

"I remember." I laughed, but it was followed quickly by a groan. "If she likes all of this so much," I waved my arm around, "maybe she should be the one getting married."

I regretted the words the moment they were out of my mouth. My cousin might drive me crazy but I loved her. And even though she was pushy and competitive to the point of totally overbearing, she was still a good person. And it wasn't a secret that Sarah was dying to be the one who was the center of attention this week.

She'd been dating her boyfriend Brent for over two years and he'd yet to pop the question. It couldn't be easy for her to bear witness to a huge family wedding that she herself wanted so badly.

"I didn't mean that." I shook my head and bit my lip.

Grandma Rose patted my cheek and smiled. "I know you didn't, dear. Not everyone loves this kind of thing."

That was an understatement.

"Your mother, on the other hand…she's in her element."

I groaned. "Is it awful of me that I don't want anything to do with all of this silliness?"

Grandma Rose shook her head. "Not at all." At barely five feet, she was a bundle of sweetness. She always smelled of baby powder and had a kind smile and even kinder word for everyone, especially her favorite grandchild. It was a private joke between the two of us that I would tease that I was the favorite, but secretly I knew it to be true.

Through the door, I heard Sarah calling my name. "I promise I'll be back," I told Grandma Rose. "But I just really need a few minutes. Don't tell Sarah."

Grandma Rose giggled. "I wouldn't dream of it."

From inside the room, I heard my cousin getting closer.

"Go." My grandma urged. "I'll hold her off."

I kissed her soft cheek. "You're the best."

Without a moment to spare, I took off down the hallway, no doubt leaving a trail of tissue in my wake. I heard the door to the meeting room open behind me, followed by my cousin's high-pitched voice, as I only barely managed to slip around the corner before getting spotted.

Safe from view, at least for the minute, I took a moment to catch my breath, squeezed my eyes shut, leaned up against the wall and listened as my grandma steered Sarah back to the party.

Grandma had bought me a few minutes, but Sarah was nothing if not committed and she hated to lose. Even if it was a ridiculous bridal shower game. I didn't have much time before my cousin would be looking for me.

I took a breath, turned, and ran—straight into a hard chest.

"Whoa. Careful."

Two big hands clamped onto my arms, steadying me before I tripped over the long toilet paper dangling all around my feet.

"Sorry," I muttered as I looked up into eyes so blue, they reminded me of a clear glacier lake. "I was…just…"

"Let me guess." His eyes sparkled with mischief, but he didn't move his hands. "You're either on your way to a very formal event, or…" He pretended to think. "The bathroom."

An unexpected laugh burst out of me and echoed through the empty hallway. I slapped a hand over my mouth, my eyes wide as I glanced behind me.

"Wait," he said. "You've been attacked by a rogue toilet paper assailant and they're after you."

Again, I laughed. "Yes," I said as seriously as I could. "You're actually pretty spot-on with that one." Behind me, I was sure I heard the door to the meeting room open. "I need to hide."

Blue eyes winked. "Come with me."

Without waiting for a response, he released me, grabbing my right hand as he spun around and pulled me down the hall to a steel door with a No Entry sticker on it. "In here."

Chapter Two

ASHER

I WASN'T in the habit of rescuing women dressed in toilet paper gowns, but there was something about the way she looked at me with those big brown eyes. And when she laughed, I knew instantly that I'd do whatever it took to hear that sound again.

I turned quickly and moved for the first door I saw. "In here." I punched my master code into the keypad and pushed through the door into the banquet prep area of the main lodge kitchen.

"What? Where?"

Once the door clicked shut behind us, I released her hand, though somewhat reluctantly. "Whoever the lunatic toilet paper bandit chasing you is, he won't find you in here."

"She," she corrected me. "My cousin. She takes her bridal shower games very seriously."

The cute blonde held out her arms and spun in a slow circle, causing the layers of toilet paper to billow up around her legs.

I let out a low whistle. "I can see that." I shook my head. "It's very impressive."

She raised an eyebrow. "I guess impressive is one word for it."

"I take it you're not a big fan of these games?"

She laughed again, and I found myself liking the sound far more than I should have. There was something completely unguarded about it. Deep, throaty, and real. It was refreshing.

"I'm not a fan of weddings at all."

Interesting. In my—truthfully—limited experience, most women loved weddings.

"What's wrong with weddings? They're a celebration of love and happiness. Family and friends gather together and have a good time. Great food, lots of drinks. Dancing." I shrugged. "How could you possibly object to a big party?"

"It's not the party I object to." She plucked at a rogue piece of tissue. "I like a good time as much as the next girl. It's everything else."

"The marriage part?"

"All of it." She shrugged. "I guess I never saw the need to prance around in a white fluffy gown in front of a bunch of people and promise myself, heart, mind, and body to a man." She rolled her eyes. "There's so much ridiculous tradition involved that doesn't make sense at all," she continued. "I mean, what exactly is the point of making all your female relatives and friends dress each other in toilet paper, of all things?" She gestured to her outfit. "I look stupid, don't I?"

I shook my head seriously. "I think you look cute."

Her eyes widened, but I didn't take it back.

"So besides the promises to another person and the silly toilet paper traditions, do you object to anything else when it comes to weddings?"

I had a feeling I was lifting the lid on a whole host of other objections, but despite myself, I was enjoying this unexpected interaction and her sassy opinions.

"Don't get me started on how much weddings cost."

I knew all about the costs, and as the owner of the hottest wedding venue in town, I was perfectly fine with it. Not that I was about to mention that.

I leaned back against a prep counter and crossed my arms. "I'm going to go out on a limb and assume you're here for the big wedding this week."

She shot me a look, and I chuckled. "But you'd rather not be?"

"No. Well…it's complicated."

"Family always is." I groaned as my thoughts flashed forward to the family dinner and meeting waiting for me later that night.

But the last thing I wanted was to taint what was turning into a very fun and unexpected moment with a very beautiful woman—crazy outfit aside. I pushed it aside.

"I'm Asher, by the way."

A slow smile moved across her lips. "Nice to meet you, Asher." She held out her hand. "I'm Noa."

I wrapped my much larger fingers around her small hand and shook, but instead of releasing it, I turned it over and covered it with my other hand. "It's been my absolute pleasure to meet you, Noa. And since you're obviously not in a hurry to get back to the bridal shower, can I show you something that might change your mind about the wedding?"

She bit her bottom lip and sucked it between her teeth.

I swallowed hard and exhaled a low groan. "Well?"

"I have to be honest, Asher." She inhaled and once more worried her lip. For a moment, I thought she might confess something serious, but then she laughed and shook her head. "I doubt you'll be able to change my mind."

"Challenge accepted."

With her hand still in mine, I turned and led her away from the quiet corner and into the heart of the busy kitchen.

All around us, preparations were underway for the wedding celebration the next day. The lodge was fully staffed, and as always, the kitchen was chaos—organized chaos.

"Asher." Gwen, the pastry chef, greeted me by waving a piping bag in the air. "Please don't tell me there have been any more changes. I can't handle it, Asher. I won't do it. I don't care if they want roses instead of—"

"No more changes." I put a hand on the icing bag and lowered it slowly to the stainless-steel counter. "They're going to love what you've created, Gwen. I promise you."

She didn't look convinced and turned to Noa. "What do you think?"

"About?"

"The cake." Gwen waved the icing bag again. "The wedding cake."

"The wedding cake?"

Noa looked to me for help.

"Here." I released her hand long enough to slide a white two-layer cake toward us, decorated with red poinsettias dusted in gold to match the colours the mother of the bride had insisted on.

"It's gorgeous," she said immediately. "Wow. You made this?"

Gwen nodded smugly, pride radiating from her.

"It's amazing," Noa continued. "The mother of the bride is going to go ape shit for this."

"The mother of the bride?" I gave her a sideways glance.

She shrugged. "Like I said, weddings are all for the families, right?"

I didn't argue. Instead, I reached for a large knife. "You haven't even seen the best part yet."

Without waiting for a response, I slid the knife straight through the cake, right through an edible poinsettia.

"Asher!" Noa grabbed my arm. "What are you doing? You can't cut the wedding cake!"

NOA

Horrified, I looked at the ruined cake, then at the baker, who did not look nearly as panicked as she should be considering she was going to have to make a brand-new cake overnight or risk the wrath of her mother—which, from experience, I knew was something she definitely wouldn't want to do. Finally, I dragged my gaze back to Asher, who was grinning.

"What on earth are you doing?"

"This is the best part." He slid the knife through the cake again, cutting a generous piece.

Gwen handed him a plate, and he easily lifted the cake and set it on top before handing it to me.

I shook my head and crossed my arms, unwilling to be part of the situation. "You just ruined the wedding cake."

As if he'd only just realized what he'd done, Asher started to laugh. "No." He shook his head. "I didn't."

I wasn't convinced.

"This is the practice cake." He set the plate down on the counter and gently spun me around. "This is the actual cake."

I blinked, and just like that, I was staring at another, much larger wedding cake on the prep table behind us. I turned back to the smaller, ruined one.

"You mean…" The dots connected, and I smacked Asher playfully. "You made me think that you—"

"I'm sorry." He didn't look apologetic in the slightest. His lips quirked beneath the scruff of his beard, and his blue eyes glittered with disarming mischief.

"I can't believe you got me like that."

"Honestly, I didn't mean to." He picked up the plate again and grabbed a fork from a nearby jar of cutlery. "I just really wanted you to taste this." I watched his fork slide through the moist cake as he lifted it into the air. "It will change your life."

"My life?" I raised an eyebrow.

He nodded with complete seriousness. "I can't explain it, but it's a fact. Gwen's cake will change your life. And your opinion on weddings."

"I doubt it very—"

My protests disappeared when he slipped the forkful of the most delicious cake I'd ever tasted between my lips.

The rich, velvety chocolate exploded across my tongue in a symphony of heavenly flavor. I'd never considered myself a chocolate lover, but with one bite, I was fully converted.

My eyes closed, and the softest moan slipped from my lips.

"See?"

My eyes snapped open to find Asher watching me intently, a grin spread across his handsome face.

"I told you it would change your life."

I finished the bite slowly, nodding as I turned to Gwen. "That is the best piece of cake I have ever had," I said honestly. "Truly. That's like magic."

She beamed. "I just hope the bride likes it."

"How could she not?" Asher said before I could respond. He turned back to me. "So?"

"Did it change my life?" I nodded. "It definitely changed my opinion on chocolate cake."

He chuckled.

"And weddings?"

"I guess if they serve cake like this, they can't be so bad. But I still think it'll take more than the most delicious cake I've ever tasted to convince me weddings aren't more for the family than the couple."

He considered that while taking a bite himself. "I don't disagree," he said after a moment. "But the cake…"

"Are you going to share any more of that?" I reached for the plate, but he moved it out of reach.

"I can't have you ruining your beautiful gown," he teased, offering me another forkful.

"I can feed myself." I put one hand on my hip and shot him a look.

"I have no doubt."

I eyed the forkful of heaven. Letting a strange man I'd just met feed me dessert that made me groan was probably ridiculous—and wildly inappropriate—especially when I couldn't tell whether it was the chocolate or the man giving me the reaction.

There were a million reasons to refuse.

The smell won.

I closed my eyes and accepted the bite.

"It's seriously good," I said once I recovered. "But I should probably—"

"Not yet." He set the plate down and took my hand. "I haven't even shown you the best part yet."

I stared at his large hand wrapped around mine, then back up into his gorgeous blue eyes. For the first time in years, I stopped thinking about what I *should* do and let myself do what I *wanted* to do.

"Okay."

His eyes sparkled when he grinned.

"You two are very cute together."

I turned to Gwen, who waved her icing bag between us. "I didn't know you were dating anyone."

Instead of protesting, Asher laughed. He didn't let go of my hand.

"Oh," I said quickly. "We're not—I'm just here for the wedding." I gestured to the toilet paper gown still clinging to me. A flash of guilt hit as I thought of my cousin, probably losing her mind trying to find me.

"Oh." Gwen straightened. "I'm sorry. I didn't—"

"It's fine," Asher jumped in. "I rescued Noa from a particularly aggressive bridal party game and made it my mission to convince her there *are* some highlights to weddings."

"The cake is definitely one of them," I said. Possibly the only one.

"Now for the best part." He winked and reached for an abandoned icing bag. "May I?"

Gwen shrugged. "Just get out of here before I end up making another cake."

Asher tugged my hand gently, leading me away.

"Thank you, Gwen," I called over my shoulder. "The cake is amazing."

He guided me back through the kitchen to the same back door we'd escaped through earlier.

"Thank you for rescuing me," I said. "Obviously you work here, but how is it you can convince the pastry chef to give you cake like that?"

"I can be very charming." He winked, squeezing my hand —still holding it.

The space between us shrank.

"You really are quite charming."

I was drawn to him in a way I couldn't explain. A complete stranger who somehow felt familiar.

"Are you sure you need to go so soon?"

I wasn't sure of anything. I exhaled slowly. "I really should be getting back to—"

"Not without trying this."

The icing bag appeared between us. After the cake, I had no doubt the icing would be just as good. I held out my hand.

"Oh no." He shook his head and gestured toward my mouth.

"What?"

He shrugged, like it was completely out of his control.

He really *was* charming. I smiled, shook my head, and stuck out my tongue.

The burst of sugary sweetness hit a second later. I pulled back too quickly, just as he did, and the icing smeared across my cheek.

"Oops." He released my hand and wiped my cheek with his finger. His voice dropped, his eyes never leaving mine. "Got it. Is it amazing?"

I looked at the icing on his finger and nodded slowly.

Maybe it was the sugar. Maybe it was his closeness. Or that smile.

For one suspended moment, I forgot myself.

I took his hand and brought his finger to my mouth, sucking the icing from the tip.

A low groan reached my ears.

I didn't have time to figure out where it came from because the door burst open.

Two hotel employees muttered apologies as they passed, and as Asher held the door, I caught a clear view down the hallway.

Straight into the stunned faces of my cousin—

And Grandma Rose.

Chapter Three

NOA

FORTUNATELY, Sarah believed my lame excuse that I'd taken the wrong turn and gotten lost on my way to the bathroom. I didn't get a chance to say thank you or goodbye to my rescuer, nor did I dare. But I didn't miss the air kiss Grandma Rose sent in his direction as Sarah dragged me out of the kitchen and back toward the party.

Somehow, I managed to make it through the rest of the festivities, where of course I was awarded the best-dressed bride. The beaming look of pride on my cousin's face was worth it, and because I felt guilty about ditching her earlier, I didn't immediately rip the tissue from my body the moment the prize was awarded.

It wasn't until I made it back to the safety of my suite that I began to tear at the toilet paper gown in earnest.

"Whoa. It looks like you let a bunch of kittens loose in a toilet paper factory."

I yanked a piece of my veil from the back of my head and looked up to see Ryan Little—my longtime best friend, and for a significantly shorter period of time, fiancé—leaning against the wall, watching me as if he wasn't about to experience the worst day of his life.

"Let me guess." He walked toward me and helped shed me of the *gown*. "Sarah? Or your mother?"

"Or yours," I snapped, and immediately felt bad. "You were right the first time. These games are ridiculous. I don't know why I couldn't go skiing with you guys instead."

"Because, my dear." He kissed my cheek. "*You* are the bride."

"Don't remind me."

I walked into the massive suite and straight to the picture window that looked over the ski hill. The sun had started to dip behind the mountain and the chair lifts were closed for the day, but dozens of people still milled around the base and a few stragglers made their way down the hill.

"We can ski after the wedding." Ryan came to stand beside me and handed me a glass of wine. "We're here until after New Year's, remember? We need to make new memories. Happy ones. There'll be lots of time for skiing."

New memories. Happy ones.

Right. After all, that was the entire reason we were here.

I lifted the wine to my mouth and drank deeply, but almost spilled it down my front when Ryan grabbed my other hand.

"Where's your ring?"

I tugged my hand out of his grasp. "It's too big."

That was an understatement. The diamond Ryan had presented me with when we'd agreed to be married was ostentatiously large. A square-cut, three-carat solitaire, it made me uneasy wearing it. And not only because it was worth more than my vehicle—but also because of everything it represented.

"It represents our love, darling."

I rolled my eyes at Ryan's over-the-top sarcasm.

"I know, I know." He wrapped an arm around me and squeezed. "But you really should wear it, at least until the wedding is over with."

Over with.

That was how we both felt about our upcoming nuptials. In any other circumstance, our overwhelming indifference to the fact that we were about to be legally joined in a marriage neither of us wanted would be a massive red flag. No—more like a parade of red flags accompanied by alarm bells blaring directly into our brains.

But there was no other circumstance. Only the one Ryan and I found ourselves in.

I dropped my head back and blinked viciously at the tears that had appeared out of nowhere. I was not a crier. And even if I were, the time for crying was long past. It was way too late for tears.

"Oh man," Ryan groaned. "Don't cry, Noa. I hate it when you cry."

My head snapped up. "I never cry."

"Ha. Got ya."

I smacked his arm lightly and laughed—but my laughter quickly turned into a choke when, to my surprise, actual tears leaked from my eyes after all.

So much for not crying.

"Shit." Ryan led me to the giant oversized couch positioned in front of the wood-burning fireplace. I downed the rest of my wine before letting him take the glass away. "If I didn't know better, Noa, I'd think you didn't want to marry me tomorrow. Don't tell me you got cold feet?"

ASHER

"We're going to need a bigger dining room table soon." I followed my brother Craig from the dining room and into the kitchen, carefully balancing a stack of dirty dishes. "I swear, this family gets bigger with every family dinner we have."

"And that's saying something, considering we do this every week." Chase, my eldest brother, joined us with the empty platter that held the remains of what had been a delicious roast beef. It had become the tradition for the men in the family to clean up after our weekly family dinners, while the women relaxed. As far as I was concerned, it was more than a fair deal. I'd way rather clean up than have to cook for such a big crowd.

"But hey," Chase added with a laugh. "I'm not adding any more family members. At least not for a while."

"Are you sure about that, brother?" Craig raised an eyebrow. "I saw the way Annie was looking at baby Poppy. She looks like she might be catching baby fever."

Annie and Chase had been an item for just over a year since my eldest brother returned to Trickle Creek after spending most of his adult life estranged from the family. Our father's will brought Chase back into our lives by forcing him to stay in town for a minimum of six months. It was also the start of what turned out to be special stipulations for all of us.

My turn was next, but there was no point in spending any energy wondering what my father had in store for me. I'd find out soon enough.

"Maybe it's Asher's turn next." Symon Scott, Charli's new husband, joined us in the kitchen, his arms full of yet another stack of dirty dishes.

"Keep dreaming, man." I took the dishes from him and started to load them into the dishwasher. "Even if I wanted a girlfriend, which I don't," I added quickly, "I don't have time."

"Bullshit." Craig called me out. "From what I see, you have plenty of time for women. Every time I bump into you around town or call you, you're with a different woman."

"That's different." I laughed, because it was true. "Those women are definitely not girlfriends."

"I don't buy it." Chase stood at the sink. "It seems to me that it would be more work."

"You guys all have it backward." I shook my head. "You all are committed, and that means spending quality time together and talking." I used air quotes. "I get all the best parts of dating without any of the time-consuming bullshit stuff. Win-win."

Symon made some sort of snorting sound, while Craig only shook his head.

It was Chase who finally spoke. "As your older brother, I think it's my duty to tell you something."

I gave him a warning look.

The two of us hadn't shared the closest relationship over the years, and although it was starting to change, I still didn't feel like taking brotherly advice from Chase.

"I was just going to say that I think you're missing the point. It's the time-consuming bullshit stuff that's the best part."

Next to him, Craig nodded. "Truth."

"Whatever." I shrugged it off the way I always did. "You guys can have it. I have enough going on at work. The lodge is packed already, and it's still so early in the season."

"Charli said it looks amazing up there," Symon said. "I need to pop in after training one day and check out the holiday decorations."

"Absolutely. I'll buy you a beer." I liked my new brother-in-law, but then again, the professional skier was an easy man to like. And I loved the hell out of my big sister, Charli. What else could a guy ask for in a brother-in-law?

"Asher, you do know that it's probably your turn tonight, right?"

"And?"

Craig had only said out loud what all of us were thinking when it came to the will reading. Still, it pissed me off. Maybe I was a little more on edge than I'd thought.

"And...I think you need to be prepared that whatever your stipulation is, things are going to change for you for the next six months."

I shook it off. "Whatever it is, I'll manage it. That's what I do."

"Are you going to manage falling in love, too?"

All four of us spun around to see Kat in the entry to the kitchen with a big grin on her face.

"What on earth are you talking about?" I looked at my baby sister as if she'd totally lost her mind—which obviously she had. There would be no falling in love for me. Ever.

"Look around, Asher. Three of us have had our turn, and all three have fallen in love." Unnecessarily, Kat pointed to Chase, Craig, and then Symon.

All three men shrugged, but I only rolled my eyes.

"You're crazy. Can we get this over with already?"

NOA

Cold feet?

How about a completely numb *body*?

I swiped at my tears and forced myself to pull it together. I could do a whole lot worse than Ryan Little.

By any standard, my fiancé was an amazing catch. Not only was he handsome in a casual surfer-boy-meets-successful-lawyer kind of way—with a smile that could make any girl melt—but he was also one of the nicest guys I'd ever met. Everyone loved Ryan. He was funny, smart, and incredibly generous. As if that weren't enough, he'd also been blessed with a sharp wit and a ridiculously high IQ. He recently gradu-ated from law school, just like I did, and together we were set to start working at Briggs & Little Law in the spring. Just as soon as we returned from our four-month honeymoon trip around the world. Compliments of our families.

On top of all of that, he was also my best friend.

Our mothers met in a Mommy & Me class with our older siblings—my brother Tom and Ryan's sister Olivia—and became fast friends. By the time Ryan and I were born, our families were already inseparable.

Years later, the children became just as tightly entwined as our parents. When Olivia and Tom started dating in high school, everyone was thrilled. After college, when they announced their engagement, both families were elated.

The elation was cut short when almost two years ago, on New Year's Eve, Tom and Olivia were killed in a drunk driving accident. After that, both families were shrouded in darkness, until six months ago when Ryan and I announced our own engagement.

And why not?

We made sense in every way. We could finish each other's sentences, we knew all the deep, dark secrets the other one had, our families already spent every major holiday—and most weekends—together.

Our parents deserved to have something to smile about again.

There was no doubt in my mind that I loved Ryan. I did. The only problem was that our love was purely platonic.

We'd tried once or twice over the years to see whether we could be more, and every time, it ended up in laughter or that one time, a very awkward morning after.

"Noa." He reached for my hand and threaded his fingers through it. "Talk to me."

I took a deep breath and then another. After a moment, I

was able to swallow back the panic that grew more profound as the nuptials approached.

"It's not you," I said after a moment. "You know that."

He nodded.

"I've never wanted to get married. Not to anyone." Out of nowhere, my thoughts flashed to earlier in the hotel kitchen and Asher trying to convince me that even if it was only cake, there were some good things when it came to weddings.

That cake *was* good. Or maybe it had been the man feeding it to me?

Either way, I should not be thinking of a strange man the night before my wedding.

"I know this whole thing isn't our scene," Ryan said. "You know I've never seen myself tying the knot either. That's why this works."

It was true. Ryan enjoyed the Playboy lifestyle far too much to settle down. Although he had promised to be more subtle about it after we were married.

"Maybe we shouldn't—"

Ryan shifted on the couch, grabbing my hand and moving closer. "Remember why we're doing it, Noa. You should have seen the way our fathers were laughing and smiling out on the slopes today. I haven't seen them like that in…"

He didn't need to finish the sentence. We both knew exactly how long it had been.

"Our moms, too. The games were ridiculous, but they were both so happy." I nodded as I spoke. Ryan was right. We'd agreed to get married for one reason only. For our families. There had been too many tears and way too much heartbreak since the accident that took our older siblings almost two years earlier. They deserved to be happy again, and if that meant the two of us tying the knot, why not? There were a lot worse things I could think of than spending the rest of my life with my best friend.

"It'll be worth it." Ryan kissed my cheek. "Besides, it won't be so bad being married to me. I've been told I'm pretty good between the sheets and as my wife—"

"Enough." He was trying to make me laugh, and it worked. I shoved him away gently. "You don't think it's weird that we agreed to see other people once we're married?"

"I think it's fantastic."

"Of course you do," I groaned.

"Hey." Ryan turned serious. "I meant it when I said it. If it means that much to you, I won't see other people, Noa. You and me. That's it."

My eyes widened. "But...we..."

"We could try harder."

Ryan had never lied to me before, and I believed him now. But was that what I really wanted? To be married to my best friend in a passionless marriage?

I looked away and shook my head. There were too many unanswered questions.

"Look." He grabbed my hand, and I looked in his eyes once more. "Think about it. Tonight is the stag and doe party. Let's go have some fun."

Reluctantly, I nodded. Ryan was right. We just needed to go out and blow off some steam. My doubts, or whatever they were, would be gone in the morning.

"That's the spirit." Ryan tugged me to my feet and pressed a kiss on my forehead. "And hey, we're not married yet. If you want to go and have a little fun tonight, you know I'm cool with it."

I groaned.

This situation was way too screwed up.

ASHER

"We're obviously going to need an extension."

I stood from my seat at the front of the wood-paneled office we all still thought of as our father's. Steven Larson, who had been my dad's assistant of many years, and William Evans, his lawyer, had just finished reading out the latest stipulation of the will.

To no one's surprise, this one had in fact been intended for me.

I turned and slowly looked at the room full of my siblings. "There's no other way. We'll have to take an extension on this one." I clasped my hands as if the matter were settled…which, in my mind, it was. "January first is probably the next logical date for—"

"I'm afraid that isn't possible." William spoke up. "The requirements are clear," he continued.

I turned around slowly as the other man spoke.

"Once the will stipulation is communicated to all family members." He lifted his head and gestured to the group. "As it has been done here." He nodded and continued speaking. "The clock starts on the required six months."

"So, we give it a few extra weeks." I could feel the uncomfortable sensation of stress start to burble in my stomach. I never allowed myself to get worked up about business things. My ability to remain calm when it came to business was a point of pride for me. And this was business.

But it was also family.

Family that was really going to fuck with my business.

"I'm sorry, Asher. That's just not—"

"You *just* did it with Charli." I whirled around and pointed in my sister's direction. "Were we not supposed to have the fourth will reading when Craig finished out his six months?"

Everyone in the room was silent as they waited for the answer. Craig had been the last sibling to complete his stipulation. He'd been required to hire a nanny. One he'd subsequently fallen in love with, a fact that I couldn't let myself think about at the moment.

"That was an extraordinary situation," Steven Larson chimed in. He'd been our father's assistant for as long as any of us could remember. "William and I have been given the power to pause the reading of the stipulations in the event of extraordinary situations. Such as the end of a pregnancy." He smiled at Charli. "We decided that it was in everyone's best interest to wait until after the baby was born, which is why we postponed this next reading."

"But now that we've read the terms," the lawyer once more picked up the thread of conversation, "the clock starts now, Asher. As of midnight, you are on a required six-month leave of absence from Carlson Corporation, which means that you will suspend all management duties of all kinds, including but not limited to, answering emails and phone calls. You are also required to cease day-to-day management of the premises and are to have limited access to all Carlson properties."

My pulse pounded in my forehead. "This is ludicrous and complete corporate suicide. I run the company. I cannot simply walk away for six months without any preparation at all." I scanned the faces of my siblings. All of whom looked as startled as I felt.

"There is an alternative, of course."

I once more spun and stared at the lawyer. Logically, I knew William Evans was only the messenger. It wasn't his fault that he had the task of reading out these increasingly stupid stipulations to our father's will.

"What's that?"

"You could forfeit the inheritance," he said simply. "All assets, including the complete holdings of Carlson Corporation, would be transferred to the charitable organizations your father—"

"And that's an option, how?" I slammed both hands on the

tabletop and stared at the lawyer, unable to keep my frustration at bay. "If I do it, I risk losing the entire company. And if I don't do it, it's gone anyway. What kind of fucking choice is that?"

"Whoa, brother."

"Calm down."

Chase and Craig flanked me, each threading an arm through mine and pulling me backward and away from the lawyer.

"It's not that bad." Kat appeared in front of me.

"Not that bad?" My mouth dropped. "I'm not sure what it is you think I do, but we're not only in the middle of the busiest holiday season we've ever had, but we're also hosting a huge wedding in the middle of everything. Never mind all the events that are coming up in the new year. That's only right now."

"We'll help." Charli stood next to Kat. She was the only other sibling who'd ever worked for Carlson Corp, but had quit recently to start her own floral business because of her stipulation from our father. Besides that, she was the mother of a newborn baby. She wouldn't be any help. Even if she could help. A fact that Steven reminded us all of a moment later.

"Please don't forget that you're required to carry out your task by yourself, without any direct help from your siblings."

I shook myself free from my brother's grasp. "And what was that about limiting my presence at any corporation properties? I live at the lodge on the hill."

"Right. Your father took that into consideration as well." William slid a manila envelope out from under the stack of papers and handed it to me. "I think you'll find that—"

"My dad is trying to screw me over from beyond the grave? Yes," I snapped as I snatched the envelope away. "I think I'll find that's exactly the case."

I needed air. I needed to think. I needed to get out of there. Of all the scenarios I'd imagined my father presenting me with, never had I considered that Michael Carlson would take away the one thing that mattered to me. My entire identity was caught up in Carlson Corp and the pride I took in running the family business so successfully. I was good at it. Damn good. And I loved it.

How could my father not have seen that?

"Asher. We can figure this out." Chase reached for me, but I shrugged him off.

"Leave him." Out of the corner of my eye, I saw Charli grab Chase's arm to hold him back as I stormed from the room. "He needs time."

But time was the one thing I definitely didn't have the luxury of. I only had a few hours to figure out how to transfer all of my responsibilities onto my managers, never mind the matter of finding somewhere to live for the next six months.

Suddenly my siblings' idea that my biggest problem was that I'd end up falling in love through this process didn't seem quite so bad now that I was faced with the alternative.

Chapter Four

NOA

"ANOTHER!" I slammed the empty shot glass down on the bar top and wiped my lips with the back of my hand.

"Are you sure?" Sarah gave me a look. "You don't think you've had enough?"

"I sure don't." I turned my back on my cousin and leaned over the bar, exposing my cleavage to the bartender who winked and set to work making me another shot of whatever concoction he'd been pouring me all evening.

The bartender was cute, and he'd definitely been flirting with me all evening. Never mind that he probably made his money in tips, I couldn't stop thinking about what Ryan had said earlier. Maybe I did need to get something out of my system. But how fucked up was it that I was even contemplating anything to do with another man only hours from my wedding ceremony?

Very fucked up.

That's what it was.

But then again, so was everything to do with my situation.

"Here you go, darlin'." Cute Bartender Man slid the shot over to me with yet another wink.

"Are you flirting with her?" Sarah snatched the shot away before I could grab it. "She is getting married tomorrow."

I didn't bother to stifle the groan as my cousin admonished the poor man.

"Have some respect!"

"My apologies, ladies."

I mouthed the word *sorry* before the man moved to the far end of the bar.

"Sarah. That wasn't—whoa." I only managed to grab the edge of the bar before I fell over. Maybe I really did have too many shots?

"You need to stop drinking, Noa. It's your wedding tomorrow. You don't want to be puffy."

"Puffy?" I threw my head back with a sharp laugh. "I don't think it'll matter."

"Of course it won't." Sarah grabbed my arm and led me to a nearby table. "Ryan obviously thinks you're the most beautiful woman in the world. Have you seen the way he looks at you?"

I raised my eyebrows but didn't bother to burst my cousin's bubble by informing her that right before we'd left our suite to go out, Ryan had told me that the silky, plum top I'd paired with my faux leather leggings and tall black boots was giving off eggplant vibes.

And he did *not* mean it in a sexy way.

Just like everything else between us, he teased me like a brother, too.

As if he knew I was talking about him, across the room, where the men were gathered around a pool table, Ryan looked up moments before taking a shot of his own and flashed a smile in my direction.

I groaned.

"Really, Noa. I don't know what's wrong with you. I would be thrilled to marry Ryan."

Before I could stop myself, I jumped up from the table. "Well then," I said to my cousin. "You marry him."

I regretted it the moment the words were out of my mouth, but only because when I spun around for my grand exit, I ran straight into my mother, who, of course, was arm in arm with Ryan's mom.

"Noa?" The bright smile that had been on her face was replaced in a flash, with the all too familiar shadow that Jeannie Little had worn since the accident.

And just like that, I wanted to crawl into a hole. The whole point of...well... everything was to keep those smiles on their faces again.

"Is everything okay?"

My own mother wore a matching look of concern, and both women glanced from me to Sarah, who was proving to be useless in the bridesmaid category. At least when it came to any duties that actually helped me out.

"I'm just..." Either I really had had too much alcohol, or I was about to have a panic attack. Or both.

I looked around frantically but found nothing to steady me.

"It's your big party, Noa." My mother reached for me, but at that moment, a surge of rebellion washed through me.

I pulled my arm backward, leaving my mother's mouth agape.

"Let's go back to the party, Noa," Janice tried.

That's what I should do. I should just down another shot, and go dance like everyone expected me to.

It was the right thing and it would make everyone stop looking at me that way. But I couldn't make my feet move. Like a petulant child, I shook my head.

"I'm not sure everything is—"

"Ladies!"

Right on cue, Ryan appeared next to me. He slid his arm around me and pulled my body into his.

Everything about Ryan was familiar. His cologne, his touch, the way he gave me a little shake as he held me tight. I knew it was meant to reassure me, but it only made me want to scream.

"What's happening?" Ryan looked to the mothers and Sarah, who shrugged and walked away before he turned his attention to me. "It looks like someone needs a drink."

I was trapped. Like an animal in a cage, the panic that had been brewing deep inside me threatened to burst out in what was sure to be an explosive scene. I swallowed hard. "What I need is to—"

"Darling?" Ryan squeezed me even tighter to his side. "I think what you need is to blow off some steam."

"That's why I thought a drink might—"

"That's not really what I was talking about."

I squeezed my eyes shut as he gave me another little shake.

"Remember what we talked about earlier?"

I sure did. But if Ryan thought I was about to pick up some random guy for a hookup the night before we got married, with all of our family members who were convinced we were madly in love lurking around every corner, he was crazy.

"Well, as long as the two of you have everything under control."

"We always do." Ryan flashed the moms his megawatt smile.

They may have been appeased, but I only wanted to scream.

"Excuse me." I somehow managed to slide out of Ryan's grasp and headed for the door. I needed a chance to breathe and pull myself together.

"Remember," my fiancé called after me. "I think you should blow off…"

Thankfully for him, I made it to the safety of the lobby before I could hear the end of that sentence.

ASHER

Somehow I made it through the lobby of the lodge without being stopped by any of my employees, or anyone else I knew. It likely had a lot to do with the *don't mess with me* vibes radiating off me in waves.

I needed to be alone to figure out what the hell I was going to do.

I would be lying if I said I hadn't wondered what my father might ask from me when it came to my turn. Of course, I'd thought about it. Chase had been required to return to Trickle Creek for six months. Charli had six months to turn a small investment into a viable business. Craig had to hire a nanny for his six-month period.

Surely, my dad had something equally easy lined up for me for my six months.

I'd run through a variety of scenarios over the last year and a half, but nothing my imagination had come up with had come close to being as awful as reality.

And it wasn't just about *me*. If I took six months away from Carlson Corp, what exactly did they think would happen to the company? Who was going to run things? I had slid into the CEO position before my father had passed, allowing him to spend more time on the golf course or the ski hill, enjoying his semi-retirement. Although my father could never have retired completely.

I was a lot like my dad in that way. I loved to work. It was my entire identity. I was good at it, too.

But, now, what the fuck was I supposed to do?

I reached the elevator bank and bashed on the buttons that would take me to the penthouse suite. The moment I did so, I once more remembered that not only did I need to find something to occupy my time for the next few months, but I also had to find a place to live.

Fuck—I punched the button one more time for good measure and then again—*this*.

"If you need to hit it, hit the sixth floor please."

I spun around at whomever had witnessed my miniature tantrum. "Noa?"

She looked different dressed in a slinky purple top and tight black leather-like pants that hugged her curves in exactly the right way.

"I didn't recognize you without your toilet paper gown."

She looked up sharply. Her frown transformed instantly when she recognized me, and I was rewarded with a bright smile that made something deep down inside me flutter to life. My current problems were suddenly more manageable in the presence of a beautiful woman.

"Asher? Hi. What are you—"

"I actually live in the hotel." I gestured to the still-closed elevator doors. As impatient as I'd been only a moment earlier, suddenly I was content to wait all night for the elevator to arrive if it meant I could be in the company of this beautiful woman who continued to surprise me. "You look like you're going to a party."

"Just leaving." She sighed and flipped her hair over her bare shoulder, drawing my attention to the exposed skin at the base of her neck, and lower.

"Too bad," I said with a small smile. "You look fantastic. I really like that color on you."

"You do?" Noa straightened, surprise written on her face. "The purple?"

"It's a great color on you."

"Huh." Her lips curled into a small smile, as if I'd just reminded her of something. "Thank you. I really needed to hear that."

"That's a shame." Without thinking, I reached for her and touched her arm lightly. "You should never doubt how beautiful you are," I said seriously. "You're stunning."

We stared into each other's eyes, and I let my fingers rest on her bare arm. She didn't pull away, and for a moment, I considered an alternative to spending my evening brooding alone in my suite. A very enticing alternative.

The chime of the elevator startled us, and I instinctively stepped back to make room for the guests who spilled out the doors. I reached inside to hold the heavy elevator open and let Noa enter first, but a young woman blocked her getaway.

"Are you leaving already, Noa?" the woman said. "I just ran up to the room for a minute and now you're—"

"I'm really tired."

I hardly knew her, and I could see she was lying. Noa flashed me a look, and I tried not to chuckle.

"I thought maybe I should get some sleep." She tried to sidestep the woman.

"Oh, that's too bad. I really wanted to buy you a drink."

Noa managed to slip away and stepped into the elevator. "Tomorrow," she told the woman, who looked visibly disappointed as I stepped into the elevator as well.

"Get some sleep, Noa. Tomorrow is a—"

The door slid shut on the rest of the woman's sentiments, and the moment it did, Noa leaned back. She pressed her head back, which had the effect of thrusting her chest out against the silky purple fabric.

The woman was exceptionally sexy, and she had no fucking idea.

I stepped toward her, about to tell her just that, when she abruptly stood up.

"What I'm about to say is crazy, but will you promise not to judge me?"

"No judgment here."

"Okay." She stepped forward and stopped herself with a little chuckle and a shake of her head. "I lied. I'm actually not going to say anything at all." With one more step, Noa closed the small distance between us, put a hand on my cheek, and kissed me.

Damn.

Whatever I'd expected, it had not been her unbelievably soft lips on mine. But when it came to this kind of surprise, I was perfectly good with the unexpected. Beyond good.

It took me a split second to recover, but that was all.

I slipped one hand around her back and splayed my palm over the thin fabric of her blouse, feeling the heat radiating from her, while my other hand cupped her cheek. I deepened the kiss as I spun her slowly around and backed her up against the wall of the elevator.

A small groan slipped from her throat and she arched her back, smashing her tits against my chest.

My cock sprang to attention and I pressed closer to her, letting one hand slip down her curves, over the satiny blouse, to her perfectly lush ass in the tight leather pants.

The space between us evaporated. I trailed my kisses down her bare neck until her sweet sounds of need drew my lips back to hers.

The chime announced our arrival on the sixth floor. Startled and disappointed, but in no way ready to end things, I reluctantly pulled back. "My suite is on the eighth floor."

"I'm…" Her eyes darted out into the hallway and back at me.

I let my fingers trail down a bare arm. Her tongue slipped out between her lips, and it was my turn to groan. This woman was driving me crazy, and that kiss held the promise of more. A lot more.

Still. I was a gentleman.

"No pressure, Noa." I squeezed the hand I still held. "But definitely an invitation."

Her eyes blazed with desire, and I once again closed the distance between us, ready to pick up where we left off.

But before my lips could touch her own soft sweetness, Noa slipped from beneath my arm and stepped out into the hall. "I want to," she said. "So much. But I…" The doors began to close. "There's…there's just something I need to do."

The doors clicked shut before I could respond, but there was nothing I could have said anyway. I leaned my head back against the wall with a sigh. It was only when the elevator once more began to move that I realized Noa had completely distracted me from the meeting I'd just come from, or the fact that my life was about to change in only a few hours.

Chapter Five

ASHER

I BLINKED HARD, willing the bright light of the morning sun to bugger off.

It was December. There wasn't even supposed to be any bright morning light with the short, winter days.

With a groan, I attempted to ignore the pounding in my head as I rolled over to find my phone on the nightstand.

12:15

That would explain the daylight. It was after noon. I hadn't slept in so late since I was a kid and I'd stayed up too late with too many drinks. Then again, wasn't that exactly what I'd done the night before?

Shit.

Recollection flooded into my consciousness as I dragged myself out of bed and into the shower. After returning to my suite—alone—reality had crashed back. I had less than twenty-four hours to find a place to live and something to do for the next six months, because my father, in some sort of beyond-the-grave, sick joke had decided to fuck me over.

Right.

I turned the shower on as cold as I could stand it. I'd already wasted too much time by sleeping off the whiskey I'd downed the night before.

The cold water had the desired effect. Not only in clearing my head a little but also in dousing the flame that Noa had ignited the night before that was somehow still burning inside me.

As much as I would love the release of allowing myself a few moments of fantasy with the sharp-witted, blonde beauty playing a starring role, I resisted the urge, instead focusing on the problem at hand.

What the fuck was I going to do?

The only thing that swallowing back tumblers full of whiskey the night before had done was piss me off. I didn't normally turn to alcohol to solve my problems, but the combination of the will reading and being blindsided by such a ludicrous stipulation, paired with Noa—and then…no Noa—was too much.

In hindsight, it probably wasn't the best way to deal with my stress, but I wasn't one to dwell on past mistakes. Showered, changed, and feeling somewhat more human, I hit the button on my fancy coffeemaker to produce me an espresso and moved to the picture window that looked out onto the busy ski hill.

Skiers dotted the runs like ants. The chair lift was full, with a lineup at the base that was moving quickly, but just long enough to demonstrate that ticket sales were brisk.

It was a beautiful bluebird day, and the picnic tables scattered around the base area of the hill were full of people taking a lunch break. I couldn't hear it through the thick glass, but I knew that upbeat music was pumping through the speakers below, creating a fun and festive atmosphere. The outdoor grill was serving up burgers for those who liked to eat outside, while their kids played in the snow nearby.

The restaurant and lounge would also be full at this time of day. Business at the Trickle Creek ski hill and lodge was booming.

I pressed my hands on the window, my arms stretched wide, and dropped my head.

I had done that.

True, my father had come into town and turned things around after the mines closed, making Trickle Creek a tourism destination. Michael Carlson had built out the world-class golf course and turned the almost-defunct ski hill into a viable business, with the lodge at the center of it all, but it had been me in recent years who'd added the condos at the base and created a resort.

And now, I had to walk away.

I slammed my hand against the glass in frustration. I couldn't just stand by and let it all fall apart while I was in exile. I wouldn't.

With new determination, I grabbed my phone and sent off a text to Penny.

> Congrats. You've been temporarily promoted. Meet me in my office in thirty minutes for details.

Penny was my best and only choice for keeping things going while I was gone.

Gone.

Shit. That was my next problem.

My phone chimed with an incoming text. Assuming it was Penny's response, I glanced at the screen.

How are you doing today?

I shouldn't have been surprised that my youngest sister would be the first to reach out. Although the others knew enough to leave me alone when I was *in a mood,* Kat never did have qualms about getting right up in the middle of my business. As the youngest, she'd gotten away with a lot. I couldn't help but smile a little despite everything, and instead of returning her text, I pushed the number to call her.

NOA

I squeezed my eyes shut, willing my reflection to be different when I opened them a moment later.

It wasn't.

My eyes were lightly lined, with a sweep of glittery gold eyeshadow. My skin was flawless, almost dewy in a radiant way that surprised me. The apples of my cheeks had been dusted with a subtle pink and my lips were painted a very pretty and feminine matching shade.

The makeup artist obviously had skills. She'd been able to cover the dark circles under my eyes to the point that not even I could tell that I hadn't had more than a few hours of sleep the night before.

I had tossed and turned, and more than once I'd strongly considered heading up to the eighth floor to knock on doors until I found Asher and his smooth hands and hot kisses that had turned me inside out.

I hadn't planned to kiss him in the elevator. But then there he was, with his smoldering eyes, that sexy smile that made my stomach flip, and his smooth compliments that made me feel exactly how I needed to feel.

Besides, Ryan had encouraged me to blow off some steam. Too bad that kiss had only generated more of it.

A lot more.

Even at the time, I knew I was going to live to regret getting off that elevator and going to my own room. Alone.

But would I really be feeling any different at this moment, had the night before played out in any other way and I'd had a little bit of pre-marital fun?

No.

The whole concept of that, and the fact that I was about to marry a man who encouraged it, only made me feel worse.

I forced all thoughts of Asher, and what could have been, from my head. I straightened up and let my gaze travel the length of my reflection in the mirror, down the fitted ivory satin bodice, to the skirt that flared out at my knees. My shoulders were bare for the moment; a white faux fur shawl would complete the look.

I had a long veil attached to the back of my hair, which I'd chosen to wear in soft curls that hung down my back.

"Oh!" My mother and father appeared in my reflection. "Darling, you look…" My mother buried her face in a tissue.

"Mom." I spun around to face them properly. "Don't cry. Please."

I knew it was a pointless plea. My mother had done nothing but cry in the last few years since the accident. At least today the tears should be happy ones.

That was the whole point. The Briggs and Little families needed something to smile about. They deserved it.

"She's just so happy, Noa." My father, Charles, took my hand. "We both are. I don't think we ever thought we'd see the day when our families would become one. Not after…"

"I know, Dad." I swallowed my own emotions down. If I let myself lose control so early on, I didn't stand a chance of making it through the day. But not for the same reason as my mom and dad. "But here we are." I forced a smile to my face.

"Ryan's a great man." Charles nodded in an effort to appear stoic. "And he's so good to you, kiddo. I have to admit, none of us saw it coming with the two of you, but I think I speak for all of us when I say that we are so glad that your friendship evolved into something deeper. We're just so happy for the both of you."

"I know you are, Dad."

"The two of you are going to be so happy." Janice finally regained control of her emotions. "And you are the most beautiful bride, Noa. I...I just..."

When she once more crumbled into tears, I looked to my dad for help.

Thankfully, he took the hint and kissed me on the cheek before steering my mother out of the room. "I'll see you soon for the big moment, kiddo."

Once they were gone, the suite felt empty. I had purposely chosen to get ready on my own. I wasn't sure how I'd handle the stress of the day, but somehow, I'd known that having a bunch of women fluttering around, no matter how much I loved them, wouldn't give me the relaxation I'd need.

I walked to the window and stared out at the skiers enjoying a beautiful day on the slopes.

"It's a beautiful day for a wedding."

I turned toward the familiar voice. "Grandma."

The sight of my grandmother, dressed in a mauve lace overlay dress, her white hair perfectly curled, and her signature pink lipstick on her face, was the unexpected trigger for the anxiety inside me that had been building.

"You look so pretty, Grandma." I walked toward the tiny woman.

"Not as stunning as you, my dear." Grandma Rose reached

for my hands and squeezed. "You are the most beautiful bride I have ever seen. Truly."

"Thank you."

"But you don't look like the happiest one."

"Are you going to tell me I should be smiling?"

"Pfft. It's your day. You smile if you want to. You can do anything you want to today, Noa." She grew serious and looked me straight in the eye. "Anything," she repeated. "I hope you know that, Noa. Today should be about you. Whatever it is that you want. Not what anyone else wants. Do you understand?"

I nodded, although I wasn't sure I did. At least not completely. Did my grandma know the truth about me and Ryan?

Before I could let my thoughts travel any further down that path, Grandma Rose reached her hand out and dropped a thin necklace in my hand. "I don't know about the whole borrowed, new, blue, and old superstition, but I wanted you to have this."

I opened my hand to see what my grandmother had placed in it.

"Your grandfather gave it to me on our wedding day," she said.

I held up the familiar necklace. A dainty gold rose, on a delicate chain. My grandmother never took it off.

"I can't—"

"You can. I want you to have it, Noa. Every day wearing that rose reminded me of the love I had with Frank. Even after he was gone, I knew how deeply loved I was and always would be because of the way he loved me."

"So why give it to me, Grandma?"

She smiled softly. "As a reminder of the love that you deserve, my dear."

ASHER

"I wasn't sure I'd hear from you today," my baby sister said the moment she picked up the phone.

"Technically, you reached out to me."

She laughed before turning serious, matching my tone. "How are you doing, Asher?"

I looked from the window, back down to the countertop in front of me. "You want the truth?"

"Always."

"I'm pissed."

"I know."

I couldn't help but chuckle. "Then why did you ask?"

"I guess I was hoping you'd tell me you were excited."

We both knew that was never an option.

"Did you open the letter?" Kat asked before I could respond. "You're the first one who got their letter early, you know? Everyone else had to wait. I wish I could have my letter right now. That's the only part of all this that—"

"Wait. What?" I shook my head and tried to keep up with my sister's ramblings. "What letter?"

"Asher! The envelope Steven gave you last night right before you took off. It's a letter."

"A letter?"

I turned slowly in my small kitchen, as if the envelope would appear. I'd forgotten all about it and only now had a vague recollection of my father's assistant handing me a manila envelope after he and the lawyer finished telling me I'd basically have to leave my life for the next six months.

In my ear, my sister was still going on and on about how could I have possibly forgotten to open such an important letter while I moved through my suite to where I'd hung my jacket the night before.

"I had a few other things on my mind, Kat."

Like a sexy woman in the elevator.

I was pretty sure my little sister would not consider that a reasonable excuse for forgetting a detail such as a mysterious envelope under such circumstances. It wasn't normal for me to forget such details. Then again, Noa wasn't a normal woman.

Just thinking about the curvy blonde with the luscious lips and the way she'd lit me up the night before filled me with regret that our night had ended early and rather abruptly. Based on the way she'd been kissing me, I'd been so sure the evening was going to end very differently.

Then again, I'd been wrong before. Even if it didn't happen very often. Still, maybe she was still in the hotel and I could—

"Asher?" Kat's voice snapped me back into the present. "I thought maybe you hung up on me. What the hell is going on over there?"

"Sorry." I scrubbed a hand over my face. "I got distracted."

"From this? Seriously. What else could be more important right now?"

I didn't bother answering her, but went directly for the closet, found the jacket I'd worn the night before, and pulled out the envelope I'd folded and stuffed into my inside pocket. "Got it."

"What does it—"

"Give me a second." I shook my head with a chuckle and slid my finger under the flap of the envelope.

"I'm so jealous you got your letter already," Kat continued to ramble. "All I want is to hear from him, and of course I'm last. I can't believe you aren't even the least bit curious."

"It's not that I'm..." I didn't bother finishing the thought. Truthfully, since hearing my terms the night before, I didn't give a fuck what my father had written about it all, because there wasn't anything he could say that would justify the move he'd pulled off from the grave.

I put the call on speaker and set my phone on the counter as I dumped the contents of the envelope next to it. "Just let me…"

"What is it? What does it say? I mean, you don't have to tell me. I just—"

"It's…" I picked up the piece of paper that was quite obviously a copy of a property deed with my name on it for an address I wasn't familiar with.

"What, Asher? What is it? Did you get your letter already?"

I ignored my sister and picked up the single key, unremarkable in every way besides the fact it was included in the envelope.

"Asher? Hello!"

"I don't…" Distracted, I typed the address for the property into my phone and my map app dropped a pin in what looked to be a rural area off a forestry service road just out of town. "I don't really know what it is," I answered truthfully. "But I guess I'm going to find out."

NOA

I could hear the soft piano strains of an Ed Sheeran song as I made my way down the hall to the top of the stairs that would lead outside to the ceremony site.

I peeked out the window to look out to the ceremony site down below that the mothers had selected. I had to admit, it was gorgeous.

The lodge itself was a massive log building with a river rock fireplace as the centerpiece of the grand lobby; it sat at the base of the ski hill. The decks and rock patios behind the lodge were surrounded by towering pines and larches that turned bright orange in the fall. The creek ran through the property, spilling into a small but picturesque waterfall, right next to the lower patio.

Benches with cozy blankets had been set up facing the now-frozen waterfall, where a large wooden arch, covered in pine boughs and holly berries, had been placed for the ceremony.

At the end of the aisle, the sign declaring **"Alessandra & Ryan Forever"** sat. My mother had insisted on using my legal name for the wedding despite the fact that I hated it. *One day you might want to go by your legal name,* she'd given as a reason. As if there was even the slightest chance of that. Or that it mattered at all.

It wasn't the big, over-the-top wedding Tom and Olivia had wanted, but there were at least seventy to eighty people out there.

So many people to bear witness to my union.

My mistake.

But it couldn't really be a mistake when I knew exactly what I was doing. It's not as if I were under any illusion that marrying Ryan was going to be something it wasn't. It was for our families. Our future. It wouldn't be awful. It wasn't like I was being forced into an arranged situation or anything like that. Ryan was a good guy. A great guy.

And it wasn't as if I were in love with anyone else. Or was ever likely to be. It had never been my dream to be tied down to a husband. I didn't believe in the whole idea of love. Not really.

So why was I hesitating?

My nerves didn't make sense. We'd talked out all the details. Together, we'd gone over the pros and cons of our arrangement and every time, both Ryan and I came out well on the side of the pros. We were going to work together, one day take over our fathers' law firm, travel together, and build a life that would be enviable by anyone.

Except me.

I slipped the faux fur stole from my shoulders and dropped it on a nearby chair. I was overheating and needed some fresh air, but the only nearby exit was the doorway that would lead to the very event that was giving me the anxiety-induced hot flash.

Instead, I walked slowly down the hallway in the opposite direction and inhaled deeply. My hand moved to my neck and the rose necklace my grandma had given me.

A reminder of the love you deserve, she'd said.

But what did that even mean?

I had no idea what kind of love I deserved. Was it different from the love I had for Ryan? I'd never even been in love. Let alone any kind of deep, connected love like my grandparents had experienced.

I blew out a breath, straightened my shoulders, and went back to the window. I was running out of time.

Ryan and his father, who was acting as his witness, had just walked up the aisle. That meant that our mothers would go next, and my dad would be waiting for me to walk down the stone steps to my new husband.

Husband.

The word caused my stomach to turn.

Even when I was a little girl, I'd never dreamed about a wedding with the big white dress and the multi-tiered cake—as delicious as it had been. A smile played at my lips as I remembered how Asher had sliced into the beautiful cake, ruining it completely, before feeding it to me.

My breath quickened and a warm flush that had nothing to do with my nerves about the wedding washed over me.

Again, my fingers went to the necklace.

Right then, Ryan looked up to the window and locked eyes with me. He grinned broadly and winked.

The smile fell from my face, and I spun away from the window.

I loved Ryan.

I could have a good life with him.

The love you deserve.

I shook my head in an effort to get Grandma Rose's voice out of my head. I squeezed my eyes shut but instantly snapped them open again when Asher's face and the memory of his lips on mine flooded my senses.

"Dammit."

I needed air.

Now.

Without another look back, I lifted my skirts and moved as quickly as I could down the giant wooden staircase into the bustle of the busy lobby. I stood for a moment and looked around, unsure of what to do next.

"Congratulations."

"You look beautiful."

"Look at the bride."

Voices were all around me. I could feel eyes on me, watching and wondering why a bride was in the lobby by herself when the wedding was set up out back.

Air.

I'd be able to think straight once I got some fresh air. With my skirts still gathered in my arms, I moved quickly to the front doors, where the bellman held them open for me with a curious glance.

The moment the cold December air hit my flushed skin, I sucked in a sharp breath. But it wasn't enough.

"Miss? Are you all right?" The bellboy's brows knitted together. "Can I get you anything? I think the wedding is—"

"Thank you. I'm fine. Just getting a little air." I forced a smile to my face and shook my head. "It was just so hot in there."

I pressed a hand to my chest in an effort to slow my still-racing heart and turned away. Behind me, the doors opened again, and I was sure I heard my father's voice call my name.

It was at that moment I knew.

I wasn't just getting some air. I wasn't fine. And there was no way in hell I could marry Ryan Little.

Without looking back, or even knowing where I was going, I once more gathered the fabric of my huge dress and took off as fast as I could safely go down the stone steps. I had no idea where I was going. It didn't matter. As long as it was far away from the wedding and my family. The only thing worse than running out on my own wedding would be trying to explain everything to my parents.

I could not bear to see their faces when I—

"Watch out!" the bellboy yelled as a horn blasted.

I froze in place as a pickup truck skidded on the ice in front of me. It came to a stop only inches before hitting me, and my eyes locked with the driver's.

Asher.

My brain computed who I was staring at, only seconds after my body did.

"Noa!"

I turned to see my father, looking equal parts handsome in his suit and worried as he stared down at his daughter in the middle of the hotel driveway in a wedding dress when he should be walking me down the aisle.

The driver's side door of the truck opened, and Asher began to climb out of the truck.

There was only one thing to do.

I moved quickly, slipping on the ice in my heels as I moved to the passenger side door of the truck and hauled it open.

"Noa? What are you—"

"Drive." In a pile of satin and tulle, I managed to wrestle myself up into the cab of the old truck. "Please, Asher." My eyes locked on his. "Drive."

I didn't have to ask again.

He slid back behind the steering wheel, and with a spray of snow and ice, peeled out of the drive and away from my wedding.

Chapter Six

ASHER

IT WAS ONLY ONCE I had swerved around a group of skiers in the parking lot, and made it safely out onto the main road, that I stopped to think about what exactly was going on, or what I was doing. It took about five seconds for me to realize that I had no freaking clue, on both counts.

"Noa?"

I glanced to the passenger seat to see the woman I'd been hot and heavy with less than twenty-four hours ago, wearing a goddamned wedding dress, on her knees, peering out the back window of the truck.

To say I had questions would be a massive understatement.

"What the—"

"I don't think they're following us."

She spun around and dropped into the passenger seat in a cloud of white fabric. *Bridal white.*

"Who?" I shook my head to make sense out of something. "Who would be following us? And why the hell are you dressed like that?"

"My dad." She brushed her hair back off her bare shoulders. "Ryan. I don't—"

"Who's Ryan?"

The dots were connecting pretty quickly, and I was afraid I already knew the answer. After all, the stupid sign had been on display in the lobby for the better part of the last week.

Alessandra and Ryan Forever.

Before she could answer, I fired a new question at her. "Is he the groom?"

Noa nodded.

"And that would make you…" I didn't bother finishing the sentence, because the answer was more than obvious.

"The bride."

"Yeah." I clenched my teeth together. "I got that. But what I don't get is…well, fuck, Noa. Is that even your name? Or should I call you Alessandra?"

She looked confused. "How would you—"

"The sign."

"Oh."

"Yeah, oh. It's kind of been all any of my staff has been talking about for weeks."

"Your staff?" She turned in her seat. "Who exactly are *you?*"

Oh, hell no. There was no way I was going to let her distract me with questions about myself. Not until she explained a few things. Starting with her name, the dress, and the fact that she was now riding shotgun in *my* truck when she was supposed to be saying her vows to some other man.

"I think it's fair that I ask the questions for now, don't you?"

She blew out a breath and crossed her arms but didn't argue. "Go ahead."

"Let's start with your name."

"My full name is Alessandra Briggs."

The bride.

"I've always gone by Noa. I hate my full name, but my mom insisted on using it for the wedding."

"That brings me to my next question." I steered the truck off onto a side road and put it in park so I could give her my full attention. "What the actual fuck, Noa?"

It might have been funny, if the situation wasn't so completely screwed up.

"I know this all seems a little…" She waved her hand in the space between us; a giant diamond flashed in the sun.

My eyes locked first on the ring and then back to her beautiful, and completely distressed, face.

She saw immediately where I was looking and covered the ring with her other hand. "I don't usually wear it."

"Obviously."

I shook my head and looked out the window at the snow-covered trees. It wasn't something I was proud of, but I'd definitely been with women before who probably wouldn't be considered available. But never before had I hooked up—or almost hooked up—with a woman the night before her wedding. That was a whole new level. And it wasn't one I'd ever sunk to.

Until now, apparently.

Shit.

"Asher, you should know—"

"That you were just trying to get something out of your system before you tied the knot?" I spat out the words and instantly regretted it when I saw the hurt on her face.

"That's not what it was, Asher. It's complicated."

"I bet it is."

I couldn't help it. I was pissed. And I had every reason to be. I dropped my head into my hands and pinched the bridge of my nose. "As if this day couldn't get any worse. Fuck."

"I wasn't trying to—"

"Well, you did. The biggest event of the year for the

Lodge, and I'm sitting here with the star of that particular show. I'm pretty sure when Mommy and Daddy wrote the check, they didn't think the events would play out quite like this."

"That's what you're worried about?" She crossed her arms over her chest, an act of defiance that pressed her full tits up to the point that they almost spilled out of her low-cut *wedding gown*.

A low groan, one I hoped she hadn't heard, slipped from my throat, and I forced myself to look away again. "Fuck, yes. That's what I'm worried about. How do you think it looks to have the bride run off with the person who's in charge of her wedding being the most spectacular day anyone has ever seen?"

"In charge?"

I ignored her question. "Do you have any idea the damage control I'm going to have to…" I realized that *I* wasn't going to have to do any damage control because in a few hours, I would officially be on leave from my duties. Which meant that the fallout from Noa's runaway stunt wouldn't be my issue to deal with at all.

I let that thought settle in for a moment and dropped my head back against the headrest of the old truck.

"I'm sorry, Asher. I didn't mean to drag you into anything. This is my mess, and I'll sort it out. I just couldn't be there. I couldn't…I couldn't do it."

Her voice shook and, just like that, any anger I felt toward her dissolved. I put a hand on her bare arm. "You're freezing." It was only then that I realized she wasn't wearing a coat, or a wrap or any of the fancy things that brides usually wore over their gowns to stay warm. "Hold on."

I reached behind the seats where I'd stashed my duffel bag and a few supplies I'd grabbed from the activity room before I'd left. I pulled out a thick flannel jacket.

Noa leaned forward so I could wrap the red and black plaid coat around her shoulders.

"Thank you."

I muttered a "You're welcome," and put the truck into drive once more before slamming the gear shift back into park. I turned toward my runaway bride again. "Where are you going? I can drop you off—"

"Where are you—"

"Oh no." I pressed my lips together. "You are *not* coming with me."

The last thing I needed was Noa, or Alessandra or whatever the hell her name was, hitching a ride with me while I went to—well, truthfully, I had no idea where exactly I was going. It was a pin dropped onto the app on my phone. All I knew was wherever it was I was headed, apparently, it was mine and it might have to be home for the next six months. The last thing I needed was a stowaway with me.

Even if she was sexy as hell, even dressed in that ridiculous white dress. Despite myself, the outfit—or, more likely, the woman wearing it—was doing something for me.

My cock twitched in my jeans, and I quickly looked away.

Things were messed up enough as it was. The last thing I needed was to complicate them any further.

Noa turned and looked behind my seat. "Are you going camping?"

"In December?" I raised an eyebrow. "Hardly. I'm going…" I trailed off. "You're not coming."

"Asher."

"No."

"Fine."

Before I had the chance to put the truck in reverse and take her right back where she'd come from, the damn woman had popped open the passenger door and hopped out into the snow.

"What the actual—"

NOA

"What are you doing?"

He called after me, but I didn't turn around. It took all my focus to keep from slipping on the snowy, icy side road Asher had pulled onto wearing my stupid stiletto heels that were even more uncomfortable than they looked.

I hadn't thought about what I was going to do, or the fact that the snow might be too deep to walk in. Or that there would be any snow at all, really. I hadn't actually given it any thought at all, which seemed to be the theme for the day.

My stockinged feet froze almost instantly in my completely impractical heels, but I had no choice. I would not go back. I *could* not.

"Noa! Dammit, woman!"

I ignored him and pressed on. But a split second later, my foot shot out from under me as I slipped on some ice.

"Oh—"

"I got you."

Strong hands caught me moments before I landed on my back in the snow. Asher put me back on my feet but didn't take his hand off my arm.

"I'm fine." I set my jaw.

"You are most certainly *not* fine."

I turned to glare at him, but the moment my eyes locked with his, desire flared through me. And it didn't help my situation that his hand was still wrapped around my bare arm, sending all kinds of heat through my body with the simple touch. "Asher."

"Where do you think you're going to go?" He tipped his

head and didn't bother hiding the smirk on his face. "Do you even know where this road leads?"

I inhaled sharply and straightened my shoulders. "If you're not going to help me, I'll find someone who will."

"You're going to freeze to death."

He had a full-on grin now, and although he was really starting to piss me off, the urge to throw myself into his arms and kiss the cocky smile off his face began to consume me.

Focus, Noa.

"I'm fine."

"You are literally shivering."

He took his time raking his gaze up and down my body, which only made me shiver more despite the flannel that was still draped over my shoulders.

"How do you feel about frostbite on your toes?"

"I'm only going to freeze to death if you don't let me—" I moved to yank my arm from his grasp, but the moment I was free, he scooped me up in his arms, so quickly I didn't realize what was happening until I was upside down, draped over his shoulder.

"Put me down." I pounded my fists on his back and wriggled in his grip, but Asher clamped a hand down on my ass and pressed me into his back, holding me in place.

I needed to be thinking of escape, whatever that might look like, but pressed up against his hard body, I could only think of one thing...and it had nothing to do with getting away from the big man with the very large, very warm hands.

"I'm not going to let you freeze to death out here." He opened the passenger door of the truck and deposited me and my massive dress unceremoniously into the seat.

My cheeks blazed with a mixture of humiliation and desire as I looked up at him. "You are not taking me back there."

"Fine." He scratched his fingers roughly through the scruff on his chin. "Just don't get out of the truck, got it?"

I crossed my arms and nodded once before facing forward.

"You're a pain in the ass, you know?" He shook his head a moment later as he returned to his seat behind the wheel.

Without asking, he cranked up the heat and a moment later, the cab of the truck filled with warmth. I desperately wanted to reach down and pull my feet up to warm them between my hands, but I wouldn't give him the satisfaction of knowing how cold they really were. That, and I wasn't sure I'd be able to reach them through the ludicrous amount of dress between me and my feet.

We sat in silence while Asher put the truck in reverse and backed out onto the main road. I held my breath until he turned in the opposite direction of the hotel.

"Where are we going?"

He handed me his phone, open to the map app. "Here. You tell me."

I looked from him to the phone in my hand. I waited a beat for him to elaborate. He didn't.

We drove in silence, with the exception of me relaying the instructions from the map. I wasn't a stranger to snowy roads, but as a city girl, I didn't spend much time, if any, on the backroads in the mountains.

More than a few times, I would have been frightened if I'd been behind the wheel, but Asher obviously knew what he was doing and less than thirty minutes later, we pulled up in front of a snow-covered cabin tucked into the forest.

"Where are we?" I handed him his phone back.

"Got me." He shrugged and turned the truck off. "Stay here for a second."

Without waiting for a response, Asher shut the door behind him and picked his way through the snow to the front door.

A million questions flashed through my head, but I was aware that I wasn't in any position to be asking much of him. Not after he'd finally agreed not to take me back to my wedding. I was also painfully aware that I hadn't given Asher much of an explanation for the night before, either. Or anything, really.

I watched while he pulled a key from his pocket and wrestled with the door for a moment before pushing it open. He disappeared inside, but a second later, reappeared and made his way back through the snow to the truck.

"Are you going to tell me where we are?" I asked the moment he opened my truck door.

"I told you, I don't know."

"Should I be worried that you're going to kidnap me, have your way with me, and leave me for dead?"

"Looks like the ship has sailed on the kidnap thing, intentional or not." He stopped and gave me a wry look. "As for leaving you for dead, if I wanted to do that, you'd currently be a bridal popsicle on that forestry road back there."

It probably would have been a wiser decision to keep my mouth shut, given the situation I was currently in, but I couldn't help but notice he hadn't addressed the third part of my question. "So you do plan on having your way with me?" I winked, feeling bold now that I wasn't at risk of being delivered back into my fiancé's waiting arms.

Asher's nostrils flared, and he sucked in a breath. A sound that may have been a low growl slipped from his throat a moment before he reached into the truck and once more lifted me into his arms.

"I can walk."

"The hell you can."

I half expected him to flip me over his shoulder again. A move I wouldn't object to, despite my previous reaction. Something about the way he manhandled me was doing all kinds of things to my insides.

This time, Asher cradled me in his arms, pressed up against his hard chest. He carried me as if I didn't weigh anything at all, despite the fact that my dress alone was probably twenty pounds.

He picked his way through the snow to the front door of the cabin and across the threshold inside, where he finally set me on my still frozen feet.

"Did you just carry me across—"

"Not a word." He spun around and held up a finger.

Again, his nostrils flared and this time his pupils were blown, clouding his eyes with desire that I could recognize even in the dim light. His gaze traveled down my body. I knew he couldn't see my feet and that even if he could, he wouldn't be able to tell just by looking at them that I couldn't feel my toes.

Still, he shook his head and muttered, "Fuck. You need to warm up."

He moved across the room, to the built-in rock fireplace on the far wall. There was a stack of wood piled next to it, along with a lighter and a bucket of kindling.

"I hope like hell this chimney isn't blocked." Asher knelt on the wood floor in front of the fireplace and got to work while I stood there, just inside the door, feeling useless and, all of a sudden, more than a little self-conscious.

Doubt flooded through me.

What was I doing?

At this moment, I should be raising a glass of champagne to a toast with my new husband.

Husband.

The word caused a visceral reaction in my body and served as a perfect reminder of exactly what it was I was doing.

"Noa?"

"Sorry, what?" I focused on Asher, who had a flicker of a flame started in the hearth.

"Come sit on the couch here and warm up."

"Right." I nodded and tried to do as I was told, but with the first step I took, I stumbled; my ankle turned on the high heel and I almost fell to the floor. But somehow, Asher was right there to catch me. Again.

"Whoa." His arm wrapped around my waist, and I had to resist the urge to lean into his warmth.

"I'm fine." I tried to take another step and faltered again.

"I get it, Noa. You're stubborn." Once more, he swept me up in his arms.

It was starting to become a habit, and I was not used to being rescued in any way by any man. To my surprise, I didn't hate it.

Asher set me down gently on the couch before pulling it closer to the fireplace. The fire had begun to catch, and the warmth I felt from it was immediate. He grabbed a wool blanket from somewhere and dropped it over my lap before sliding onto the couch next to me.

Without a word, he lifted my feet into his lap and, with gentle hands, undid the tiny clasps of my shoes. "Holy shit, woman. Your feet are ice cubes."

"I don't actually feel them anymore."

He shot me a look of concern. "Why didn't you say something?"

It didn't feel like a question that needed an answer, so I simply watched as Asher wrapped his big hands around my feet. It wasn't long before I started to feel the warmth from him seep into my frozen toes, followed by painful tingling.

"Dammit, woman. You could have gotten frostbite." His words were sharp. But his eyes were full of worry. "What were you thinking?"

ASHER

I expected her to fire back with another quick retort. I was very quickly getting the impression that she was the type of woman who wouldn't back down easily. That was evident from the fact that I had to haul her out of the snow and into the truck before she froze to death just to prove her point.

Stubborn. She was also very stubborn.

And dammit if both of those traits didn't make her look even hotter in my eyes. I had spent my entire adult life actively avoiding anything that would even vaguely resemble a relationship, so it had never been important to consider a woman's qualities beyond the incredibly superficial. Until very recently.

"I was thinking that I would rather lose a toe, or ten, than get married today."

I sat back, her feet still in my hands, and assessed my runaway bride. "You're going to have to help me out," I said after a moment. "I brought you here because the alternative was that you freeze to death. But I still deserve some answers about the crime I just became complicit in."

She tilted her head and rolled her eyes a little. "Crime? Driving me out to…wherever the hell we are is hardly a crime." She glanced around the small room and back at me. "Where are we, exactly?"

Noa had provided an interesting and somewhat entertaining, if not frustrating distraction, and I hadn't had much time to actually check out my new home. I took a moment to scan the small, sparsely furnished room.

There wasn't much to it. The cabin looked old but well made. It had obviously been cared for, judging by the condition of the fireplace and chimney. As well as the well-stocked wood supply stacked neatly beside it.

The couch was old but clean. Just like the rest of the room. *My* room.

I finished my quick survey of the room and looked at Noa with a grin and a shrug. "This is my house."

"You don't sound so sure."

"It's a long story."

"I have time."

"Oh?" I pretended to look shocked. "You have questions for me?"

"Okay, okay."

She tried to tug her feet away, but I held them firm. Maybe they weren't frozen solid anymore, but they still needed warming. Besides, I liked touching her. And for the life of me, I couldn't think of any other reasonably appropriate way to do it. After all, she was betrothed to another man.

"That's fair." Noa glanced down at my hands on her feet but didn't try to move them again. "How about this? For every question you ask me, I ask you one."

I didn't know about fair. After all, I wasn't the one who had just taken off moments before exchanging vows with someone else. Never mind the way she'd been kissing me the night before. I could still taste her on my lips.

Dammit. No.

I forced myself to think about anything else besides the soft give of her mouth on mine and the small little noises she made when I—

"I'll go first." I cleared my throat. "Why the hell did you run out on your wedding?"

She shot me a look. "That's a pretty big question."

"That's why I asked it."

"I told you." She looked to the fire as a piece of wood crackled. "I couldn't marry him."

"Right." I drew out the word. "But he wasn't abusive and

really, he's a great guy." I paraphrased what she'd told me in the truck. Not that it clarified anything.

"He's my best friend."

I had no right to the feeling, but her words stung.

"Isn't that usually a good thing? I thought that was a whole thing?" I tried to shrug off the cloud of jealousy for this man I'd never met who knew this woman well enough to be considered her best friend. "I thought women wanted to marry their best friend?"

"Not this woman."

She fixed her beautiful brown eyes on me and for the first time, I realized she wasn't sad.

"Shouldn't you be crying?"

Her head tipped back, exposing a length of creamy white, and very kissable, neck. "Why should I be crying?"

"Because…" I waved one hand in the air futilely. "You just ended your relationship? Well, I assume you ended it."

"I did."

The two simple words sent a flash of satisfaction through me. I forced myself to ignore it.

"So, if you just ended your relationship," I continued. "A relationship I'd say was pretty serious." I gestured toward her huge dress that was bunched up around her waist and only half covered by the woolen blanket. "Shouldn't you be sad about that? I mean, I'm not an expert in serious relationships, and I really know nothing about how marriage is supposed to work. You know, except for the whole, walking down the aisle, declaring love for each other, and then living happily ever after."

She looked away, clearly trying not to smile. "I agree, that's how marriage works. But as I told you, I didn't want to marry Ryan. So, no. I'm not sad about it, and I'm definitely not going to cry about it. I don't cry."

I wasn't sure I believed that, but there didn't seem any

point to argue it with her. "So are you going to tell me *why* you didn't want to marry him?"

Noa shifted on the couch so she sat up straight. "It's my turn to ask a question. You've asked way more than one."

"You didn't answer it."

"I did, too. Maybe you should ask better questions."

She winked at me, and the grin she'd been trying to hide flashed in my direction, sending a hot shot of desire directly to my groin.

I groaned. I knew when I'd been beaten.

"Tell me the story about the house. You obviously have never been here before. Why? Why today?"

"That's more than one question."

She shot me a look, and I ran a hand over my face.

"Fine. But let me put some more wood on the fire first. You're still shivering."

Chapter Seven

NOA

WITH THE FIRE ROARING, the wool blanket, and Asher's hands holding my feet long after they'd thawed out, I started to warm up halfway through his story about the cabin.

When I'd met him the day before, I had assumed he was a manager of some sort. Especially considering he'd walked through the kitchen like he owned it.

Which, apparently, he did.

"So, you actually run the whole thing? The ski hill and the hotel and—"

"Technically, I don't run it. I'm acting CEO." He turned away and stared into the fire. "Correction. I used to run it."

"It sounds like a little break might be kind of nice, and you have this cabin to hang out in."

"I never said I wanted a break, Noa. I love what I do. Work is my life. He knew that."

I could hear the hurt he was trying to hide laced through his words. I sat up so I could reach for him, but he turned to face me before I could, the mischievous grin back on his face.

"Your turn."

"My turn?" I sat back and wiggled my toes, which were still in his lap. He'd gone from warming my feet to slowly, absent-mindedly tracing a finger along my arches. It was a good thing I wasn't ticklish.

"Your turn for a question." His fingers slid higher up my stockinged foot. "That's how this game goes."

"I didn't realize we were playing a game."

His gaze locked on mine. "Didn't you?"

I swallowed hard. It was easy to be comfortable with him. And flirty. Despite the circumstances. Because something about this man made me feel things—made me feel like I was balancing on a precarious edge and could tumble at any moment.

Without waiting for my response, Asher asked his next question. "Why did you kiss me last night?"

He held my gaze with an intensity that reminded me exactly why I kissed him the night before.

I shifted on the couch and decided to go with complete honesty. It wasn't as though I had anything to lose. "Because I think you're sexy as hell."

"You do, do you?" The corner of his mouth curled up.

"You know I do."

He chuckled and his fingers traveled a little higher up my foot to my ankle. "But that still doesn't answer my question. Why the night before your wedding? It doesn't seem like something a bride should do."

I groaned and attempted to pull my legs away, but Asher tightened his grip.

"I've already tried to explain this to you. I didn't *want* to marry Ryan. In fact, I'm getting really sick of that word." I held my fingers up in air quotes. "I *should* do a lot of things. I should go to law school. I should work at the family firm. I should get married."

"Oh, so your marriage was arranged?"

"Not at all." I tried to pull my hair back in a ponytail and caught my fingers on the veil that was still fastened to the back of my head. With a groan of frustration, I dropped my hands back into my lap. "It's complicated. Our families have been friends for years. Like, really close friends. I grew up with Ryan and—" I stopped myself. I didn't want to talk about my brother and Olivia. Not today. "Like I said, it's complicated, and getting married just felt like the thing we *should* do."

"So you don't love him?"

Of course I loved Ryan. I inhaled slowly and my fingers drifted to the rose necklace.

"It's complicated."

I nodded. "I'll always love Ryan. But, not in the way you should when you get married." I laughed at myself. "There's that word again. Truthfully, I never wanted to get married. I never saw myself as a bride."

"You make a fucking gorgeous bride."

The compliment was delivered with such sincerity that it took me off guard. "You think so?"

"I'll be honest." Asher shrugged, and his fingers stilled on my feet. "Brides aren't really my type, but you make a very sexy one."

I laughed. "I'm not a bride."

He raised an eyebrow and used his head to gesture to the piles of satin and tule peeking out from under the blankets. "You sure look like one."

Maybe it was the heat in the room, or more likely, in Asher's gaze as he looked at me, but I grew suddenly and completely uncomfortable in the massive dress. I shrugged the flannel I was still wearing off my shoulders, and before he could stop me, pulled my feet from his grip and stood, shaking the blanket from my lap as I did so. "Maybe you could help me change that?"

I spun so my back was facing Asher.

"You want me to take your dress off?"

I looked over my shoulder at him. "Well, I can't do it myself. And I don't know if you noticed, but it's not really very practical clothing for a cabin in the middle of nowhere." When he didn't move, I groaned and twisted my arms around my back in an effort to reach the approximately eight million tiny buttons that held me prisoner.

"What are you doing?"

"I told you, I'm taking this dress off. It's incredibly uncomfortable. Not to mention heavy." I twisted and turned while I spoke. "Whoever came up with the idea of wedding gowns should be—"

"Given a medal."

His voice was laced with desire, and when I stopped what I was doing and turned to look at Asher, he wasn't even bothering to hide the look in his eyes.

"No," I said simply. "Now, are you going to help me with this, or just stand there gawking all night?"

ASHER

I stroked my scruff of a beard and considered my options. Either way, she was determined to take her dress off. If she continued her attempts to do it on her own, it looked as if she might put her back out or pull a muscle.

I stepped forward.

Noa turned away, presenting her back and a ridiculous number of tiny buttons.

I meant what I said. The designer of this dress had obviously understood the assignment. Noa was friggin' stunning.

The right combination of classy and devastatingly sexy. Her groom was a damn lucky man.

No.

I corrected myself. It was I who was the lucky man because, for reasons I still couldn't understand, it wasn't her groom helping Noa out of her dress, but me.

Oh yes, I was definitely the lucky one.

I let my fingertips skim her bare shoulders and slid the veil to the side. She shivered under my touch; was that a little gasp I heard?

Damn.

There were a million reasons I should turn and walk away before things went any further. Or at most, help her out of her dress and retreat to the opposite side of the room. What I most definitely should not be doing was entertaining any thoughts at all of what was under the dress. Or the kiss we'd shared the night before and what could have happened between us.

No. I shouldn't be inhaling her sweet scent and wondering about how she would taste, or the sounds she would make when I laid her down on the couch and buried my head between her legs.

No.

That would be inappropriate.

Just like it probably wasn't a good idea to trail my fingers slowly down her back to the first button. Noa didn't speak, but her breath came a little faster while she waited for me to slip the satin button through the tiny hole and move on to the next one.

I took my time, enjoying every second of the process. Between buttons, I let my fingers travel over her heated skin, enjoying the little gasp and intake of breath she took every time.

When the dress started to loosen, her arms went up to hold the front in place.

"Still a few more to go." I continued to work methodically. One button at a time. "There really are a lot of buttons—"

The words died on my lips as I exposed her undergarments. For whatever reason, I hadn't considered what Noa might be wearing under the gown. But the moment my fingers came in contact with a lacy bustier, my cock thickened in my pants to the point of pain and a groan slipped from deep in my throat before I could stop it.

"Fuck, Noa."

"What?" Her voice was laced with innocence, which I knew was bullshit.

This woman knew exactly what she was doing to me.

I swallowed hard and let my hands slide under the fabric of her gown to span over her rib cage as I slowly moved them down to her hips, where I rested for a moment.

Her body quivered, but she worked hard to hold herself in check.

I leaned forward. I held my body mere inches from her heated skin and whispered in her ear. "Just a few more."

Fuck. Her scent filled my senses until I couldn't think straight. The urge to kiss her, to taste her surged through me with an intensity that was difficult to control.

Somehow, I managed to put my hands on the buttons once more and finish my task of undoing the dress. "There you go."

Reluctantly, I moved back, giving her space to step from the dress.

Noa didn't turn as she released her hold on the dress and let the fabric pool around her feet. But I wasn't looking at the floor. My eyes were locked onto the vision in front of me.

If I thought Noa was sexy in the dress, out of it, she was a goddamn miracle of nature.

The white lace bustier hugged her curves and nipped in at her waist before flaring out over her hips to showcase two perfectly round, luscious, and very bare ass cheeks.

I sucked in a breath and let my eyes travel down the length of her legs and the garters holding up the scraps of stockings I'd let my fingers slide over earlier.

"That's so much better." Noa breathed out a sigh and shook her hair out. The veil, still fastened to the back of her head, fluttered into place, covering my view with a sheer curtain.

"It *really* is better."

She turned to face me.

I ran my hands through my hair and let out a low whistle. "I feel sorry for the poor bastard you left at the altar, Noa. Because…" I shook my head instead of finishing the thought.

"Trust me," she said with a little frown. "He wouldn't have cared."

"What?" My feet moved involuntarily toward her as if she were a magnet with a powerful pull I was too weak to deny. "Is he not into women?"

"Oh no." She lifted her arms to reach for the veil behind her head. The action made her breasts strain in their confinement, giving me a delicious view of her cleavage. "Ryan's very much into women," Noa continued. "Just not me. I told you, it's—"

"Complicated," I finished for her. "Yeah. You've mentioned it. But I'll tell you what's not complicated."

She dropped her arms by her side, the veil now in her hand. "What's that?"

As if she didn't know.

"What I'm feeling right now."

It was a lie. The feelings slamming through my body and brain were very, *very* complicated.

She was someone else's bride who I'd all but kidnapped and brought to a deserted cabin in the middle of nowhere on a night when all I'd planned to do was drink too much whiskey and forget about my problems for a minute.

Complicated didn't even begin to describe things.

Still, I moved closer to her until I stood only inches away. My eyes locked on the lips I'd very much enjoyed kissing less than twenty-four hours ago.

"And what are you feeling?" Her voice was all but a whisper.

I brushed a lock of hair from her cheek and tilted her chin up so she was looking at me. "I'm feeling like I'd very much like to kiss you right now."

A *kiss*. That was it. I could leave it at that. Hell. I *would* leave it at that. No matter how badly I wanted this woman, I needed to remember she'd only hours ago left a man standing at the altar. There would be feelings mixed up in that, and I didn't do feelings. Not of any kind. Not when it came to women.

"Then what exactly have you been waiting for?"

NOA

I thought he might never kiss me. That maybe the stupid white dress had been a turn-off after all. But the moment his lips pressed to mine, all such thoughts vanished.

He kissed me as if he needed me to breathe.

I had never been kissed with such need, such desire.

His hands slid down my sides, his fingers spanning over my lace-clad rib cage. I'd forgotten I was wearing the sexy lingerie until Asher had started the torturous process of undoing the tiny buttons.

His reaction had been worth every moment of wearing the tight-fitting bustier under the dress. And I hadn't been lying when I told Asher that Ryan wouldn't even have noticed. Not really. The most he might have done would be to tease

ELENA AITKEN

me about my choice of lingerie, akin to snapping my bra strap.

The one thing I knew for sure was that if things had played out the way they were *supposed* to on my wedding day, I would not be currently feeling like the sexiest woman alive.

And, oh shit, did I ever.

Asher nipped at my bottom lip as he pulled his mouth away. "Damn, Noa. I don't know why they say white is a pure color, because you are positively, fucking sinful in this outfit right now." He dropped his mouth to my neck and the sensitive spot right below my ear.

"Holy shit, Asher." My knees buckled, but his hand was right there cupping my ass, holding me in place as he took his time kissing, licking, and nibbling until his mouth hovered over the swell of my cleavage.

My eyes opened, and I looked down to see why he'd stopped when the very last thing I wanted was for him to stop. Ever.

A moan slipped from my lips, and I put my hands on either side of his face to drag his mouth back up to mine.

His hands were all over me, sliding down my side, squeezing my ass before again moving up my body, to where my breasts were only barely contained in the lace. With every breath, each one coming quicker and harder than the last, they heaved upward, threatening to spill from their captivity in the bustier altogether.

His fingers grazed each swell; his hand cupped my breast through the lace and he dragged his thumb roughly over my nipple, making me gasp. A flood of heat rushed between my legs.

When he dipped his head to my chest and used his teeth to tease my nipple into a hard nub of pulsing pleasure through the lace of the lingerie, I was sure I would explode.

My hands found the hem of his T-shirt, and I slipped my

hands under the fabric to feel his hot skin. My fingers clawed over the hard ridges of his chest as I tried to pull his shirt up and over his chest, but he twisted from my grasp and pulled my hand away, using my arm to spin me around. He pulled me roughly back so I was pressed against his chest.

I could feel his desire, long and hard, against my backside. I wiggled backward into him, grinding myself against his need.

"Careful, sweetheart. You don't want to start something you can't finish."

I tried to twist in his grasp to look at him, but he held me firm. "What makes you think I can't finish it? Because I assure you, I'm fully prepared to—"

My words were lost to a gasp as he nudged my legs apart and his free hand found the heat between my legs.

Need and lust swirled through me in waves so intense that I thought I might come with only a simple touch through the lace of my panties. But instead of giving me the pleasure my body craved, he stopped. His breath was hot on my neck, and I could feel his hard cock pulsing with a need of his own against my back.

I tried to jerk my hips, in an effort to urge him on and let him know how much I wanted him, but his arm around my waist held me tight.

"Asher?"

His grip on me relaxed enough for me to spin and press the front of my body against him. My mouth found his, and he returned the kiss with renewed fervor. His hands were big and strong, holding me tight against him.

"I need you," I said between kisses. It was an understatement, but for the life of me, I couldn't think of any other way to express how badly I needed this man to bend me over the couch and make me forget the bad decisions I'd almost made. "Please."

He jerked backward. This time he released me completely.

The cold air hit the heat of my body the moment he stepped away.

Asher stalked across the room to the farthest point away from me. He put his hands on his hips and faced the wall.

I watched, confused as he sucked in deep breaths.

"Asher? What—"

"It's late." He turned to face me; his handsome face was twisted in a mask of indecision and frustration. "If you won't let me take you back, then—"

"Back?" I shook my head. Back? After that kiss, that… everything? He thought I was going to let him take me back? "I thought we were past that. Way past that. I'm not going back, Asher."

"It's your wedding—"

"Don't." I held up a finger, and he wisely shut his mouth.

I had no idea what had caused the shift between us, but I didn't like it. Not at all.

He inhaled deeply. Even with the distance between us, I saw his nostrils flare and the catch of his breath when he looked at me. He moved across the floor, bent, and snatched up the flannel jacket I'd discarded earlier. Without even looking at me, he tossed it to me. "You need to put this on."

I caught it and held it against my body. "And why is that?"

Asher spun on his heel. His pupils were blown, and he swallowed hard. "Because if you don't," he said through clenched teeth, "I'm afraid I'll push you up against the wall and tear that sexy fucking lace off your body with my teeth before I sink myself so deeply inside you that we both see stars."

Fuck.

I swallowed hard, dropped the flannel, and stood up tall, thrusting my tits out toward him. "And?"

A low growl rumbled from deep in his chest. "Noa." My name was a warning. "The flannel."

My eyes defiant, I dared him to make good on his threat—or should I say, promise. I didn't move.

Instead, I tilted my head, just a little, and let my tongue slip between my lips to taste the deliciousness he'd left behind.

"Dammit."

He moved so fast, I didn't realize what was happening until his mouth crushed mine and he had me pushed up hard against the wall, his arm behind me, taking the brunt of the force. His kiss left no question that he would make good on his threat, and my body thrummed with delight.

His hands were everywhere, pulling, pinching, and driving me wild while his mouth worked mine. With his body pressed hard against mine, he pulled away from my mouth. "I won't do this, Noa. Not tonight."

I opened my mouth to protest, but he stopped me. "I meant what I said. Tonight was supposed to be your wedding night, and whether you think it means nothing or not, I won't be the guy who makes a hard situation even harder."

"What do you—"

"I want nothing more than to finish what we started here. And we will." He ran his thumb along my swollen bottom lip. "When you're ready."

"I *am* ready." In an effort to try to prove it, I thrust my hips up at him, grinding into his hard, thick cock. "I think that's clear."

"Not tonight, Noa." Somehow he managed to grab the discarded flannel and without hardly backing away from me, he pressed it against me. "The flannel. Or I take you back right now."

There was no mistaking the intention in his voice or the seriousness in his gaze.

"Fine." I took the jacket from him, and he backed away. For whatever reason, Asher felt he needed to be noble. But he truly didn't understand where I was coming from in this situation. Either way, it didn't matter. I quite clearly wasn't going to get what I wanted.

And if I wasn't going to get it, that meant he wasn't. And I had every intention of showing him exactly what he was missing.

I took my time putting the heavy jacket on. I pretended to drop it, and bent over slowly, putting my ass on full display as I retrieved it. Self-satisfaction flowed through me when he groaned. Good. Slowly, arm by arm, I slipped it over my shoulders and, leaving it unbuttoned, turned toward him.

"Happy?"

He ran a hand roughly over his face. "Not even one fucking bit."

ASHER

I was wired tighter than a set of guitar strings that were set to snap with the slightest wrong move. I needed to put as much distance as possible between myself and Noa. Just breathing the same air as her was turning out to be an excruciating test of will, and I wasn't sure how long I'd be able to hold out.

I'd left her in the living room by the fire to stay warm while I went to investigate the rest of the house.

The cabin was old and needed some TLC, but just like the living room that was ready to go with firewood, the rest of the house proved to be equally clean and prepared.

The kitchen was tucked into the back of the house with a table and chairs and well-stocked cabinets that held cooking supplies and a complete set of dishes.

There were some non-perishable groceries in the cupboards, and when I checked the expiration dates on a few cans, I was surprised to see that everything was current.

The freezer even held a section of frozen foods, which turned out to be a good thing considering my plan to stop at the grocery store before heading out to the cabin had been thwarted by my unexpected passenger.

There was basic electricity in the cabin, but so far, the only source of heat I'd been able to find was coming from the fireplace in the living room.

Just beyond the kitchen was a door that led to the bathroom. Indoor plumbing was also a welcome discovery.

I moved through another closed door and found a mostly empty room. There was a desk pushed up against a large window, a big trunk against another wall, and an overstuffed easy chair in the corner. Maybe it was used as an office of some kind?

I had so many questions about the cabin and although Noa's presence had been somewhat of a welcome distraction, I hadn't forgotten about my current situation. However, any further questions were going to have to wait for the light of day. It wasn't even very late, and I was exhausted.

The last door led to the bedroom. A double bed, neatly made with a plaid comforter, sat in the middle of the small room. There was a dresser, an empty wardrobe, and two small bedside tables. That was it.

One bed.

One. Small. Bed.

"Shit." It was going to be a long night, with my six-two frame folded onto that tiny sofa. I blew out a breath. I might as well get started and try to get some sleep.

I turned to return to the main room and ran directly into Noa.

Instinctively, I reached up and grabbed her by the arms to keep her at a distance, but it was too late. My body had already reacted to her touch, as slight as it was. My dick hardened, and I sucked in a breath.

"What are you—"

"Is this the bedroom?"

She slipped past me, rubbing her breasts against my back as she moved.

I hadn't figured her for a tease; then again, I hadn't figured myself as the type to turn down the sexiest woman alive, who was clearly as into me as I was into her.

"There's only one bed," I said when she moved into the room. "I'll take the couch."

She turned, her hands on her hips. Her eyes flashed with mischief. "You're going to sleep on the couch?" She raised an eyebrow. "Don't be stupid."

I shook my head. What would be stupid would be laying only inches away from her with the expectation that keeping my hands to myself wouldn't be torture.

"Okay." Noa blew out a breath and moved to shut the door. "Goodnight."

I stood, frozen in place for a few minutes after she'd disappeared behind the bedroom door. I rubbed a hand roughly over my face and finally exhaled.

More than once, I questioned myself and my decision not to follow her to bed. There had never before been a time, or more specifically, a woman who had me questioning myself the way Noa did.

And that was the most troubling thing.

Chapter Eight

NOA

TO MY SURPRISE, the stress of the day caught up with me, and I fell into a fast and hard sleep. I woke at some point in the night and it took me a moment to remember where I was. As soon as I did, I rolled over, half expecting that Asher would have joined me in the bed after all.

His nobility…stubbornness…or whatever the hell it had been the night before, when he'd walked away from me instead of taking me to bed and finishing what we'd started…had been beyond frustrating. Truthfully, if I considered it from his point of view, the whole runaway bride thing might be a little off-putting. And he didn't know that I didn't have that kind of relationship with Ryan. Hell, he was probably feeling relieved that we didn't go through with it, too.

I squeezed my eyes shut in an effort to block out thoughts of Ryan or my family. At least for a few more hours.

A groan, followed by a thud, came from the living room, so I threw back the blankets and went to investigate.

The fire had burned down to only a soft glow. I could make

out the sofa with the cushions in disarray, but Asher was nowhere to be seen.

Another groan alerted me to his presence. My eyes adjusted in the dim light and I saw his legs sticking out from the front of the sofa.

I stifled a giggle and walked closer until I found him, stretched out on the floor, his head awkwardly beneath the coffee table.

"Asher?"

He sat up with a start and slammed his head on the table. "Shit."

"Oh." I crouched next to him and slid the table over to free him. "What are you—"

"The couch was too short." He rubbed his head and sat up. "Flannel." He turned away.

I looked down and remembered I'd taken the bulky jacket off when I went to sleep. I was still wearing only my wedding night lingerie.

"Enough of this." I ignored his comment. "You can't sleep on the floor."

"I can't sleep with you." He rolled over and faced the fire.

"Suit yourself." I was way too tired to argue with him. Besides, he was a grown man. If he would rather sleep on the cold, dirty floor than next to me, I'd try not to be offended and leave him to his choices.

I was almost back to sleep when I felt the mattress sink with the weight of him climbing into the bed next to me.

My body tensed in anticipation of his touch, but he turned so his back was pointed toward me; a moment later, I heard the rhythmic sound of his breathing when he fell asleep.

ASHER

The lace was rough under my skin, but she was soft in all the right places as I let my hand travel over her curves. I had only a vague memory of waking in the night to see her sexy shape outlined by the glow of the fire, but that one look fueled my dreams.

I'd had enough of being the good guy. It was definitely not all it was cracked up to be.

My hand slipped lower until it was cupping the smooth skin of her bare ass.

A groan slipped from her lips, and she wiggled backward into me, encouraging my touch.

"Good morning." I brushed the hair from her shoulder and whispered into her ear.

Noa turned her head to face me. "I see you got tired of the floor."

I pressed a kiss on her lips instead of answering the obvious.

"Bold." She wiggled her face away from me, but at the same time pressed her ass back against my hand. "What makes you think I'm still interested?" She turned away completely. "After all, a girl doesn't like to be rejected, Asher," she teased as she slowly rolled her hips under my touch.

"You think that's what I did, Noa?" I pressed a soft kiss on her neck, under her ear. "You can't believe for a second that I rejected you, sweetheart. I think it's clear that I want you just as badly as you want me."

I pulled her up against me, so she could feel for herself that the need I had for her last night had only intensified during the night. My dick strained against the jeans I still wore.

"I think you sent me to bed alone, Asher. When I made it pretty clear that I wanted company." She sighed as my hand slipped around her waist and traveled up to her breasts.

"Yesterday was a lot for you. I didn't want to add to that."

"And today?"

"Now…" I tweaked her nipple between my thumb and forefinger, eliciting a gasp. "You've had a chance to sleep on it and it's your call. If you want me to stop, I will. I'll get up right now and never touch you again. But if you feel the same way as you did last night, then we finish this. Now." I let my thumb casually flick over her nipple as I spoke. "So, tell me, Noa. Do you regret running away from your wedding and getting into bed with me?"

Her answer was immediate. "Not for one second." Her sweet ass ground against me as she arched her back to press her tits into my hands. "But if you don't finish what you've started, there might be a few things I do start to regret."

It was all the answer I needed. I pulled her easily to her back and in the next moment was over top of her. "Fuck, Noa." I took in the sight of her with her hair tousled from sleep, breasts heaving, only barely confined in the bustier, her lips swollen from our kissing the night before. I hadn't thought it possible, but she was even sexier than the night before. "You're so fucking gorgeous."

"Less talking." She reached up and pulled me down in a rough kiss before releasing me again. "Less clothes."

"And you are wearing just the right amount." I bit my lip and shook my head with an intense appreciation for whoever designed such undergarments.

I'd already wasted too much time with her. The need to taste her and pull more of those sexy noises out of her consumed me. I dropped my mouth to hers and kissed her thoroughly until she was gasping for more, and then I turned my attention to her beautiful breasts. I kissed and suckled them through the lace until I was sure I'd tear it with my teeth.

Slowly, I moved lower until I found the scrap of fabric she called a thong. My tongue traced the elastic band before moving lower to kiss her core through the thin barrier.

She cried out and her hips bucked against me, but I

clamped an arm down to hold her still. "You like that, do you?"

"Asher." Her voice held a warning, but I had her exactly where I wanted her.

The panties, however, were going to have to go. With my free hand, I slipped two fingers under the elastic and pulled. They snapped easily, and then she was perfectly and completely exposed to me. "So much better."

Without further hesitation, I kissed and licked and swirled my tongue along her seam, focusing on her hard bud. It didn't take long for Noa to cry out as pleasure consumed her.

I continued to kiss and taste until finally, with a smile, I lifted my head. "I was right." I looked up to see her now flushed, satiated face. "You are every bit as delicious as I knew you'd be."

Noa's eyes, clouded with desire, fluttered open and her gaze locked on me. "You are still wearing far too many clothes."

NOA

My entire body vibrated with the orgasm that I hadn't even begun to recover from when Asher hopped from the bed and finally stripped out of his clothes.

I propped myself up on my elbows and watched while his jeans fell to the ground to reveal his very hard cock that was every bit as impressive as I'd expected it to be.

"You like what you see?"

Damn. He was so cocky and self-assured that it made me crazy. But hell yes, I liked what I saw. Very much.

In response, I crooked my finger and beckoned him to me.

Asher grabbed a condom from the pocket of his jeans and

quickly sheathed himself before climbing back onto the bed, between my legs.

He notched himself between my legs and leaned forward to take my mouth in his again. I had never been kissed like this before, as if he needed me to breathe. Asher held my head in his hand while his tongue tangled with mine until we were both gasping with need.

Despite the earth-shattering orgasm he'd just given me, I was hungry for more. I was hungry for anything and every-thing he would give me.

"You are so fuckin' delicious, Noa." His voice was rough with desire. "I don't think it's possible to get enough of you."

I felt the same, but if I didn't get more *soon*, I was going to go insane.

My hips bucked up to meet his, and my legs fell open as he pressed his hard length inside my heat.

"Oh!" My body stretched to accommodate him, but he didn't pause or wait until I'd adjusted to his size. A small mercy I was grateful for because the last thing I wanted was for him to slow down in any way.

My hands reached around to claw at his back as he pulled out before once more thrusting deep inside me.

"You feel so fucking good."

My only response was a groan. Words were beyond me as he continued his deep thrusts. I dropped my head back against the headboard, as another climax teased. And just when I thought I might explode into another kaleidoscope of heat and color, Asher pulled back and my eyes flew open.

Before I could protest, Asher wrapped an arm around me and easily scooped me up to flip me around so that he was now on the bottom and I straddled his strong hips.

"Fuck yes." He grinned as he leaned back against the pillows. "This is exactly the view I wanted."

I took a moment to resettle myself on him, filling myself

completely. I sat up and tossed my hair back over my shoulder, giving him every bit of the show he wanted.

His pupils were blown with desire as he reached up for me, letting his hands travel down the length of my body to rest on my hips.

I rocked my hips forward and he matched my every move until finally, I couldn't hold my climax back any longer. His eyes rolled back and I felt him tense beneath me at the same moment.

I cried out, unable to hold back, and Asher did the same, driving up into me as he took his own release.

When I came back to my senses, I rolled off him to my side, and Asher immediately pulled me up tight against his chest.

"Umm," he murmured in my ear. "That was well worth the wait." He left lazy kisses on my neck, and I snuggled back even tighter against him. "Careful, sweetheart. I think I'll be ready for round two before you know it."

"Round two?"

"After that…" He nipped and sucked at my neck playfully. "There is no way one time will ever be enough."

Chapter Nine

ASHER

I FINALLY DRAGGED myself out of bed and away from Noa a few hours later. The beautiful blue-sky day we'd enjoyed the day before had been replaced with heavy clouds and the threat of snow. Still, with the fresh morning light, I could finally get a good look at the cabin I was going to call home for the next few months.

My initial impression the night before had been accurate. The house was old, but obviously well kept. Given that it was in my name, I assumed that Steven Larson had been tasked with the upkeep of the house since my father's death.

But why?

With Noa in the shower, I took my time to explore the cupboards and closets of the cabin. It was stocked with extra blankets, towels, and even some spare clothes in the bottom bedroom dresser drawer. I didn't recognize the jeans and flannel shirts as my father's, but truthfully, I'd rarely seen my dad in such casual clothing.

In the kitchen, there were plenty of dishes and cooking

supplies, along with the canned goods and items in the freezer I'd found the night before.

I was still going to have to make a run to the store for some perishables at some point, but I had what I needed, at least for a little bit.

What *we* needed.

I glanced at the closed bathroom door. The mere thought of Noa naked and wet just beyond the thin piece of wood that separated us was enough to light up my body with a fresh surge of desire.

I'd meant what I'd said earlier: once was not enough. Our connection was fire in a way I hadn't experienced with another woman since—well, ever.

I shook my head and forced myself to look away.

The last thing I should do was join her in the shower. What I really needed was space from her because when she was near, the only thing I wanted to do was push her up against the wall and do dirty things to her. All kinds of delicious, sexy—

No.

What I really needed to do was take her back to the lodge and her family, who was no doubt losing their minds over the wedding that didn't happen.

"Shit." Noa's family wasn't going to be the only ones losing their minds. Guilt flared through me. From the moment she'd jumped into the cab of my truck, I hadn't given any thought to anything else. Including the business I was walking away from.

I retrieved my phone from my jacket pocket and powered it on. The screen lit up almost immediately with dozens of texts and missed calls.

Half of the messages were from my siblings. All of whom expressed varying degrees of concern for me *during this transition.*

I laughed. If they only knew exactly how I'd been *transi-*

tioning, they wouldn't be too worried at all. Or maybe they'd be even more concerned.

Either way, it wasn't my problem.

I ignored my siblings and looked at the messages from Penny. I didn't bother listening to her voicemail, but simply pushed the button to call her.

She picked up on the first ring. "I'm not supposed to talk to you."

"Good morning to you, too."

"Good morning, Asher." She sighed. "I'm not supposed to talk to you. It was made very clear to me that you are no longer the CEO of Carlson Corp, at least for the next six months, and if I help you circumvent the boundaries put in place by Michael Carlson's estate, I will face disciplinary action."

"Are you reading that from something?"

"A letter from your family lawyer," she admitted.

I wasn't surprised. "I'm only returning your call," I said after a moment. "I'm not trying to get you in trouble."

"I shouldn't have called you." I heard a door shut and the background noise dulled as Penny obviously moved somewhere more private. "Seriously, Asher! The bride? The friggin' bride!"

"It is a bit—"

"For the biggest wedding of the year. A wedding you left me pretty much high and dry on."

"That wasn't my—"

"And *you* helped her? What the actual—"

"Wait a minute. I didn't help her." I stopped myself. "Well, I didn't mean to help her."

"She climbed into a marked Trickle Creek Lodge truck and you drove her away, Asher. Three bellmen and her *father*, of all people, saw you."

Penny was on the verge of hysteria, and I had to admit, it did look bad.

I took a deep breath and exhaled slowly. "If it helps, I certainly didn't mean to help her. It's not like I planned it or anything, Penny. Hell, I didn't even know Noa was the bride until the moment she got into my truck."

Penny muttered a string of expletives under her breath before refocusing on the conversation. "I don't suppose you know where she is now, do you?"

I turned toward the bathroom at the same moment the door opened to reveal a very naked and very wet Noa wrapped in only a towel. I swallowed hard. I couldn't lie to Penny. I'd *never* lied to her. It was part of why our work relationship worked so well. And I needed her more than ever now to keep things running smoothly while I was gone. But…Noa.

When she saw that I was on the phone, her expression shifted. "Do I know where the bride is?" I repeated the question for Noa's benefit.

"Yes. The runaway bride that you took off with, Asher. *That* bride."

Noa shook her head slowly. She mouthed the word *no*.

I took a breath and turned away. "I'm sorry, Penny. I can't tell you—"

"To hell you can't, Asher." Her voice vibrated with anger, and I knew the woman was likely only holding on by the thinnest of threads under all the pressure she had to be under.

"I'm not even supposed to be talking to you, Penny. I don't want to get you in trouble."

Penny laughed, but there was no humor in the sound. "That ship has sailed. The family is…well, they're worried." Her voice softened. "Just tell me she's okay."

"She's okay." I didn't look at Noa when I spoke but I didn't think that letting her family know that she was at least safe would be a problem. "They don't need to worry."

"Right." Sarcasm laced Penny's voice. "I'll be sure to let them know."

I couldn't help but chuckle. I turned around and saw Noa, still in her towel, leaning against the doorframe and watching me carefully, as if she didn't trust that I wouldn't turn her in.

"The families are all staying through to New Year's," Penny said. "They decided not to leave early just because the wedding…well, because there was no wedding."

"The families are staying?"

"I just said that."

"Through New Year's, you say?"

Noa groaned and dropped her head into her hand.

"Are you drunk?" Penny said on the other end of the line. "Why are you repeating everything I say? You know what," she added quickly. "I don't want to know. I don't have time for this. If you can't help me, and I know you can't, I shouldn't be talking to you."

"You really are doing a great job, Penny. Thank you," I said sincerely. "I owe you."

"You bet your ass you do."

Penny ended the call, and I dropped the phone on the counter before facing Noa.

"So they're staying," she said simply.

I stepped closer and tucked my hands into my pockets to keep from yanking her towel away. "Sounds like it. Does that change things?"

We hadn't discussed Noa's desire not to go back to the lodge since the night before, and although there was no way she could stay with me in the remote cabin, I was surprised to find that I wasn't in a hurry for her to leave either.

Her fingers danced along the edge of the towel before it slipped to the floor. "Looks like I'm going to need something to wear."

She walked naked past me and into the bedroom, stopping only to look over her shoulder and wink before disappearing inside.

I groaned and sucked a breath through my teeth. "I don't know what you're talking about." I followed her into the room. "I like what you're wearing just fine."

NOA

I lifted my arms over my head and stretched out my muscles with a very satisfied groan. I ached in the most delicious way all over.

It had been a long time, a *very* long time since I'd had such amazing sex. And so much of it.

Okay, if I were being truthful with myself, I probably had never had the kind of sex I'd been having with Asher.

It was…the kind that you only read about. It wasn't real.

Only it was.

I rolled over to watch Asher as he searched the bedroom floor for his clothes—for the second time that morning.

"What's the hurry?"

He tugged his jeans over his bare ass and turned to face me. Another shot of electricity fired through my body at the sexy sight of his hard, bare chest. With the scruff of a beard that had seemed so well-manicured only a few days ago in the hotel, Asher looked every bit the mountain man standing in the middle of the rustic bedroom.

My tongue slipped between my lips almost involuntarily in appreciation of the sight.

"Trust me, sweetheart. My motives are purely selfish."

I watched as he reached for his T-shirt.

"When was the last time you ate something?"

My stomach growled in response to the question, and Asher laughed. "Exactly. We need to keep your strength up."

His words held the promise of more. So much more.

"Besides, I'm going to have to run into town later and I'd like to do it before the sun goes—"

"Town?" I shot up in bed, the sheet falling from my exposed breasts. "Why?"

We hadn't discussed my return to the hotel and my family, and as far as I was concerned, I didn't plan to. I needed space from all of them. At least until I figured out what to say to them. "I was under the impression that you weren't going to take—"

"I didn't say I was taking you with me, did I?"

I narrowed my eyes and crossed my arms over my chest. "Good, because I'm not going anywhere."

The mattress sagged under the weight of him as he sat on the edge of his bed and reached for me. I didn't put up any resistance as he pulled me into his arms. "You still owe me an explanation that makes sense." He held my chin between his thumb and forefinger and stared into my eyes. "But you're a grown-up, and you seem to have your reasons for not marrying him. It's not for me to tell you what to do."

I felt like there was a *but* coming, but when he didn't add it, I nodded. "Good."

He chuckled. "Besides, it turns out I'm quite enjoying having you exactly where you are." He kissed me hard until I was breathless and once more gasping with need for him.

"Damn, Noa." He pulled back. "I don't think I should so much as look at you if I plan on getting anything done." Asher stood abruptly from the bed and headed to the dresser where he'd unpacked his duffel bag. He rifled through the drawers and handed me a T-shirt and a pair of sweatpants. "They'll be too big, but they'll have to do until I can get you something more appropriate."

He disappeared without turning around, and a few minutes later, dressed in the T-shirt that fell to my knees, I joined him in the kitchen, where he had pancakes cooking on a griddle and sausages sizzling in a pan.

Again, my stomach growled angrily. I hadn't eaten since very early the day before and only a bowl of yogurt before putting on my dress. "This smells amazing. Was all this here?" I started to open the cupboards to locate plates and cutlery while Asher finished up cooking. "I thought you said you'd never been here before?"

"I haven't."

I looked over my shoulder at him, and Asher shrugged.

"I can only assume my dad's assistant kept everything stocked and ready."

He tried to hide it, but I could see the hurt on his face when he spoke about the cabin and how he'd come to be there. It was the same the night before when he'd given me the brief explanation of his father's death and the strange stipulations of his will.

"Well, however it came to be," with the plates in my hand, I moved across the kitchen and kissed him on the cheek, "I think it's perfect." I spun away from him before the kiss could turn into anything deeper. After all, we *did* need to eat.

A few minutes later, we each had a plate full of pancakes and sausages in front of us, along with a steaming cup of coffee.

I took a big bite of the fluffy pancake I'd drizzled with maple syrup and immediately closed my eyes and moaned.

Asher laughed, but I didn't care.

"This is *so* good, Asher." Maybe it was the fact that I hadn't eaten in twenty-four hours, or maybe it was because I'd had help working up an appetite. Regardless, the pancakes were the most delicious thing I'd ever eaten and before I knew it, I'd cleaned my plate.

I pushed back from the table and put my hands on my stomach. "Whoa. I think I was hungry."

"I thought maybe it was because my cooking was irre-sistible." He winked at me, and I laughed.

But the laughter died a moment later, when he asked, "Are you sure you don't want to come back with me?"

I swallowed hard, the pancakes sitting like a rock in my gut. "Are we going to keep doing this, Asher? I told you, I don't—"

"I know." He held out his hand in defense. "You don't want to marry him. You told me. And I'm just…" He dropped his head and shook it a little before looking up. "You can't stay here forever. Your family—"

"Will be fine."

But would they?

The guilt that I'd been trying to keep at bay pushed through. Truthfully, I had thought about my mom and dad more than once. What were they thinking? Were they angry with me? Were they worried?

I already knew the answer. They would be worried. Ever since Tom and Olivia's accident, they'd become obsessed with knowing where I was, who I was with, and if I was safe. It had been oppressive and overbearing, but at the same time, with everything they'd been through losing their firstborn, I couldn't bring myself to tell them to back off.

Until now.

There was probably a better way to express my need for independence than dramatically running away from my wedding. But…

"I just wanted to put it out there." Asher pushed from the table and took his empty plate with him to the sink. "Last night…"

He dropped his head, and I wished I could see the look on his face. Did he want me gone? I'd go. As much fun as we'd had together—and we *had* enjoyed ourselves, multiple times—the last thing I wanted was to overstay my welcome.

"I get it." I pushed my chair back. "Maybe you could drop me off at—"

"You don't have to leave." Asher spun around quickly. "I wasn't saying that."

I scanned his face for any trace of dishonesty. Was he just saying what he thought I wanted to hear? The problem was, I didn't know him well enough to know. My instincts told me that Asher was the type of guy who wouldn't hesitate to say what he was thinking. Still, I knew deep down I couldn't hide from the world or my problems forever.

But maybe a few more days…

"Asher, I know you didn't plan on having a runaway bride on your hands, so I don't blame you for one minute if you—"

His hands gripping my upper arms stopped me. "Noa. Look at me."

I did.

"I'm not trying to force you out. Quite the opposite. I just wanted to know if I could pick anything up for you?"

ASHER

It had been some sort of miracle that I hadn't run into anyone I knew at the grocery store as I filled a cart full of whatever I could think of. Including a few bottles of wine. It wasn't that I was planning on any romantic dinners with Noa. But I also wasn't *not* planning on it.

For the first time in my adult life, I had no plan at all. And I still wasn't sure how I felt about it.

I got lucky at the grocery store, but when I pulled into the parking lot for the plaza in the center of town, I knew I wouldn't be so lucky. The week before Christmas, the pedestrian-only strip that included a variety of shops and restaurants, including three of four of my siblings' businesses, was bustling with people.

I pulled my knit toque down over my ears and tried to hide in the collar of my jacket as I headed directly for Summit Style.

Although I would happily have Noa wear only my T-shirt or the ridiculously sexy bustier around the cabin, neither were very practical options for the end of December in the mountains.

Especially if she was going to stay with me.

It was definitely the question that hung in the air between us. No one had been more surprised than I was earlier when I insisted she stay longer. Everything about having Noa in my cabin was a bad idea.

Almost everything.

Having her in my bed was most definitely *not* a bad idea. My dick twitched just thinking about the moments we'd already shared between the sheets, and I had to force myself to focus on the task at hand.

I moved quickly through the busy store and grabbed a stack of things, including a warm winter jacket, boots, socks, some leggings and sweaters before heading to the checkout desk.

"Asher? Is that you?"

Reluctantly, I looked up with what I hoped was a friendly, but not encouraging smile. "Hi, Krysta. Pretty busy in here today."

"All the last-minute Christmas shoppers." She started to fold and scan my pile of items. "What about you? Shopping for...Kat?" She held up a sweater. "Because I think she probably takes a different size." She moved to the boots next. "And I know for a fact that she wears the same size as me. These are—"

"Those are fine." I didn't have a lot of experience with

women's shoe sizes, but I had held Noa's feet in my hands for quite a long time the day before, and I was pretty sure I had their size right. Not that I was going to explain that to Krysta Nelson, the owner of the shop.

It was a small town, and Krysta and I had been out a few times in the past. Although we'd never pretended to be anything more than friends with benefits, I didn't feel like explaining to her who I was buying everything for.

Krysta eyed me suspiciously but thankfully didn't press the issue. "I'll just put a gift receipt in just in case."

"Perfect." I handed over my credit card and paid for my purchases, grabbing the bag from her hand before she could ask any more questions.

"Merry Christmas, Asher."

"You too, Krysta. Don't work too hard."

I was almost through the plaza and back to the safety of my truck when I heard my name called. I froze and muttered a string of expletives under my breath. But there was no help for it. With a sharp exhale of breath, I pasted a smile on my face and turned around to face my sister.

"Hey, Kat."

My little sister held a pair of sharp scissors in one hand, the other on her hip as she stared at me with raised eyebrows and, no doubt, a million questions for me on the tip of her tongue.

"So you are alive?"

I shrugged, going for a smart-ass approach. "Looks that way."

"Don't get smart with me."

She pointed the sharp scissors at me, and I held up my hands. *So much for that approach.*

"We've all been calling and calling. You don't know how to answer a phone anymore?"

I pressed my lips together and sucked in a breath of air. "About that. I—"

"Don't lie to me, Asher. We've been so worried."

"I spoke to you yesterday, Kat. I'm fine." Had it really been only yesterday morning that I'd talked to my sister and opened the envelope with the key and the address to my cabin? In so many ways it felt like much longer.

Kat dropped her arm and, with a quick look behind her at her salon, where she'd very obviously left a client mid-haircut, approached me. "You didn't tell me what was in the envelope and then we all heard what happened at the lodge yesterday evening."

Of course they had.

"You kidnapped the bride?"

"Hardly." I burst out laughing. "More like she…" I thought better of sharing any more details. "Never mind. But whatever you heard, I'm sure it was far more dramatic than the truth." I wasn't really sure how that could possibly be true, but it didn't seem like a good idea to feed Kat any more details than were strictly necessary. "At any rate, I'm fine, Kat. Honestly."

She crossed her arms over her chest and looked me over carefully. Satisfied I was telling the truth, she asked, "Are you going to tell me what was in the envelope?"

That much I *could* tell her. "It was a key and a property deed with my name on it. Apparently, I am the proud owner of a tiny, rustic cabin in the middle of the woods." I shrugged, and the effort lifted my giant bag in the air. "I just popped into town for supplies."

When she tried to look in the bag, I tucked it behind my back. There was no reason she needed to know exactly what kind of supplies I'd rounded up.

"A cabin? I didn't know Dad had a cabin. I've never heard of one."

"Well," I turned to walk away, "we didn't know he'd decided to play games with us after his death either, did we?"

My sister's face crumbled, and I instantly felt bad. Out of

all five of us, Kat was having the hardest time with our father's passing.

"I'm sorry, Kat." I reached for her and pulled her in for a quick hug. "I guess I'm still a little pissed that he booted me out of the business." *Understatement.*

"It's not permanent." Her voice was muffled by my shoulder. "Six months will go by before you know it."

"And then it will be your turn." I released her in time to see the hope shining in her eyes. It wasn't a secret that Kat had been waiting, not so patiently, for her turn with our father's will stipulations. "You're freezing. You should get inside." I pointed with my free hand to her salon.

She didn't disagree. "Mrs. Bradford is probably wondering where I went." She laughed. "I'm glad I saw you though, Asher. Please don't be a stranger, okay? We all love you and we're worried about you."

"No need to worry." I put a smile on my face and found that the moment I thought about Noa waiting for me in my little cabin, there was nothing forced about it. "Like you said, six months will go by before we know it, and then I can pick up right where I left off."

Kat looked like she was going to protest, but a knock on the window of her shop pulled her attention. "Okay, I've got to go. But you make sure you answer when I call, okay? Christmas is only a few days away."

Chapter Ten

NOA

"DO YOU KNOW WHAT YOU NEED?" I trudged through the deep snow behind the cabin, directly for a small fir tree. I patted my gloved hands together and turned to see Asher right behind me, dragging a sleigh we'd found in the shed when we'd finally pulled ourselves from the bed—and each other—and headed outside for some fresh air.

It had only been two full days since we'd been at the cabin, but in some ways, it felt as if I'd known Asher for years. I continually reminded myself that it wasn't serious, and he was only providing me with a fun distraction until I gathered up the courage to face the mess of my life I'd run out on.

Still.

I couldn't remember the last time I'd laughed or smiled so much. Not to mention the orgasms that had my body in a perpetual state of buzzing pleasure.

I was absolutely not in a hurry to end whatever was going on between us.

"What do I need?" Asher caught up to me.

His beard had grown out a bit more in the days since we'd been together. Dressed in his winter coat, wool toque, and mitts, he looked every bit the sexy mountain man. I blew him a kiss before I answered him. "A Christmas tree."

I waved my arms to showcase the little tree in front of me. "It's perfect for the living room."

"A Christmas tree?" Asher chuckled. "No way. I don't think so."

"Christmas is only a few days away." I batted my eyelashes, and he shook his head. "It'll be cute."

"You're cute."

I froze, temporarily taken aback by his easy affection. It was too early for there to be any actual feelings between us. Still, whatever was happening between us, I was enjoying it. And that was good enough for now.

"I'll look even cuter laying naked under a Christmas tree."

"Say no more." He charged past me to the tree in question and assessed it.

"You don't plan on ripping it out by its roots, do you?" I laughed. "I think I saw an axe in the shed next to the wood pile. I'll grab it."

"No way. I'll get it. You guard your tree."

He smacked my bum lightly with his mittened hand as he went by. I was cozy and warm in my own mittens and jacket that Asher had bought for me on his trip to town earlier that week. It hadn't even occurred to me to ask him for clothes, but he'd taken care of it all on his own. And he'd done a really good job of it, too, nailing my sizes almost perfectly.

Asher returned a few minutes later with an axe and made short work of the tree. He dropped it on the sleigh and together we headed back to the house.

"Thank you."

"For the tree?" He looked over at me and winked. "Not a

problem. I agree that you are going to look damn good under the tree. But I would prefer you unwrapped."

My body flushed with the constant desire he stirred in me. "No. I mean, yes. Thank you for the tree. But also, for—"

"Don't."

The smile slipped from his face; he faced forward and pulled the sleigh with a little more force.

"Don't what?" I rushed to keep up with him in the snow.

"Don't thank me for rescuing you."

Rescue?

Stunned, I froze in place.

Oh hell no.

If Asher thought for even one minute that he'd rescued me like a damsel in distress about to marry the big bad king who would lock me away in a castle, he had another thing coming.

Before I could stop myself, I bent down and formed a perfect snowball. I took aim and hurled it toward the back of Asher's head, where it hit its mark perfectly.

"Shit." His hand flew up to rub his head and he turned, startled. "What the—"

Maybe I shouldn't have done it, but both the sound of it hitting his head and the response it garnered made me feel better instantly.

"Did you…"

I shrugged and, before he could process the shock, bent and scooped up another snowball that I threw in his direction.

Asher dodged the second one and recovered quickly. It was his turn to scoop up snow to attack, but I grew up with a big brother. There was no way I was going to wait around for him to retaliate. I charged through the snow toward him, wrapped my arms around his waist, and knocked him backward into a giant snowdrift.

"Noa! What the—"

I straddled his body, pinning his arms next to him, filled my hands with snow and held them over his head. "I don't need to be rescued."

"What?"

I repeated myself. "You didn't rescue me, Asher."

He looked up at me and laughed.

I let some of the snow drop onto his face.

"Okay, okay."

"I mean it." I still didn't lower my snow-filled hands. "You happened to be in the right place at the right time. That's it. I was leaving that wedding with or without you. It just so happened that you got lucky."

"Lucky?" His lips twisted into a very sexy grin.

"Yeah." I dropped my hands and dumped the snow next to his head. "Pretty damn lucky that you happened to be driving by at the exact right time."

He appeared to think about it for a minute. "I can't disagree with that."

"You can't?"

He wiggled enough to free his arms and rested his hands on my hips. "I sure can't."

Something about the way he looked up at me warmed me inside. Again, I reminded myself that nothing about what we were doing in the little cabin in the woods meant anything. But it didn't matter. For the moment, it made me feel good.

I bent and kissed him thoroughly on the lips until finally, Asher groaned and insisted if we didn't get inside, we would end up melting the snow altogether.

ASHER

Even as a child, I hadn't been one to get very excited over the Christmas tree. When I was young, it had been Chase and our father's tradition to pick out the family tree. And then when we were older, my sisters would take over the decorating, leaving very little for me to do at all.

After a while, I would take for granted the fact that we had a family Christmas tree at all. It just sort of happened.

In only one afternoon, Noa had changed my mind about Christmas trees altogether. After lugging the fir tree through the snow, I'd stopped in the shed to construct a rustic type of stand that would hold the tree in place and brought it inside.

Noa decided the perfect place was in the corner by the window, with the fireplace nearby. Once it was in position, even I had to admit, it did look pretty good.

With no actual decorations, we got creative and made paper snowflakes and strung popcorn with string. Noa found some red yarn in one of the kitchen drawers and wove long braids with it to use as garland.

"I like it." She finished placing the last paper snowflake and stepped back to admire her work. I caught her in my arms and held her tight. "I think we did a pretty good job." She looked up at me, and I had to force myself to look away.

It was too easy to fall into something comfortable with this woman. And that was saying something, considering I had never had anything longer than a night or two with any woman, let alone anything *comfortable*.

It had only been a few days since we'd been together in the little cabin. Maybe it was the forced proximity, or the super-hot sex—but whatever it was, I found myself more and more thinking about what happened next. And those weren't safe thoughts to be having. Not for a man who preferred to live life alone and a woman who'd only *very* recently run away from her fiancé and her entire family.

And had yet to address any of those particular details.

"We don't have a star." I gazed up to the top of the tree. "What could we use?"

"The tree topper should be something that finds you," Noa said.

"What does that even mean?" I tried not to chuckle when I saw how serious she was.

"What it means is that you'll know the topper when you see it. It can't be rushed."

I assessed the tree with the bare top and shrugged. "I'll have to take your word for it. I've honestly never given much thought to the Christmas tree. But I have to admit, this was pretty fun. And even without a topper, I think it looks pretty great. But it's still missing something." I spun her out of my arms and looked her up and down knowingly. "You're wearing far too many clothes to be unwrapped under the tree."

Noa laughed and spun herself right into the kitchen. "Maybe we should have dinner first?"

Right on cue, my stomach growled, and I followed her into the kitchen. "Have I told you that you're such a tease?"

Her laughter filled the room. "I don't know if that's the right way to describe what's going on between us." She opened the freezer. "Pizza or tortellini?"

Avoidance was one of my favorite techniques, too. "Pizza."

"Perfect. I'll make a salad to go with it."

NOA

The fire burned low, and I rolled to my side with the Christmas tree and Asher at my back so I could watch the glowing embers.

"I should put some wood on," Asher murmured in my ear, but made no move to get up.

We'd eaten our dinner on the floor next to the tree before, true to my word, I'd unwrapped myself. If I were being truthful, it was a gift to both of us. Asher was a skillful lover and my body responded easily to his touch.

Now, satiated and warmed by the fire and our lovemaking, I stretched my arms over my head and rolled to my back. "Let's play a game."

"A game?" His fingers trailed down my side to my bottom. "I like games." His hand slipped over my hip, and I swatted it away.

"Not that kind of game, you horn dog."

He raised an eyebrow. "Pot. Meet Kettle."

"Fair." I laughed. "But I'm serious. Let's play twenty questions. You can only answer with a yes or no."

When Asher didn't respond right away, I was afraid I'd made a mistake. Everything between us had been light and easy up until now. Besides that first night when I'd reassured him that I hadn't made a mistake and wasn't hung up on my fiancé, we hadn't spoken about our personal lives. It had been easy and simple. And…not real.

"Okay," he said after a few minutes. "If you think you're ready for it."

I swallowed hard. I didn't know whether I was or not, but what I did know was that whatever it was between us, I was enjoying it and there only seemed to be one way forward. We were either going to like what we found out about each other… or not.

"You can go first."

His eyes widened with surprise but he was ready. "Once and for all, I need to know. Are you in love with your fiancé?"

I'd been expecting that one. "His name is Ryan. And no. Like I said before, I will always love him, but I'm not, nor have I ever been *in* love with him."

I rolled onto my other side so we faced each other. Asher was incredibly sexy with one arm propping up his head, the fire glowing enticingly on his hard, naked chest.

I was ready with my own question. "Are you dating anyone?" I was pretty sure the answer was no, but given my own recent history, I needed to know for sure.

"No. I don't date."

My mouth fell open before I could stop it. "You don't—"

"No."

"Ever?"

"No." He shook his head. "I've never been interested in everything that goes with that."

"With dating?"

Asher blew out a sigh. "You're not going to change my mind on this."

"I'm not trying to." I held up a palm. "Honestly. I'm just curious because I feel the same way."

Asher pushed up to sitting and didn't bother trying to hide his laughter. "That's rich, coming from the woman who had a ring on her finger and a white dress, only minutes from walking down the aisle."

I narrowed my eyes but ultimately sighed. "I guess I can see how that might look."

"I'm glad you see it, too." He squeezed my thigh. "Are you ever going to tell me how that came to be, anyway?"

"Yes." I returned to the format of the game we'd all but abandoned, and it was Asher's turn to look unimpressed.

"To be fair, I think you owe me a few questions, Noa. So we can either—"

"Okay, okay." I pulled myself up to a sitting position and pulled the blanket up over my naked body. "But I'm going to need a glass of wine first."

Asher returned to his spot in front of the fire a moment later with a bottle and two glasses. He poured us each a glass and grabbed a blanket for himself before he sat across from me. "All right, tell me then. How does a woman like yourself, who tells me that she's never been interested in everything that goes with dating, and claims she loves her fiancé, but is not *in* love," he added quickly before continuing, "get to the point where she runs out of her wedding and into the truck of a virtual, but very handsome stranger?"

Somehow I managed to swallow the sip of wine in my mouth. "Handsome, huh?"

Asher shrugged casually and winked. "At the very least."

I shook my head with a laugh and set my glass down. "Okay. I'll tell you the whole story, but I'm afraid it's not nearly as exciting as you're expecting it to be." If anything, it was sad. *Very* sad. But I didn't say that to Asher. He'd find out soon enough. "I already told you that Ryan and I grew up together."

He nodded.

"Our families are best friends in every way. In fact, our dads are partners in a law firm together, and Ryan and I are lined up to start working there, too, just as soon as we get back from the honeymoon we won't be taking." I'd need to talk to him about the round-the-world tickets we had. Maybe there was someone else he'd like to take with him? I blew out a breath and shoved those thoughts from my mind for the moment in order to finish my story.

"So you guys are all going to work together like a big happy family?"

"Were," I corrected him. Although I hadn't given much thought to pretty much anything that was going to happen next, I'd never wanted to work for the family law firm. "I don't think that will happen now."

"You don't think Ryan will want to work with you, or will your dad be upset?"

I chuckled. "Oh, I'm sure Dad's upset, and I kind of don't think Ryan will care. But it's me. I don't want to practice corporate law. I never did."

Asher blew out a breath and took another big sip of his wine. "So let me see if I have this straight so far. You didn't want to marry Ryan but didn't say anything. And you also didn't want to work in the family law firm, and also kept quiet about that."

I nodded. That was pretty much the gist of it. I'd been pretty quiet about what it was I wanted for far too long.

"Don't take this the wrong way, Noa. But you don't really seem like the type who wouldn't speak up. I mean, I've met a lot of women."

A flash of completely unreasonable jealousy shot through me.

"And most of those women aren't nearly as…" He searched for the right word. "Strong." He said the word almost like a question. "You don't seem like the type of woman who will do anything she doesn't want to do. So, honestly, I'm a little confused."

"You and me, both." I picked up my wine and looked deep into the glass. "And I never used to be this way."

He scooted closer to me on the floor and put his hand on my leg through the blanket. "So what happened, Noa?"

Chapter Eleven

ASHER

AS A RULE, I typically avoided difficult or serious conversations with women. After all, I'd meant it when I'd told Noa I wasn't interested in dating or any of the things that came with it, and that definitely included intense conversations of any kind.

But I wanted to know her story. Especially because there seemed to be such a contrast between the woman I saw and what was going on in her personal life.

I held my hand on her leg, and it didn't take long for me to feel her relax under my touch.

"What happened?" She repeated the question and gave me a sad smile. "They died and everything changed."

Of all the things I'd expected her to say, I wouldn't have guessed that. Before I could ask who had died, she continued talking.

"Not only were our parents best friends, and Ryan and I, but our older siblings, too. But they were more than friends. Tom was my older brother, and Olivia was Ryan's sister."

Was.

I watched Noa carefully as the pieces of her story started to come together.

"They were so in love." There was a faraway look in her eyes, and she looked past me into the burning fire. "I think they fell in love as babies, if I'm being honest. They were just always so perfect for each other. So when they announced their engagement, no one was really surprised at all. Our families were so excited, and I'm sure both of our mothers were already imagining the house full of all the grandbabies they were going to have."

She looked at me and smiled a little. "Ryan and I thought it was great, too. By then, we'd tried dating a little bit but there really wasn't much chemistry between us, so we decided to stay friends, which worked for both of us because, even at that point, I knew I didn't want to get married like Tom and Olivia. I've always wanted to travel and see the world. I knew I wanted to be a lawyer; that was my choice. But my plan was going to be working in family law, and maybe taking some pro bono cases for women who needed help leaving desperate situations."

"That sounds like a good plan."

"Right?" Her face changed. "And then, two years ago, on New Year's Eve, they died."

She said it so matter-of-factly that it took me a moment to register the words.

"They were hit by a drunk driver and killed instantly."

"Holy shit, Noa." I moved so I could pull her into my arms, wrapping myself around her from behind. "That's awful."

She sank backward into me and let her head drop back to my chest. "It was." Her voice was soft, almost a whisper. "The sadness was almost suffocating. It was unbearable. And then, one day, I made an offhanded comment to Ryan about how we should just get married to see them all smile again. And…"

"The rest is history, as they say?"

She nodded. "Maybe it was crazy, but it started to sound like a good idea. We talked about all the logistics and what it would mean to have an open relationship, even if it was secret."

"Open relationship?"

"Like I said, we didn't have any chemistry." She shrugged, as if it were no big deal. "Not like that. Although Ryan offered to…anyway, I could think of a lot of things a lot worse than marrying my best friend."

"Even if you didn't love him."

"Right. After all, I never wanted to get married anyway, so what was the harm? And then when we told them…Asher, you should have seen their faces." She twisted in my arms to look at me. "We knew then that we had to do it. They were all so happy. It was like the first time since Tom and Olivia died that they felt anything other than sadness, and we'd done that for them. It felt…well, it felt right."

"Until it didn't."

She nodded. "Until it didn't." Noa exhaled slowly and turned back to face the fire. "I can't even think about how upset they all are right now." She shook her head slowly. "Not Ryan. He'll be fine. But Mom and Dad, and Jeannie and Brad." She fell quiet for a moment. "I'm a terrible person."

"What?" I jumped up and moved so I was in front of her. I took her hands in mine and held them. "Are you kidding me? How can you sit there and tell me that you're willing to sacrifice yourself for your family and think for even the slightest moment that you're a terrible person? It's okay to look after yourself, too. And holy shit, woman. Marrying a man just to put a smile on your parents' faces…damn. That's as unselfish as it gets."

Over the last few days, I'd thought of a few possible explanations for why Noa had run from her wedding, but my imagination could never have written that particular story.

I handed her the glass of wine, and she drank deeply. "Does it make sense now?"

I chuckled but shook my head. "I think I have even more questions. But yes, I think I understand why you did what you did. I think you're crazy, but I get it."

I winked, and she laughed. After the story she'd just told me, it was a very welcome sound to hear again.

"I probably am a bit crazy."

I pulled her into my arms. "No probably about it, sweetheart." I kissed her deeply until she wiggled backward.

"Your turn."

I eyed her sideways. "My turn for what?"

"Tell me what your story is."

I rocked back on my heels and shook my head. "I answered your questions already."

"We're done with that game." Noa waved away my protest. "You owe me."

I laughed and jumped to my feet. Still naked, I moved through to the kitchen and started to dig through the fridge for the makings of a charcuterie board for dinner. "I think if anyone owes anyone anything, it might be you."

I was teasing, but when I looked over my shoulder at her, Noa had wrapped the blanket tightly around her shoulders and had dropped her head onto her knees.

Was she crying?

Shit.

"I was only kidding, Noa." I abandoned the fridge and crossed the floor quickly. "You know you don't owe me anything. I was just—"

"It's not that." She looked up at me with dry eyes, but the distress on her face was clear. "It's just...I haven't even called them."

Oh.

"Do you think they're worried?"

I nodded. "I'm sure they have questions. Yes." There was no point lying to her. If Kat had pulled a move like that and then disappeared from the face of the earth for a few days, I knew without a doubt we'd all be worried. "Use my phone."

NOA

The call was long overdue, but that didn't make it any easier. I almost hung up the second I heard the ringing on the other end of the line.

I'd dressed in leggings and an oversized sweater, and I had the blanket wrapped around my shoulders as I sat by the fire. But still, I shivered the moment Ryan answered the call.

"Hello?"

"Ryan." My voice shook. "It's Noa."

He didn't speak right away. "You're okay?"

"I'm okay."

I heard him exhale a breath that he'd probably been holding in some capacity since the day of the wedding. "That's all that matters." He was silent for a moment, and we both started speaking at the same time.

"Ryan, I'm so—"

"That was a pretty ballsy move—"

I stopped. "What did you say?"

On the other end of the line, he laughed. "Damn, Noa. That was a pretty ballsy move, running from the wedding like that. Dramatic. Even for you."

The sound of my best friend's laughter, after everything I'd just put them through, almost made me cry with relief. "I'm so, so sorry, Ryan. I know I shouldn't have done it like that. I just…" My fingers fiddled with the gold rose around my neck. "It all just felt really real, all at once, you know? I wanted to talk to you, but you were out there already and…I didn't know what else to—"

"It's okay."

"It is?"

"I mean, no." He laughed again. "It's not. But it will be. You know I love you, Noa."

I didn't know what I'd expected, but to hear Ryan's voice and know that he wasn't angry with me filled me with relief.

"And the parents?"

"Oh, that's a different story. They're upset for sure."

My heart clenched.

"I figured you'd just gotten cold feet and needed a bit of space. To be honest, I wasn't too worried about it all. I did my best to calm everyone down. Mom wanted to leave and go home, but I convinced everyone to stay. After all, there was no point in canceling all the reservations. Besides, the skiing has been great."

I rolled my eyes. Leave it to Ryan to turn a botched wedding into a fun, family ski holiday. I listened while he filled me in on how the mothers were taking the news, and he made me laugh a few times until I'd forgotten the reason for my call completely.

Asher had gone outside to give me privacy, and through the kitchen window, in the porch light, I could see him behind the cabin, chopping firewood next to the woodshed. Being with Asher felt different. On some level, I knew what we were doing wasn't real and we couldn't stay hidden away from reality forever.

But I couldn't help but hope for a few more days at the very least. Asher made it clear that he also never wanted a relationship, which made what we were doing kind of perfect, because I didn't have any expectations either.

"So, are you going to tell me where you are?"

I shook my head but before I could answer, Ryan continued. "There are rumors that you're with the hotel guy."

"The hotel guy?"

"He's an owner here. Carlson, I think his name is?"

Again, my eyes traveled to the man in question.

"Some employees reported you getting into his truck, but the manager isn't confirming or denying anything. Honestly, I think it's great, Noa. I told you to blow off some steam and get it out of your system."

It struck me at that moment just how screwed up the entire situation actually was.

"You did tell me that…"

"Great. So when you're done with that, do you think we can get this done?"

"When I'm—"

"Maybe New Year's Eve? It would be a good new memory for—"

"Oh no." I stopped him. "Ryan. We're not getting married. I thought I made that clear when I…well, when I didn't show up for the wedding."

He was silent for a second. "I thought that maybe you just needed to blow off a little steam. You can't be serious about not going through with it." The laughter had completely vanished from Ryan's voice.

I fingered the gold rose. "Ryan, I really think—"

"Don't give me an answer right now."

"I already—"

"Sit on it." He interrupted me. "Really think about it, Noa. And what it will mean to everyone. Our families need this. And you know it doesn't matter to us. Not really."

I let my gaze travel out the window again.

It was ridiculous to think that what I was doing with Asher was anything important or serious in any way. It wasn't. I knew that. Ryan was important and special to me. So what was I doing?

"Remember what I said about seeing other people, Noa. You can do as much of…whatever it is you're doing, as you want. You know I don't care."

"I know. But that's not why I ran, Ryan. I just…it doesn't feel…"

"You'll be back for Christmas, right?"

Christmas. I nodded. "Of course." I couldn't stay away forever, and I'd never forgive myself if I missed what could be Grandma Rose's last Christmas. After everything, I knew better than to take time for granted. "But I think we need to tell them the truth, Ryan. When I get there. We just need to—"

"Noa. Just wait. A lot can change in a few days. Don't make any decisions you can't come back from."

Chapter Twelve

ASHER

I'D DONE my best to avoid looking at my phone for the last few days, which, in any other circumstance, I would have considered some sort of miracle.

We'd spent our days playing cards, making love, and talking. I found myself opening up about things in my life that I'd never shared with another person before. How I wished I could travel more, but I'd been too tied down with Carlson Corp to leave for long. How I'd wanted to make my father proud of me for as long as I could remember, and how, despite all my best efforts, I'd never heard the words. And in return, she'd talked about her life and her hopes and dreams. It was effortless to talk to her, and she made it so easy to open up in ways I never had before.

Noa had been a pretty decent distraction. Okay, better than decent. She'd been an absolutely perfect distraction from the fact that my entire reason for being had been ripped away from me.

I didn't want to think about what that little fact told me

about my life. Or how on earth I would distract myself from the reality of the next six months without work to focus on once Noa went back to her life.

Because she would go back to her life.

I glanced toward the bathroom door and listened to the sound of the shower I'd only very recently vacated so that she could finish her shower while there was still some hot water left.

As much fun as we were having together, I wasn't stupid. I knew it couldn't last forever, even if I wanted it to. Which I didn't.

I shook my head clear of the conflicting thoughts and focused on the matter at hand. It was Christmas Eve, and—as every one of my siblings had pointed out via half a dozen text messages and voicemails—the baby's first Christmas, and I "better not miss it."

I had plenty of faults, but being a dick to my family wasn't one of them. As much as I'd prefer to stay cuddled up with Noa under our rustic little Christmas tree, I knew I'd be heading into town for a big family Carlson Christmas.

I picked up my phone and fired off a text to Charli.

> You know I won't miss it. What can I bring?

A moment later, my phone rang.

"Good morning, sis."

"Is it still morning?" Charli sounded exhausted. "I swear, this little girl's internal clock is seriously off schedule. I've been up for hours."

"Procreator problems." I tried not to laugh. "I guess that answers my next question," I added. "How are you doing?"

"So great. Really. I love being a mom, Asher. Poppy is the sweetest thing."

"Despite the early mornings?"

"And the late nights...and the times in between." Charli chuckled. "But we'll figure it all out."

"If anyone can, it's you." I glanced toward the bathroom door again, but the shower was still running. Now I was sure I could hear Noa singing the strains of *Santa Claus Is Coming to Town*. "What time do you want me at the big house tonight?" I asked. "Do I need to bring anything?"

"Chase and Annie put themselves in charge of dinner this year," Charli told me. "And last I heard, they said they have it totally under control, so just bring yourself." Her voice softened. "You know we're all a little worried about you, Asher. Truthfully, I'm just really glad you'll be there. I miss you."

"It's only been a few days since I've seen you, Char. I'm fine."

Was I?

"It's okay to talk to us about all of this, you know? It's a lot, Asher. None of us expected this for you, and I know it's a big—"

"It's fine." I cut her off. I didn't want to hear any more about how worried they were about me, as if I couldn't function without work.

Is that what they all truly thought of me? That I had nothing else in my life besides running the family business? There was more to me than that.

I just didn't know what it was yet.

I turned at the sound of the bathroom door opening as Noa appeared, wrapped in only a towel. Instantly, and despite the fact that I'd only very recently been *in* the shower with her, my body reacted to the sight of her. Never had I spent this much time with a woman before and not grown tired of her.

And not just that. With every minute that went by, I found myself looking forward to the *next* one, too.

What the hell was that about?

"Asher? Hello?"

"Sorry, Charli." I forced my attention back to the phone call. "I'll see you in a bit."

Noa winked and disappeared into the bedroom.

"Hey, Charli?"

I caught her just before she ended the call.

"Can I bring someone tonight?"

"Someone? As in a woman?"

"Yes."

"As in the woman you kidnapped from her wedding day?"

"I did not—"

"I'm kidding." My sister laughed. "Mostly. But of course you can bring her. I'm sure I won't be the only one with questions."

NOA

"Are you sure this is a good idea?"

We'd only been in the car for ten minutes, but already I was doubting my decision to join Asher at the Carlson family Christmas celebration. It had seemed like a good idea in the moment, but the farther we got from the cabin, the more anxious I felt.

"I don't really belong at your family function." I turned away from the snowy landscape out the window to look at him. "I mean, we're not…we're only…we hardly know each other."

He gave me a look that made me blush. "I wouldn't say that."

"You know what I mean." I swatted at him, but he'd made me laugh.

He reached over the seat and took my hand. "Besides, it's just dinner."

"It's Christmas dinner." I looked at him pointedly. "They're going to think we're…"

"They're going to think that you jumped in my truck on your wedding day and we've been hanging out together," he finished for me.

"Hanging out?" I lifted an eyebrow, and he laughed.

"Hey, I don't plan on giving them any more details than they already think they know. Which is pretty limited. Besides, there isn't any more to give, is there?"

I inhaled slowly and shook my head. "Nope. I guess that is what we've been doing."

"Besides, I'm not letting you spend Christmas by yourself. They're all super easygoing," he continued. "Except for maybe Chase. But he's not as bad as he used to be, and he'd probably say the same about me. At any rate, it won't be too bad. Just a few hours and we'll get out of there, okay?"

I nodded. I'd powered through my share of family events over the years. How bad could it be? Besides, Asher had a point. I didn't want to be alone on Christmas Eve, and despite what I'd told Ryan, I wasn't quite ready to face my own family.

ASHER

I pulled up in the big circular drive of the *big house*, my childhood home. My father had built it just outside of town, on a huge piece of land that looked out over the valley below. Chase and Annie, along with Grady—Annie's nephew—lived there full-time now, but it would always be the family home and was, more often than not, the gathering place for weekly family dinners.

"This is where you grew up? It looks so…"

"Big?"

"I was going to say festive." Noa laughed. "But yes, it's obviously a much bigger house than anything else I've seen in Trickle Creek so far. To be honest, it kind of reminds me of the house I grew up in."

Beyond the tragic story about her brother, we hadn't discussed our childhoods, but it shouldn't have surprised me that Noa grew up in a big home, too. After all, her father was a lawyer, and I'd seen firsthand the bill he'd paid for the wedding at Trickle Creek Lodge.

"It *is* festive." I put the truck in park but wasn't in a hurry to go inside. "Chase really outdid himself this year."

"You and your brother... are you..."

"It's complicated." We also hadn't discussed much of my childhood either. "Chase left home fairly young, and we missed a lot of each other growing up. After a while, I just assumed he resented me, and he thought the same."

"And now?"

"Now...it's getting better. Ever since he moved back, we've been getting to know each other again. But sometimes, we still fall into those old patterns."

Noa reached across the cab of the truck and squeezed my hand. "You're really lucky to have so many siblings."

It was true. I knew that. Even on days when they made me crazy. "You're right. I *am* lucky." I returned the squeeze. "And you're about to be lucky, too." I laughed. "They are going to pepper you with questions. I apologize in advance."

I knew she was a little nervous about joining me, and why wouldn't she be? It wasn't like we were dating or anything, and all they knew about her was that she'd run away from her wedding, right into my truck—and arms. But Noa was tough. She'd be able to hold her own.

"Just a few hours, right?" She nodded toward the house and the door that had cracked open.

Annie's nephew Grady and Craig's daughter Meri poked their heads out, and I knew we were out of time.

"I guess we better get in there."

NOA

"Merry Christmas, kiddos." Asher bent down and ruffled the boy's head and scooped up the little girl, who wrapped her arms around his neck. "What are you doing outside? You weren't watching for Santa, were you?"

"No, silly," the little girl said. "We were waiting for you, Uncle Asher."

I couldn't help but smile at the easy way he had with the kids.

The little girl peeked over his shoulder and, with wide eyes, stared at me. "Is she your girlfriend, Uncle Asher?"

Asher, the child still in his arms, spun to wink at me. "This is Noa," he introduced me. "Noa, this is my niece, Meri." He waved a hand toward the little boy. "And this is Grady. These are our resident rug rats."

"We are not rats." Meri wiggled out of his arms, and the two children took off in a fit of giggles.

"They're cute." What I really wanted to say was how cute he was with the children.

I followed Asher into the foyer and was immediately greeted by the rest of the family.

"It's about time you got here." A petite redhead threw herself into Asher's arms. "I was about to send Craig out searching for you."

A man, who looked a lot like Asher, appeared. "Not that it would do much good," he said as he gave his brother a hug. "Since I don't know where the hell you've been hiding."

Before Asher could respond, the redhead turned to face me. "You must be the woman he's been hiding out with." She wiggled her eyebrows dramatically and burst into laughter. "Just kidding. I'm Kat." She thrust her hand out. "I'm the baby of the family, and Asher's favorite." She leaned in and stage-whispered, "I'm everyone's favorite—they just won't admit it."

I couldn't help but like her immediately. "My name is Noa." I shook her hand. "And you must be…"

"I'm Craig." He extended his hand as well. "I'm Asher's youngest brother. It's very nice to meet you, Noa. I'm glad you could join us."

"Especially since we're way overdue for some good gossip," Kat added. "And you two are the talk of the town." She wiggled her finger between the two of them.

Asher took my coat and gave me an apologetic shrug. "I'm sure we're not—"

"Stop torturing her." Another woman appeared in the foyer. "She's our guest," the woman admonished Kat before turning in my direction. "Merry Christmas. I'm Charli."

"Noa."

"Welcome, Noa." Charli looped her arm through mine and, after blowing a kiss to Asher, led me out of the foyer and into the kitchen, where there were even more people to meet.

I was sure I wasn't going to remember anyone's names after meeting Annie and Chase, Craig's fiancée Lucy, and Charli's husband Symon, along with their new baby, Poppy.

At some point, Asher handed me a glass of wine and then, like magic, the men disappeared into the living room with the children, leaving the women in the kitchen to prepare dinner.

"Don't worry," Annie said to me. "I know it looks like gender roles are truly alive and well here, but the men do a killer job cleaning up while we relax."

"Besides," Charli chimed in. "We're better cooks."

The women laughed, and I found myself joining in with them easily.

"What about you, Noa?" Lucy asked. "Do you cook?"

"I have a few specialties." I shrugged. "My fiancé did all the—" I stopped abruptly when I realized what I'd said out loud. "I mean…my…"

"It's okay." Charli put a hand on my shoulder. "We're not going to judge you. And you don't need to talk about it if you don't want to."

"I was only kidding when I said you were the talk of the town earlier." Kat frowned. "Honestly. No one is talking about you."

"It's okay." I smiled. "I'm sure plenty of people are talking. Why wouldn't they be? After all, I ran out of my wedding and jumped into Asher's truck."

Silence fell in the kitchen, as everyone stopped working to stare at me. I almost clammed up, but there didn't seem to be much point.

"It wasn't my finest moment." I blew out a breath. "But I have chatted with Ryan about it all—that's my…well, you know. And he's not mad. We're really great friends more than anything else and…well, now I'm just rambling."

"It's okay." Charli offered me a kind smile. "I can't imagine anything about the last few days has been easy."

I bit my tongue before I could tell the woman just how easy it had been to be with her little brother. There had been nothing difficult about the time we'd spent together.

"Are you and Asher…"

"He's been great about letting me stay at the cabin, and I just want you all to know, it's not like…well, it's not what you think. I didn't run away from my wedding because of him. I'd only met him the day before and honestly, he just happened to be in the right place at the right time. But I'm sure it must look like…"

"It doesn't look like anything." Lucy shrugged. "Noa, you should know that this family is pretty understanding of pretty much everything." She glanced around at the other women, who all nodded in agreement.

"It's true." Annie stepped forward. "You don't have to tell us anything you don't want to."

"But if you want to…"

I nodded in Charli's direction. "Thank you." I looked to the others. "All of you. It's been a very weird time. I really appreciate all of you being so friendly and welcoming."

"Well, if you can put up with Asher, you'll have no problem getting along with the rest of us." Kat laughed. "I'm teasing. We like to give him a hard time because he's the most uptight of all of us. But we love him."

"Uptight?"

"Oh, yeah." Kat fell into the chair next to me and reached for her own glass of wine. "Asher is a total workaholic. Worse than Chase used to be. That has to be why Dad gave him the task of taking time off. To be totally honest with you, we were all pretty worried about how he was going to handle things but you've been a pretty good distraction for him."

"He hasn't said much about that situation," I admitted. "Except for how he's been forced to take six months off. I didn't realize it was so difficult for him." I felt a flash of guilt for not recognizing it when he'd been so understanding about my situation. I should have asked more questions to try to understand all of it better. Truthfully, I'd been more than a little wrapped up in my own issues.

"He's not historically been much of a talker," Charli said.

"But he's also not historically been the type to kidnap runaway brides." Kat wiggled her eyebrows. "So who knows, maybe this is a whole new side of Asher. I, for one, look forward to seeing what happens next."

Me too.

I swallowed a mouthful of wine before I said anything more, or let myself go down a line of thought I shouldn't.

"Enough serious talk." Lucy reached for my arm and gave me a wink. "Let's get this dinner on the table." She pulled me to my feet. "You can help me with the salad."

ASHER

"Noa's cute."

Ninety seconds. That's all it had taken for one of the guys to say something to me about Noa the moment we were left alone. In a strange way, I was impressed they'd waited so long.

"She is." I tried to keep my tone as neutral as possible, but there was no point in denying the obvious truth. Noa was cute. Very cute.

I settled into a dining room chair with the misguided hope that the conversation would shift to pretty much anything else.

Not that there was any real hope in that regard.

It was Craig who pushed the issue. "Are you going to offer up details willingly, or are we going to have to pull them out of you?"

"Because you know we will pull." Symon, the baby in his arms, grinned at me.

I looked to Chase for assistance, but my eldest brother wasn't saying a word.

"You know we're not letting this go," Craig confirmed. "Not after you pulled the whole disappearing act for the last week."

"Not to mention the whole bride kidnapping," Symon added.

Chase shrugged. "They're not wrong."

I knew when I'd been beaten. "Fine. But you're all going to

be disappointed when you learn it's not nearly as dramatic as you're thinking."

"Doubtful." Symon settled back into the chair.

For the next few minutes, I gave the men the abbreviated version of the story. From how I'd met Noa, not knowing she was the bride, all the way to her running out in front of my truck in her gown as I was making my own getaway.

"So, it wasn't planned?" Craig asked. "She wasn't running away from her wedding for you?"

I almost spat out my mouthful of water. "Hardly. It was definitely a case of right place, right time. Or maybe, wrong time. Either way, I was the getaway driver. That's all."

"But she's still with you."

Leave it to Chase to point out the obvious.

"So, that's not *all*, is it, brother?"

All three sets of eyes focused on me, and I blew out a breath. "Like I said, it's not at all what you're thinking. She needed a place to stay for a few days and I…well, I guess I found myself with a little cabin in the middle of nowhere. Maybe we should talk about that?"

When none of the men spoke up, I continued. "Seriously, none of you want to know about the secret cabin in the woods that Dad had?"

"Of course we want to know," Craig said after a moment. "There's a lot we want to know, Asher." He ran his hand through his hair. "Not important, though. I think we should all back up for a minute and ask the really important question."

I sighed. "What's that?"

My youngest brother took the seat across from me and looked me straight in the eyes. "How are you doing with all of this?"

I groaned in frustration.

"It's a fair question, Asher." Chase joined us at the table, sitting next to Craig. "I mean, none of this is easy and for you…" My brothers exchanged a glance. "This really can't be easy."

"Because I'm the workaholic?" I knew what they thought of me. That work was my entire life and the only thing that I found meaning and joy in. Every single one of my siblings had approached me about their concerns at some stage. And yes, work was important to me, but I didn't do it just for myself. That's what they couldn't see. I did it for all of them. The whole family. I worked my ass off to keep Carlson Corp running and thriving after Dad died, because if I hadn't, our legacy would have died along with him.

"Asher, that's not what—"

"That's exactly what you're saying." I stopped my younger brother. "It's what you always say. What all of you always say. And yes, I like to work. Hell, I even love working. So obviously having Dad kick me out of the job I take pride in from beyond the grave…well, yes. That's a bit of a blow." I looked at each of my brothers in turn. Symon had turned away and was focusing a little too intently on the baby in order to give us space. "Even if I tell you that I'm fine, you're not going to believe me."

"That's not true."

"Isn't it?" I focused on Chase. "All of you are so deeply entrenched in the idea that I have nothing without work that you can't stop for a second to consider that there might be more to me."

Neither of them spoke for a moment. It was finally Craig who sighed and nodded. "You know what? You're right. I'm sorry, Asher."

Chase stood and rounded the table to put his hand on my shoulder. "I'm sorry, too. Damn. I didn't realize we were all being so closed-minded."

"We weren't trying to be." Symon finally spoke up, and I knew he spoke for Charli as well. "It's just that you've always been so focused that I don't think anyone bothered to stop and realize that there was more."

"Of course there's more." I hoped I sounded convincing, especially after my outburst. The problem was, I was full of shit. Even if I'd somehow managed to convince my brothers differently, I knew there wasn't anything more.

I didn't have anything in my life besides my work at Carlson Corp and my family. Nothing except Noa. And I didn't even really have her. She wasn't real or permanent or anything more than just a temporary distraction. In fact, spending the last few days with Noa, although they'd been a lot of fun, had also made it clear to me that I'd been missing out on a lot of life.

I swallowed hard and reached for my glass of water in an effort to calm my racing thoughts before I blurted out that particular realization. I drank deeply and then set my drink on the table. "So do you want to know about the cabin?"

I grinned as the men quickly switched gears and peppered me with questions about the little house I'd inherited. Thankfully, before the conversation could swing back to the topic of Noa again, the women entered with platters of food, the kids arrived with a burst of energy, and the Carlson family Christmas officially began.

Chapter Thirteen

NOA

AS PROMISED, the men cleaned the dinner dishes and kitchen while the women relaxed. As soon as the men joined us, Kat jumped up from the couch and announced that it was time for the annual family Christmas photo.

I followed everyone as they filed into the foyer of the house and jostled for position by the big Christmas tree and tried not to feel out of place because there was no way I could be part of Asher's family Christmas photo.

Chase set up the camera on a tripod, and Asher gestured for me to join him.

But I shook my head. "I'm just going to—"

"Noa." Chase noticed me trying to sneak away. "Get in the picture."

"But I'm not—"

"Come on, Noa!" Charli called. "Let's do this before the baby cries."

I looked around in a bit of a panic, but finally, when it

seemed there was no other choice, I blew out a breath. "Tell you what?" I said to Chase. "Let me take the first one, and then I'll get in one."

He looked like he might argue with me, but ultimately, he grinned and ran into position while I crouched down and looked through the viewfinder of the camera.

"Got it!" I called after taking a handful of pictures. "You all look great."

I started to slip away, but Asher appeared next to me. "Your turn," he whispered in my ear. "Go stand next to Kat. I'll set the camera."

There didn't seem to be any point in arguing. Besides, they had plenty of photos of their family, so my crashing one shot wouldn't tarnish the memories of Christmas. Resigned, I took my spot and smiled for the group shot.

Just when I thought things would start to wind down, and we could sneak away back to the cabin, where I could give Asher the gift I'd worked on while he was out chopping wood earlier in the day, Annie made a new announcement.

"Now we have a surprise for everyone." All eyes turned to Annie and Chase, who looked at her and smiled. "It's time for the first annual Mistletoe Madness."

"The what?" Asher raised an eyebrow.

"Mistletoe Madness," Annie repeated. "We decided that since our family has done so much growing and changing recently, we should start a new tradition."

"Okay." Charli grinned. "I like where this is going."

"Am I the only one who's confused?" Kat scanned the group.

"I promise I'll explain everything," Annie said. "Grady? Meri? It's time."

A moment later, Grady and Meri appeared with a big red sack.

"The kids are going to act as helpers this year since this first game is more suited to the adults."

"A game?" Lucy clapped her hands together like a child. "Fun."

"I hope so." Annie looked pleased, but behind her, I heard Asher groan.

I twisted my neck around. "You're not a fan of games?"

"He hates *losing* games," Charli told me with a wink.

Asher bent down and whispered in my ear. "I can't help it. I don't like to lose."

The scent of him filled my senses, and I had to remind myself that we were surrounded by his family and I couldn't kiss him the way I wanted to.

"Put your team uniform on." Annie was explaining the rules from the front of the room. "And since we have an uneven number, maybe Charli can sit out and Kat can take her place? Is that okay, Charli? Some of the activities might be a bit physical for you this year, but I didn't want to assume…"

"That's fine." Charli held up a hand. "I'm happy to let Kat be on team…" She reached into the bag Grady held out to her and pulled out a set of antlers. "Team Reindeer!"

Charli handed a set of antlers to Kat, who agreed to the team switch-up and went to stand with Symon.

Next, the kids moved to Craig and Lucy, who pulled out Santa hats. "I think you make a very cute Mrs. Claus." Craig put the hat on his fiancée before kissing her.

The kids cried out in protest, and everyone laughed before Meri took the bag over to me to choose our team uniform.

I reached in and grabbed a set of headbands with green hats and oversized elf ears.

"Looks like we're Team Elf." I slid the headband on Asher's head before donning my own.

"You make those ears look damn good." He wiggled his

eyebrows and gave me a quick kiss while everyone was focused on Annie and Chase, who were putting on their team costumes of black top hats and carrot noses.

"That was cheeky," I whispered when Asher pulled away.

"Sorry. I couldn't resist," he said under his breath. "Besides, no one saw."

But when I straightened up and faced the front of the room again, I didn't miss the grin on Kat's face, or the wink the other woman gave me.

ASHER

The games turned out to be an elaborate and completely chaotic obstacle course of sorts that had the four couples racing through the house. First up was *Rudolph and the Sleigh*. An event where the men were to drag their female partners on a blanket through the great hall, into the kitchen where they rounded the island, and then made their way back to the front door.

After that, we moved on to the *Wrapping Station*. The goal was for one person to wrap a gift while blindfolded, using only the instructions from their partner.

Once the present was wrapped, it was time to *Deliver the Gifts*. In the pool room, we raced to find floating rings in the middle of the pool. We took turns tossing small balls through the rings while Grady kept count. Once the team successfully delivered four gifts, we raced into the kitchen and the last station.

Claus's Cookies involved assembling a small gingerbread house before decorating three sugar cookies. The first team to finish was the winner.

It didn't take long for the competitive spirit of the Carlson family to shine bright. It was true that I hated to lose, but I wasn't alone in that. Chase and Craig were equally competitive Carlson family members, and as a former Olympic skier, Symon didn't know any other way.

The house filled with shrieks of laughter as the men ran full speed down the polished wood floor and swung their "sleighs" around the kitchen island. Chase took an early lead and was the first to cross the finish line. He grabbed Annie and together they sprinted to the study to begin wrapping.

I slid across the line shortly after Chase, followed by Symon and Craig. I all but picked Noa up and threw her over my shoulder in order to beat the others to our station for wrapping.

"You do the wrapping," Noa instructed. "I've got this." She tied the blindfold tightly at the back of my head. "Listen care-fully to my voice." Her fingers lingered at the back of my neck.

I reached up and grabbed her hand, squeezing it before she guided my hands to the wrapping paper in front of me.

"Asher."

Her voice cut through the noise, and I focused on the sweet sound.

"Use your left hand to find the edge of the paper."

I did as I was told.

"Good. Now lift it up and fold it over the box."

I focused on the task and followed the rest of her directions and soon, she was guiding me to put a piece of tape on the box.

"That's it."

I could hear the excitement in her voice, and more than anything, it was that alone that motivated me.

"Now the bow," Noa instructed. "It's right in front of you. Put it on top. There! We're done!"

I ripped the blindfold off and laughed at the most terribly

wrapped present I'd ever seen. I looked to Meri and Grady, who, along with Charli and the baby, were the judges. They all gave us the nod and with a whoop of celebration, I grabbed Noa's hand and we raced to the pool room.

We were in the lead, and easily aced the *Deliver the Gifts* portion of the game before heading into the kitchen.

Craig and Lucy were right on our heels and took the spot across from us at the table.

I handed Noa the icing bag and held the gingerbread pieces in place. "We got this, sweetheart."

"Sweetheart?" Craig stopped what he was doing and gave me a wide-eyed look.

I glared at my brother and refocused my attention on Noa and the task at hand. "I'll hold them and you—"

The words died on my lips as Noa used the piping bag to drop a dollop of icing on my nose. I was so shocked, I didn't know how to respond for a moment. Slowly, I brought my finger up to my nose. When I pulled it away, covered in icing, I looked at Noa, who was grinning wildly.

"Gotcha."

I glanced around the table at the rest of my family who'd caught up and were now all decorating their own houses and cookies. Each pair was focused intently on the task, each pair more competitive than the next.

In that moment, I had a choice: Focus and win. Or…

I smeared my icing-covered finger across Noa's cheek. And with my free hand, pinched up some colored sugar to flick on her.

"No, sweetheart. I got *you*."

She shrieked and then, the fight was on. Noa and I ignored everyone else intently focused on their decorating task and chased each other around the table with icing and sugar.

"Hey!" Annie lifted her head after I bumped into her, and I retaliated by dabbing her with icing. "Asher!"

Annie responded by throwing her bowl of candies at me and by then, the kids were screaming with joy and it was too late to stop the chaos that ensued.

It took me a few minutes to locate the instigator in the mess, but when I did, I wrapped my arms around Noa and spun her around. She looked so delicious with white icing all over her face, and I had to force myself not to lick it off her. "Look what you started," I teased. "Now there can't possibly be a winner."

"Don't tell anyone." She leaned in close to whisper in my ear. "That was kind of the point. I've never seen such a competitive family."

"You did this on purpose?"

Her eyes glittered with mischief.

"You're evil."

Noa threw her head back and laughed. "Truthfully, I really just wanted to smear icing on you."

She winked, and I could no longer resist this gift of a woman in my arms. It didn't matter who saw us; I didn't care. All I cared about was kissing her. I closed the distance between us and was about to kiss her when a sharp whistle split the air.

Everyone froze and turned their attention to Charli. "Okay, I think that's the end of our first annual Mistletoe Madness games. And it truly was madness." She laughed. "Did anyone actually finish decorating their cookies?"

"We did!" Across the room, Kat and Symon waved their arms in the air triumphantly. "While you guys were busy decorating each other, we nailed this."

Sure enough, to everyone's surprise, Symon and Kat had a plate of decorated cookies in front of them, as well as a completed gingerbread house.

"Congratulations," Charli declared. "I think the prize might be that the winners get to help the losers clean up. This place is a disaster."

Considering we'd been mostly responsible for the mess, I moved to find a garbage bag, but before I could slip away, Noa kissed me on the cheek and said, "Maybe we could take some of that icing back with us for later?"

The craziness of the room fell away and the only thing I could focus on was the image of Noa wearing only icing as I licked every bit of the sweetness off her body. I groaned and, very reluctantly, forced myself to move away from her before I forgot completely that I was surrounded by my family.

I watched after her for a moment when she winked and turned to start helping with the cleaning effort. When I was finally able to pull myself together enough to look away, I turned and my eyes locked on Chase and Craig, who stood shoulder to shoulder, both watching the interaction with raised eyebrows and questions on their lips.

Questions I didn't want to hear, because I wasn't ready to even think about the answers.

NOA

"That was fun." I meant it. I'd been a bit apprehensive about spending Christmas Eve with Asher's family, but everyone had been so warm and welcoming, it hadn't taken me long to get over any awkwardness and have a really good time.

"My family can be a lot." Asher pulled the truck up to the cabin and put it in park. "But it was fun to have you there. We would have won the games, too, if you hadn't gone rogue."

"That was the point." I laughed. "We couldn't win."

"Why not?" He looked at me in genuine confusion.

"Asher. I'm not part of your family. Every year, you'll talk about and remember who won the first Mistletoe Madness games. How would it be if it was some random woman you brought home after she jumped in your truck?" The thought had occurred to me when we were in the kitchen assembling the gingerbread house.

As nice as the Carlsons were, I wasn't part of their family. I didn't belong there, and I didn't want their new family tradition to be forever marred with me claiming the very first win. Which was why I'd incited the sugar and icing fight.

The look on Asher's face when I squirted the icing on his nose had been an added bonus.

"Besides," I added. "How would your future girlfriend or wife feel knowing that you'd already won with someone else?"

The smile fell from his face, and I felt a shift in my chest as my words settled around us in the cab of the truck.

"Noa. That's…" He shook his head slowly and blew out a breath. "Let's go inside."

It was ridiculous, and I had no business feeling any kind of feelings for Asher. Not when we'd both made it so clear to each other that neither of us wanted anything more than a little distraction and the fun we'd been having. Still… I was feeling something. And it was definitely more than just some distracted fun.

I tried to shake my feelings, and by the time Asher had a fire going in the fireplace and poured us each a glass of wine, I'd mostly convinced myself it was just the heightened emotion of the holiday season and everything that had happened over the last few days that had my feelings all mixed up.

Mostly.

"Come sit." Asher noticed me standing in the doorway to the bedroom. "I have to admit that while I'm not a big Christmas tree person, I think this one might be my favorite one."

It was just the opening I needed. As much as I'd enjoyed myself with his family, I couldn't help but feel out of place, and the feelings that had been gradually creeping in had left me feeling unsettled and more than a little unsure of what was happening or whether I should go ahead and give Asher the gift I'd worked on for him.

"One second." I held up a finger and disappeared into the bedroom. I took the gift that I'd wrapped carefully in some old newspaper to the couch. "I was going to give you this tomorrow morning, but I think it's better if you open it now."

"You got me a gift?" He put his glass of wine down and took the present gently from my hands. "You didn't have to—"

"I know I didn't have to," I said. "I *wanted* to. It's not a big deal. It's just—"

He stopped me with a kiss. "Thank you."

"Open it."

I picked up my glass of wine and sat back on the couch, suddenly unsure whether he'd like it.

Asher took his time with the newspaper as if it were fine wrapping paper, and finally lifted his gift up.

"A star?" He looked at me and then back to the star I'd constructed with branches and tied together with twine. It was a rustic and rough star, but it felt right. "For the tree? Noa...I love it."

"I told you the tree topper is special and it should be—"

He stopped me with a kiss that was so sweet and soft that all the feelings I'd held at bay rushed forward.

"This is so special." He stood from the couch and reached for my hand. "I don't think anyone has ever given me such a special gift. Seriously."

"Put it on the tree." I couldn't keep the smile from my face as I watched his reaction to my gift. I held the star while Asher pulled a chair over to the tree and stood on it. I handed the topper to him and then retreated to the other side of the room to check that it was straight as he put it in place.

"It's perfect."

"No." Asher stepped down from the chair and pulled me into his arms. "You're perfect."

He kissed me then, and for a moment everything did feel perfect. And not at all as if I'd just totally imploded my life by running away from my wedding and then gone and made it all so much worse by starting to fall in love with Asher.

Chapter Fourteen

ASHER

THE LAST THING I wanted to do the next morning was anything that didn't involve Noa naked in bed next to me, but when she asked whether I could drive her back to the lodge so she could see her grandmother for Christmas Day, there was no way I could refuse her.

We didn't speak much on the drive through the woods. Noa spent her time staring out the windows, lost in thought. I was lost in my own thoughts, the same ones that had been occupying most of my waking hours for the last few days.

Never in my life had I come close to such a thing, so I really had no idea what it felt like to fall in love, or even what that meant…but I was starting to get concerned that my increasing feelings for Noa might be dangerously close to something more than just a casual fling.

"I'm sorry I hijacked your Christmas." Noa spun in her seat and, for the first time, faced me. "The holidays don't really mean much to us anymore," she continued. "Not since Tom and Olivia…well, we don't really celebrate and with the whole…" She waved her hand. "Anyway, I didn't even think about it, but you should be with family today."

"I was with family yesterday. Remember?"

Her smile was sweet, if not a little shaky. She was nervous. I looked away from the road as she worried her bottom lip between her teeth.

"Besides," I continued. "My family tends to do a big thing on Christmas Eve and then everyone scatters on Christmas Day. I've spent the last few holidays mostly working and making sure everything goes smoothly at the lodge." Just like every other day of the year.

It hit me then that I was about to enter the Trickle Creek Lodge for the first time and not be able to go to my office or my suite. I hadn't stopped to consider what that would look or feel like. "I'll just drop you off at the front and—"

"You're not coming in?"

"I…well…I'm not really supposed to…"

"Are you dropping me off because you're…" She swallowed hard and looked away.

I reached across the cab of the truck and squeezed her thigh. "I'm not trying to get rid of you, if that's what you're asking." I meant it, too. For the first time in my life, I wasn't trying to get rid of a woman but was instead dreading the thought of returning to the cabin alone.

"So, you'll come in?"

I sighed.

"If it's about Ryan, I…shit. This is weird."

"Is it ever," I laughed.

I parked the truck in the staff parking lot, and together, we walked through the snow to the front doors, hand in hand.

Before we went up the steps, I stopped and pulled her into my arms. "It's going to be okay." The words felt inadequate. "Your family loves you, and I'm sure they'll have a lot of questions for you."

"They certainly will." She tried to laugh, but I could see the worry on her face. "But it's Christmas, and I know they'll just be happy to see me."

"Of course they will." Obviously, I had no way of knowing how her family would react. I knew how my family would respond if I ran off from my wedding to shack up with a stranger in a secluded cabin, and I couldn't help but think that it wouldn't be all that dissimilar to how Noa's family would be.

She leaned in and put her head against my chest. I stroked her hair gently and tried to ignore the tightness in my chest.

"Whatever happens, Noa, I want you to know that these last few days have been—"

"Merry Christmas, Mr. Carlson." The bellboy at the top of the stairs spotted me.

Reluctantly, I pulled back, the moment over, and together we walked up the steps.

The bellboy pulled the door open for us, and we walked into the warmth of the bustling lobby.

Maybe it was because I'd spent more holidays at the lodge than anywhere else, but as far as I was concerned, there was nowhere else quite as festive as Trickle Creek Lodge. My staff outdid themselves every year, and as I stepped into the middle of the room, a sense of pride filled me.

"Oh. There they are."

Next to me, Noa froze in place. I followed her gaze to the family who sat in the couches and wingback chairs next to the huge fireplace in the center of the room. I squeezed her hand and made a decision. "I'll be in the lounge whenever you're ready."

She looked at me, and her expression was impossible to read.

"If you decide you want to stay, Noa, it's okay. You don't owe me—"

"I owe you a lot, Asher. But that has nothing to do with why I plan on leaving with you later."

"Noa? Is that you?"

She glanced over her shoulder and then back at me.

"Go," I urged. "I'll be in the lounge."

She mouthed the words *thank you*, and without another look back, pulled away from my hand and ran across the lobby. "Grandma. Merry Christmas."

I hesitated for a moment, curious about the reunion, but ultimately the last thing I wanted was to get caught up in it in any way. Noa had a lot to discuss with her family. A lot. She really didn't need to attempt to explain our relationship to them on top of it all. Especially when neither of us were able to explain it to the other.

Or ourselves.

NOA

I ignored my mom and dad for the moment and went straight for Grandma Rose. "Merry Christmas, Grandma. You look fabulous."

My grandmother was dressed in her traditional holiday vest, white blouse, and matching red slacks. Her hair had been freshly done and little jeweled Christmas trees dangled from her ears.

Warmth flooded me. I'd made the right choice by returning.

"I missed you, Noa." Grandma squeezed me tight, with remarkable strength. "And I think it's you who looks fabulous. You're glowing," she whispered so only I would hear. "Being on the lam looks good on you."

"The lam?" I pulled away and stared at her with wide eyes, but Grandma Rose only laughed. "I've been—"

"Yes, Noa."

The sharp judgment in my mother's voice grabbed my attention. I swallowed hard and turned to face my parents and the inevitable questions they had for me.

"Where exactly *have* you been?"

"Hi, Mom. I'm fine. Thank you. Merry Christmas."

"Is it a Merry Christmas, Noa? Are we having a happy holiday right now?"

I'd expected to be challenged. How could I not be? After what I'd put my family through, I expected nothing less. I swallowed hard and looked to my dad, who rose from his seat and gave me a kiss on the cheek.

"Merry Christmas, Noa. It's good to see you, kiddo. We've been worried."

"We haven't been worried." My mother shot my dad a look. "We've been pissed off is what we've been."

"Mom, I—"

"I don't want to hear about it—"

"It's Christmas." My father put a hand on each of our shoulders and stepped between us. "I don't know if we need to talk about this right now. Why don't we have a nice Christmas drink and we can all just be together right now? With everything that…" My dad swallowed back his tears.

My chest ached with the knowledge that I'd brought any heartache to my parents at all after everything they'd already been through. I knew my mom was putting on a tough act to protect her heart, which was already so badly bruised. And that was the only thing that stopped me from offering a sharp retort in response.

Instead, I inhaled deeply and took a seat next to my grandmother, with my father in between and my mom across from me. It might not have been the best decision to have her in eyesight, but it felt safer than having her in arm's reach.

We sat in silence for a moment, and I worked hard not to let my eyes drift to the hotel bar where Asher had retreated. I'd been overwhelmed with emotion the moment I'd seen my grandmother, but now that the moment had passed, I couldn't help but think about Asher and our last few days.

"See?" Grandma Rose grabbed my arm. "You are absolutely glowing, my dear."

I swallowed hard and wouldn't meet my mother's gaze. Not that it mattered.

"Why is that, Noa? Is there a reason that you are glowing after the last week, when any glow you have should be coming from being a brand-new wife?"

I had a few choices. And none of them were great. Still, I chose the lesser of two evils. "Mom, I know you're upset with the way things went last week, but—"

"I think Charles is right." Grandma Rose jumped in. "We shouldn't talk about this right now. The only important thing is that Noa is here and we're all together." She reached over, and I took my grandmother's hand.

The moment I squeezed her hand, emotion rose up in my chest. "I'm sorry. I didn't mean to—"

"We're not talking about it right now." Grandma Rose put her foot down. "I mean it." She stared at each of us in turn. "Today is about family. No fighting today."

My mom looked as though she might fire back, but swallowed hard before a word came out. "Okay," she conceded. "But we *will* talk about this, Noa."

"I would expect nothing less, Mother." I forced a grin. "But for now…."

"For now, I just want to hear that you're okay, sunshine."

Grandma Rose smiled so sweetly that I almost cried. There was so much to tell and, at the same time, nothing I could say.

With my free hand, I reached for my necklace and rolled the golden rose between my fingers. "Of course I'm okay, Grandma. And I'm really sorry that I worried you. I really didn't mean to. That wasn't my intention. I just needed to—"

"Worry us and waste all our money."

"Janice. That's enough."

I smiled in my father's direction.

"We said we weren't going to talk about this right now, and we won't. Let's just enjoy our time with Noa while we—"

"While she's decided to grace us with her presence?" Janice jumped up from her chair. "I'm sorry. I know you told Ryan you wouldn't make a scene about anything today. But I didn't make that agreement."

Ryan? An agreement?

"I have questions, and I think I deserve answers. We all do." Janice focused her attention on me. "And it's not just us who deserve answers, either. Ryan and his family have been so patient while you're doing..." She waved her hand in a sporadic flip. "Whatever it is you're doing. With whoever you're doing it with. So yes, I think I deserve some answers, Noa. And I can't sit here and pretend that everything is okay, because I'm just not capable of ignoring the elephant in the room."

"Aren't you?"

I regretted the words the moment they were out of my mouth. I watched my mother's face contort into a mixture of shock, anger, and then finally sadness as she realized what I was referring to.

"Alessandra Briggs, that was just cruel." My mother shook her head. Worse than anything else I could have said, she pressed her lips together, and, without another word, turned and left.

For a moment, I considered going after her, but my father stopped me.

"Let her go."

"But, I—"

"She's feeling a lot of emotions this week, kiddo. It's been...well, it's been rough. When you disappeared..." He dropped his head, unwilling to meet my eyes, and the guilt I'd been trying to push down and not think about all week flared to life.

"Oh, Dad. I'm so sorry. I hope you didn't think that—"

"We didn't know what to think, Noa." He looked me in the eyes again. "It wasn't until we got some confirmation that you were okay that your mother could sleep again."

Guilt and sadness crashed through me. It had never been my intention to cause my parents any actual worry. If I were being honest, I hadn't even given any thought to what it might mean for my family and what kind of emotions would be brought up. All I'd thought about in that moment, and for all the days since, was myself. I'd been so selfish.

"Dad, I'm so sorry." I reached for him, but he pulled away as he stood.

"It's probably best to give her a little bit of space for the moment."

His smile didn't come close to reaching his eyes, and it broke my heart that I'd done that to him again after all this time. They'd only just started to recover from losing Tom and then I'd gone and—

"I'll talk to her, sweetheart." He reached for my hand and squeezed. "I'm glad you came. I can't tell you how good it feels to see your beautiful face again. I don't know if you're staying now or...well, I'm just glad to see you, kiddo." He gave me a sad smile and then he was gone.

Chapter Fifteen

ASHER

I WOULD HAVE PREFERRED to hide in my suite, but because that was no longer an option, I retreated to the only other place that felt like home. The lounge.

I took up my familiar end spot at the bar and it didn't take long before Brian appeared with a cup of coffee.

"I didn't expect to see you here, boss. Merry Christmas."

"Merry Christmas, Brian." I reached for the mug and lifted it to my mouth. "I'm not really here. Just killing a few minutes before…" There was no real way to explain why I was there.

"Just wave if you need anything, boss. I'll leave you to it."

I nodded, thankful that Brian was a perceptive man.

Old habits died hard, and after a few sips of coffee, I felt fortified enough to turn around and survey the room and the lobby beyond. It didn't take long to see that everything was running smoothly. It was one of the busiest days of the year, which meant there was the most potential for something to go wrong: an employee to call in sick, a shortage of something in the kitchen, lost luggage, or even a broken water pipe.

All catastrophes that I had dealt with at various times. But if anything was going wrong behind the scenes, my staff was doing a good job of hiding it.

My staff.

Were they still my staff, when I'd been stripped of my role? And even if they were still mine, did they even need me anymore?

It sure didn't look like it.

I turned around and focused on my cup of coffee before I accidentally caught a glimpse of Noa and her family. When she'd walked away from me and gone to them without so much as a glance behind her, it had sparked something deep inside me that I didn't even know I was capable of feeling.

Jealousy? Longing? Hurt?

I couldn't even begin to name the feeling that was so new to me. And at the same time, I didn't think I should search too hard for what it might mean. The last few days with Noa had been unexpected, but I wasn't naive. It couldn't last. Not forever. And walking through the doors of Trickle Creek Lodge and watching her walk away from me to her actual family had been a sharp reminder of that.

"A beer please."

A voice next to me pulled me from my thoughts. Brian poured a draft beer and slid it across the bar to the man who'd taken up the seat next to me.

"Merry Christmas." The man raised his glass in my direction. "Are you celebrating?"

"Christmas?" I shot him a look. "I wouldn't say that." I lifted my coffee mug. "Merry Christmas to you, though."

The man shook his head and took a deep pull on his beer. "I'm not much for the holidays," he said. "Not anymore. And especially not this year."

I wasn't looking to get into a conversation with anyone, let alone a stranger at the bar who needed to talk, but given that I didn't have a lot of other options, I turned slightly to face the man and give him the option to open up further.

"The holidays can be a lot."

The man blew out a puff of air and shook his head. "Especially when women are involved. Am I right?"

I didn't have a lot of experience in that particular area, but if recent events were anything to go by, I quite liked the addition of having a woman around during the holidays. I kept that little piece of information to myself and nodded noncommittedly.

"I should be celebrating with my bride this year. But that didn't happen."

I almost choked on my coffee.

"Oh, you must have heard about it, too." The man laughed and lifted his glass to his lips.

I swallowed hard and raised my hand for Brian. "I think I'll take a beer after all." I nodded to my seat mate. "And one for my new friend here."

"Cheers." The man I now realized to be Ryan tipped his glass and swallowed back the rest of his drink.

I probably should have walked away and pretended I wasn't sitting next to the man Noa had been about to marry. That would have been the best decision, for so many reasons. Yet I couldn't seem to help myself from being consumed by curiosity. I had to know whether everything Noa had said was true. Of course, I wanted to believe it was, and that the two of them weren't in love. *But what if…*

"I think I did hear someone talking about it," I lied. "So, she's not here with you then?"

It was an innocent enough question, and apparently the right thing to ask because Ryan chuckled, shook his head, and started talking. "Oh, she's here. At least for the moment." He glanced over his shoulder toward the lobby, and I had to force myself not to follow the man's gaze. "But she's not my wife. Yet."

Brian passed us each a fresh pint glass of beer.

Ryan nodded a thank-you and took a sip. "It seems my bride had a little case of cold feet last week and took off right before the ceremony."

"Oh?" I watched the other man carefully.

"Dramatic, right?" Ryan laughed. "It's funny, because Noa isn't really the dramatic type."

"It does seem a bit drastic," I said. "But, and excuse me for saying this, but you don't seem very upset about it."

Ryan chuckled again.

"I would think most men would be pissed. Or...sad."

"I don't disagree." He nodded. "But nothing about my relationship with Noa is normal or traditional in any way." He leaned closer to me. "Can I tell you something?"

This was the moment I should just walk away. I had no right to listen to this man confess anything about the woman I was currently developing very strong feelings for.

But I didn't walk away, excuse myself, or confess that not only did I know Noa but had spent the last few days getting to know her very, very well. Nor did I stop to think about what it meant that I'd just acknowledged, at least to myself, that on some level I had feelings for Noa. Strong ones.

Instead, I nodded. "Go ahead."

"Noa and I aren't a normal couple," Ryan began. "Sure, I'm a little pissed that she ran off without any heads-up, but also..." He shrugged. "I'm not worried about it because I know she'll be back."

"You think so?"

"I know so." Ryan sat up straight, full of confidence. "We're meant to be together. There's no doubt about that. Our families are already so close that this is just a formality at this point. No one knows her the way I do."

"So do you know why she ran then?"

"Of course." Ryan scoffed. "The whole big wedding wasn't her dream. It was all for show. Our mothers wanted a big production. We were doing it for them."

"The wedding or the marriage?"

Ryan looked at me sideways and, for a moment, I thought maybe I'd pushed it too far, but then he laughed.

"Both," he confessed. "In a way, all of it is for them. But also for us. The thing with Noa and me is that we've been through everything together. We know each other inside and out and still like each other."

"You mean you love her?" I wanted to pull the question back in the moment it slipped from my lips. Especially when Ryan answered without hesitation.

"Sure." He shrugged. "I mean, I love her the way I can love no other. She's my best friend." A smile crept across his lips. "She just has to sow some wild oats or whatever."

I sipped at my beer, unable to quite believe what I was hearing. "And you're okay with that?"

"The thing is," Ryan continued, "Noa and I aren't like that. We'll end up with some sort of arrangement."

"Arrangement?"

Ryan shrugged. "It's complicated."

Where had I heard that before?

"Like I said, we're meant to be together, and we've already discussed sealing the deal by New Year's."

New Year's?

The half pint of beer in my stomach soured at the idea of Noa saying yes to this man, or any man who wasn't me. I pushed the rest of the glass away and stood abruptly. "That's quite a story." I forced the words out. "I wish you the best of luck, man. But I really need to go."

"Thanks." Ryan extended his hand. "I have no doubt things will…"

I didn't wait for him to finish the statement before I turned and walked out of the bar, and the lodge.

NOA

"Do you think they'll ever forgive me, Grandma?"

Grandma Rose and I shared a pot of tea and a plate of scones while we waited for my parents to return. I'd expected them to be upset with me. They had every right to be. But I hadn't expected them not to return at all. After all, it was Christmas.

"Of course they'll forgive you," Grandma Rose said without hesitation. "They're upset right now, sweetheart. And you know this time of year is difficult for them as it is."

The familiar sensation of guilt clutched my heart and squeezed, increasing the ache in my chest that had settled there the moment I'd walked through the main doors of the lodge.

"They just need a little time," Grandma continued. "I'm sure they'll be down for dinner."

"Dinner?" I glanced around, half expecting to see Asher, but not surprised when I didn't. He'd made himself scarce the moment we arrived, which at the time I'd been grateful for. The thought of explaining to my parents who he was—and what he meant to me when I didn't even know how to put it into words myself—was more than I could handle.

But now that he'd been away from me for a while, I found myself missing him. There was something reassuring about his presence. Almost protective. Not that I needed protecting. I never had. Still, it felt good knowing he had my back, even after only knowing each other for such a short time.

"Who are you looking for, my dear?"

I turned to see Grandma Rose's eyes glittering with mischief. "No one." My fingers went to the rose at my throat.

"You've never lied to me before, Noa." She held up her hand. "And before you try to tell me again that you're not looking for that handsome young man you walked in here with, you should know that I may be old, but I'm not stupid. And I see a whole lot more than you all give me credit for."

I opened my mouth, but she kept going.

"Like, for example, I also noticed that the young man from earlier today looked a whole lot like that handsome hotelier you ran into in the hallway the other day while you were escaping your cousin. Who, by the way, has returned home, along with most of the guests."

Another wave of guilt washed through me as I realized I hadn't even thought about Sarah or the rest of the family who'd expected to attend a wedding. I'd been so selfish.

"I forgot about Sarah," I said quietly. "I forgot about—"

"Hush." Grandma Rose put a surprisingly strong hand on my leg. "Of course you forgot about everyone else. You weren't thinking about anyone but yourself."

I opened my mouth to defend myself, but she continued before I could.

"And that's okay, Noa," she said gently. "You had—and still have—every right to put yourself first."

"But Mom and Dad. They—"

"They'll get over it." She pressed her lips together in a perfectly applied line. "So will everyone else. Because the only reason you should get married is because you are desperately, madly in love with your person."

Something deep inside me sparked. And it had nothing to do with Ryan.

"What you don't do," Grandma Rose continued, "is get married for any other reason." She looked me straight in the eye. "And you definitely never get married for other people or to make them happy."

Grandma knew.

I shouldn't have been surprised. I'd always had a special connection with my grandmother.

"That's not why…" I stopped myself before the lie slipped out. "I do love Ryan."

"But you're not in love with him."

It wasn't a question. Still, I shook my head.

"Ryan is a good man," I said slowly. "He's thoughtful and kind and…" My thoughts drifted to Asher. To the last few days. The way he'd drawn things out of me I'd never said aloud. The passion. The laughter. The way I felt when he was near. The way he'd driven me here even knowing how hard it would be for him.

I imagined him driving back to the cabin alone. What it would mean if I didn't go with him—if I stayed instead and tried to pick up a life I could no longer imagine living.

My throat tightened, and swallowing was suddenly hard. My fingers found the gold rose again.

"Did I ever tell you I married your grandfather two weeks after meeting him?" Grandma Rose asked.

"What?" My mouth fell open. "I didn't know that."

She laughed softly. "It's true. Much like you, I was engaged to another man. Unlike you, I thought he was the one."

The look she gave me told me she knew exactly why I'd agreed to marry Ryan.

"I didn't have cold feet," she continued. "Everything was planned for the fifth of May. It was to be a lovely garden wedding. But two weeks before the wedding, Mother sent me to your great-grandfather's office with his lunch. That's where I met your grandfather. He was an intern across the hall." She squeezed her eyes shut, lost in the memory. "It only took one look and I knew. My stomach fluttered. And when he introduced himself, I couldn't even say my own name."

"And that was it?" I asked.

She smiled. "Well, it wasn't quite as simple as that. But I knew that day that I couldn't marry George. He was a good man. Kind and thoughtful. He would have been an excellent provider and an excellent father. I would have had a good life with him. But it wouldn't have been fair. Not to either of us. Because I had never, not even once, felt the way with him that I felt the very first time I met Frank. And I knew, even back then, that kind of magic doesn't come along every day. And it can't be ignored."

"Wow."

"Wow indeed. I broke George's heart, but he went on to have the life and love he deserved."

"And you?" I already knew. I'd seen that love with my own eyes before my grandpa passed.

"Frank felt it, too. We spent the next two weeks courting, and it didn't take long before I knew everything I needed to know. We were married on the fifth of May in that lovely garden ceremony."

I pressed a hand to my chest.

"Sometimes you have to take a chance," she said softly. "And it's okay to be selfish. You only get one life. Live it well. And live it for yourself."

Her words settled deep as I scanned the busy lobby. Movement near the oversized wooden doors caught my eye. A bellboy opened them for a guest—and that's when I saw him.

Asher was outside, sitting on a bench in the cold.

"Grandma?" I turned. "About dinner…"

She smiled knowingly. "There will be more Christmas dinners, my dear. Follow your heart."

I kissed her cheek and hugged her tight. "I love you. Thank you."

I didn't look back as I crossed the lobby, headed straight for the doors and the man who made it hard to breathe.

Asher looked up, surprised.

"Can we go?" I asked. "Back to the cabin? Can we go?"

The tension drained from his face, replaced by a broad smile.

He stood and took my hand. "Absolutely."

Chapter Sixteen

ASHER

WE DROVE BACK to the cabin in silence. Noa stared out the window, obviously lost in thought, and I was consumed by my own thoughts—none of which I seemed able to untangle into anything coherent. And definitely nothing I could put into words.

After I'd left the lounge—and Ryan—I spent the rest of my time waiting for Noa walking around the hotel grounds. I followed the pathway through the trees that led to stunning viewpoints over the valley; I ventured close to the base of the ski hill and watched happy families and couples make their way down the slopes, laughing and having fun.

Everywhere I went, I saw happiness and laughter and people together, enjoying themselves. It was Christmas; that was to be expected. But I'd never really stopped to notice it before. Not in a real way. Not beyond the fact that I wanted all my guests at the lodge and the ski hill—and in the summer, at the golf course—to be happy customers.

It wasn't until today, as I waited for Noa and observed all

of those around me, that I ever stopped to consider my own happiness and what it might take for me to be participating in that kind of joy instead of just facilitating it.

The problem was, I was afraid that I might already know the answer to that question and that it might end up slipping away from me before I had a chance to figure it out.

When we were about halfway back to the cabin, I reached across the space between us and took Noa's hand in mine. I didn't say a word. It was enough to have the touch of her while we drove.

It was silly and maybe it didn't make any sense—because Noa had never been mine and she didn't owe me anything—but the longer we drove, the more I felt like she was slipping away from me.

Something had changed.

Was it the conversation I'd had with Ryan? Or something her family had said?

Or both?

She fell asleep as the sun went down. Still, I held her hand in mine until I pulled the truck up in front of the cabin I'd already come to think of as ours.

I moved around to the passenger door and lifted her carefully from the seat. I held her close against my body, and she snuggled up against my chest, still half asleep.

I moved slowly and carefully over the icy path and up the steps into the cabin. I slipped her boots off and took her back into the bedroom, where I laid her gently on the mattress.

Noa's arms locked around my neck.

"Don't go."

"You're exhausted." I kissed her chastely on the forehead and tried to untangle her from me, but she pulled me down to the bed.

"I don't want you to go."

I couldn't argue with that. Especially because there was nothing I wanted more than to lie next to her.

I shucked my own boots and coat and slipped into the bed beside her. I pulled the quilt up over us both, and she snuggled into my chest.

Her hair was soft under my touch. I stroked it rhythmically, moving down her shoulder to the fuzzy sweater she still had on. My body reacted instantly to the feel of her against me, the same way it had from the first time I'd met her.

Soon, Noa's hand slid down my chest and rested on my dick, still trapped in the confines of my jeans. She lifted her head and her mouth found mine in a slow, sensuous kiss.

It wasn't hurried, but there was an intensity to it that had never been there before. We hardly disconnected from each other as somehow we managed to strip each other of our clothes, until we were finally naked together.

I rolled us over so Noa was on her back, looking up at me.

Her eyes were full of emotion, but I didn't need to ask what she was feeling, because I was feeling it too. Something had changed between us. Something neither of us could say—or were willing to say. Not out loud.

I sighed against her mouth as I kissed her again. She wrapped her arms around my back and pulled me down to her.

We came together, eyes wide open, emotion neither of us was willing to voice on the tips of our tongues. And when we were finished, we fell into a deep, almost immediate sleep, still tangled up together.

When I woke hours later, the moon shone through the window and illuminated the room. I rolled and gently pulled Noa up against my chest, trying to hold onto everything I knew was slipping away. The last week with her had been unlike anything I'd ever experienced before. It was unlike anything I'd ever *wanted* to experience before.

I didn't know how it had happened—or more importantly, how I could possibly hold onto it—but I did know that at some point yesterday, after visiting the lodge, something had shifted between us.

I inhaled deeply and nuzzled into her neck, filling my senses with the scent of her. I needed to memorize everything I could. When the sun came up, things would be different. I didn't know how I knew it. Only that I did.

"Asher?" Noa wiggled in my arms, but I held her tight.

"You're awake." Her voice was still heavy with sleep. "Why? It must be late."

"I just…" I stopped myself and went with the truth. "I didn't want to miss anything."

She managed to turn so she was facing me. I draped my arm over her hip.

"What did you think you'd miss in the middle of the night?"

"This." I let my fingers lazily trace the curves of her body. "All of this."

The smile slipped from her pretty face. She reached for my face. I closed my eyes as Noa took her turn memorizing parts of me. I knew it was goodbye. It had to be. There was no other way forward. She was going to go and marry Ryan because they were meant to be together, and that was that. There was nothing I could do about it. No matter what I was feeling.

"Asher?"

I swallowed hard and exhaled slowly before I opened my eyes.

"What are you thinking?"

Even in the dim light, I could see that her eyes held a storm of emotions.

I reached for her hand and laced my fingers through hers. More than anything, I wanted to tell her exactly how I felt. I wanted to tell her that the last week I'd spent with her had been the best of my life. That never before had I connected with a woman the way I'd connected with her. I wanted to hold her in my arms and let her know that the thought of her walking away from me was unbearable, and despite my best efforts, I couldn't begin to imagine what a life without her would look like.

I wanted to tell her how thankful I was that she had jumped into my truck on what was probably the worst day of my life and turned it into the best one. How I'd been able to forget about my worries—and the fact that without my work, I had nothing and *was* nothing—because when she was near, somehow it felt like I had everything.

But I couldn't. It wasn't fair. Much to my surprise, I cared about her too much.

"I met Ryan."

"What?" The shock registered on her face at the same moment she tried to pull away, but I held her hand tight in mine. "You *met* him?"

"I bought him a beer."

She blinked hard. "You…were you going to tell me this?"

"I'm telling you now."

My chest ached, but there was no other way. I wasn't stupid enough to think this—whatever it was—could go on forever. It had already gone on too long. I never should have let things get carried away.

She squeezed her eyes shut, and it took all my self-control not to pull her close and kiss away the doubt and confusion she must have been feeling.

Instead, I waited, and when she opened her eyes again, I could see things had changed.

Gone was the raw vulnerability of a few minutes ago.

She was steeled for what was to come.

She knew.

NOA

For a few minutes when I'd first woken in his arms, I let myself believe that things were going to be okay. That the shift I'd felt in him last night had only been in my own overactive imagination.

The entire drive back to the cabin, I'd been lost in my own muddled thoughts. Maybe I should have tried to talk to him about what I was feeling. About how crazy it was, but how I felt in my gut that there was something between us. Maybe I should have told him that when I thought about leaving him and the cabin, it ripped my heart out in a way I'd never felt before. That I couldn't swallow down the lump in my throat.

But instead, exhausted by a flood of emotion, I'd fallen asleep.

And when he'd carried me inside and kissed me…the way we'd made love…hadn't that communicated everything that needed to be said?

The way he was looking at me now, the words he'd just spoken—the reality of it all crashed down. We hadn't been communicating our feelings. Not at all.

It had been a goodbye.

I squeezed my eyes shut.

How had I been so stupid? He'd never wanted this. Never wanted me.

I'd started this. I'd created this chaotic mess we were in.

So I'd end it.

I'd had a lifetime of pushing my feelings down and compartmentalizing them. So I did what I knew how to do. I put the lid on my heart that was threatening to shatter into a million pieces and opened my eyes.

"Why are you telling me this now?"

His fingers were still laced through mine. It felt like a last, tenuous connection, and I wasn't ready to let go. Not yet.

"I thought it was best to be honest."

Honest.

"And?" I asked. "What did the two of you talk about?"

I didn't want to know. I didn't care.

I already knew.

"You, of course." Before I could ask anything else, Asher added, "He didn't seem to know who I was."

Or what he meant to me.

"I don't know if that makes it any better."

We stared at each other in silence for a moment.

"He told me the two of you are meant to be together. That no one knows you the way he does."

I opened my mouth to object, but closed it again. It was true that Ryan and I had been through a lot together. But there was so much he didn't know. Things I'd told Asher instead. It didn't feel like the right time to bring it up.

"Ryan's always been a pretty confident man." What I wanted to say—what I should have said—was that it didn't matter what Ryan thought because I didn't want to marry him. Not then, not now, and not ever. But the words didn't come out. "He told me the same thing the other day when I spoke to him on the phone."

Asher nodded, as if I'd just confirmed his suspicions.

"He said it wasn't too late to make things right, but—"

"To make it right?" Asher's eyebrows lifted. "And that's what you're going to do then?"

"I didn't say that."

"You didn't *not* say it, Noa." He smiled, but there was no humor behind it. "You know what else you didn't say?"

He tried to laugh, and I could tell he was trying to keep the conversation light when there was nothing light about it.

"You didn't tell me how things went with your family today. Not that you need to. I just…it doesn't matter."

"Doesn't it?"

He sighed. "No, it doesn't matter, Noa." His fingers slipped out of mine as he pulled himself up into a sitting position. "We both know what's going to happen here."

"We do?" My voice shook. The emotions were too strong. The carefully constructed compartments I'd shoved my heart into were starting to crack, and I struggled to keep my composure.

Maybe I knew it would happen. But there was a huge part of me—maybe the biggest part—that hoped it wouldn't. Nothing about us made sense, and we were never supposed to be anything anyway.

"We do." Asher wouldn't look me in the eyes. "We always knew this was just a fun little fling, Noa. You were always going to go back to Ryan and your family." He chuckled, like it was some big joke we were both in on.

I wasn't laughing.

After a moment, Asher reached for me. "Don't look so serious. I was just kidding." He kissed me, but I couldn't bring myself to kiss him back.

"Noa," he said. "I'm sorry. I thought you'd know I was teasing. It's late. Let's go to sleep."

Everything felt wrong. The shift between us was too big to ignore, but he was right. It was late. We could talk about it in the morning.

I lay down next to him, and Asher immediately pulled me in tight. The heat of his body warmed me. His hand came to rest on my hip, as if it were the most natural thing in the world, like we'd been together for years.

It took a few minutes for his breathing to slow, to fall into the steady rhythm of sleep.

I was sure he was asleep when I finally whispered, "You don't know how I feel."

He tightened his grip on me, and I stiffened—worried and hopeful that he'd heard me. But again, his chest rose and fell in a gentle rhythm.

I'd almost fallen asleep myself when I heard his voice.

"I know how I want you to feel."

More confused than ever, a tear slipped down my cheek and soaked into the sheet beneath me.

But I'm afraid, I wanted to scream. *I'm afraid to feel this.*

The words stayed lodged in my throat.

A few minutes later, exhaustion finally won, and I drifted to sleep.

Chapter Seventeen

ASHER

I WOKE EARLY, before Noa, and made coffee. I needed a chance to clear my head after the horrible asshole I'd been the night before.

I'd already replayed the midnight conversation a million times in my head. Each time, I hated myself a little bit more for the way I'd handled things.

What was it about me that didn't allow me to just say how I felt? Why couldn't I just look her in the eye and tell her that I didn't want her to marry Ryan? That I wanted her to stay with me in whatever way that made sense? That I was developing feelings for her? Real ones. Why couldn't I just say that to her?

What was wrong with me?

The cabin was too small and I needed to move.

I grabbed my coat, stuffed my feet into my boots, and as quietly as I could, slipped out the back door to the shed behind the house.

It was hard for me to believe that this place was mine and I still didn't know anything about it. I'd been a little distracted.

Okay, more than a little distracted.

Maybe that was a good thing.

I pulled the old wooden door of the shed open and let the daylight spill into the dark room. I'd only ventured in far enough to find an axe and the old wooden sled we'd used a few days earlier, but there was a lot more to discover.

The room was large and organized. Tools were hung up on the pegboard, and cans of various screws and fasteners were lined up along a workbench. Toward the back of the room were a few pairs of snowshoes and cross-country skis that looked as if they hadn't been used in years.

I ignored them and turned my attention to an old notebook I'd found tucked in between two old coffee cans of nails.

I recognized my father's handwriting immediately, and my breath caught in my throat.

All my siblings had processed our dad's death in different ways. Each one grieved him in a way that was just as unique as their relationship with him had been. All five of us were so different, it never occurred to me until recently that we must have been a challenging group to raise.

Dad had prided himself on being as fair of a father as he possibly could. Even when I expressed interest in taking over the operations of Carlson Corporation, he called a family meeting to make sure everyone was okay with me assuming control. Of course, they all were more than fine with it. Only I had ever shown any real interest in the family business; the rest of my siblings always had other interests and things that drove them.

For me, it had always been the family business. Even while I'd been away at college for my degree in business management, every single thing I'd studied, I'd done it with an eye to how I could apply it to Carlson Corporation. I was constantly thinking about how I could increase profits and employee satisfaction. What could I implement to improve the guest experience, or to give back to the community?

For almost ten years, every single day had been devoted to Carlson Corporation. I'd hardly even taken a holiday. Not a real one, anyway. And definitely not one where I hadn't taken my laptop.

Now that I stopped to think about it for a minute, not only had I not been working for the last week, but I'd also hardly given work a thought.

That had never happened before. Ever.

And it wasn't likely to happen again. Not once Noa left.

And she was going to leave.

I squeezed my eyes shut against the intrusive thought and focused my attention on something I could control. The notebook in my hands.

I fanned through the pages to take a cursory look. The book was full of lists and bullet points. There were a few longer entries where my father had noted the projects he'd tackled, along with the challenges he faced. By the looks of things, he'd faced many different kinds of setbacks while he restored the little cabin.

The first entry in the notebook was dated six months after our mother, Angela, had passed away.

"How had we not known about this place?" I lowered the book and looked around the shed. Judging by the dates scribbled in the book, Michael had been visiting the cabin alone for years. There was no mention of him having any help with the various projects on his lists.

"Why me, Dad?" Again, I fanned through the book. I'd have to sit down and properly go through it when I had time to figure out what it all meant.

I could only just make out the cabin through the grimy shed window. Noa would be up soon and there was no way I could pretend that last night hadn't happened.

With a sigh, I tucked the journal and all the answers it might contain back on the shelf. I only had the bandwidth these days for one problem at a time.

NOA

He was gone when I woke up. For a moment, I didn't know whether I should be upset or relieved by that.

Maybe that feeling told me everything I needed to know.

I'd only slept fitfully after our…what could you even call what had happened the night before? A fight?

It wasn't really.

A reckoning?

A reality check?

Maybe that was the best way to describe it.

Whatever it had been, it had left me feeling unsettled and…for lack of a better word, sad.

I poured myself a cup of coffee from the pot he'd made and turned as the front door opened and Asher came inside.

"Morning."

"Good morning." I leaned back against the counter and watched as he shrugged out of his parka and kicked his boots off.

"Is the coffee still warm? I could make more if it's—"

"It's perfect." I lifted the mug to my lips and took a sip. "You're up early."

He moved through the room, into the kitchen, and pulled me into his arms for a quick kiss. In that moment, when his lips pressed to mine, everything felt *normal* again. Not that we had a normal. Not after less than two weeks. Still. The weirdness of the night before vanished, and it was just Asher and me again.

I squeezed my eyes shut, wanting to savor the moment, but

the instant he pulled away, the cold reality of the day slapped me in the face.

Something had shifted between us. It couldn't be ignored. Even if that's exactly what I wanted to do.

"What were you doing outside so early?" I asked his back as he poured himself his own cup of coffee.

"I needed to think."

I exhaled deeply before blowing out the breath slowly. "And?" I hated myself for even asking, but I'd never been the type of woman to shy away from a difficult conversation—with one notable exception.

"And I meant what I said last night, Noa." He squared off across from me, in a move that felt so confrontational that a trickle of ice spiraled down my spine.

It was a good thing I was leaning up against the counter; I needed the support. "Which part?"

"We both know what's going to happen here, Noa."

He glanced out the window before fixing me with a gaze so full of indifference that it caused me physical pain to look at him.

"No." I put the cup on the counter and crossed my arms over my chest. "We absolutely do not know what's going to happen, Asher." He tilted his head and raised his eyebrows, and I couldn't keep looking at him. My gaze fell to the floor for a moment. "I don't know why you think you know me well enough to know how I'm going to live my life, Asher."

"I know your type."

"My type?" I once more looked up. This time I narrowed my eyes and glared at him. "What the hell is that supposed to mean?"

He took a sip of coffee and dragged out the moment. "Look, Noa. This was—"

"No." I stopped him. "You don't get to say something like that and then not follow through." I stepped toward him, closing the distance that suddenly felt cavernous. "What does that mean? My *type*?"

He sighed, as if speaking to me was a huge effort. "You have your whole life laid out for you. A family who loves you. A good man waiting for you. And don't forget, I met him, Noa," he added. "I saw firsthand exactly how he feels about you and what you left behind."

I shook. "You don't even know what you saw."

"Not true." He pressed his lips together smugly, and I wanted to scream. "I saw a man who knows you a whole hell of a lot better than I do, and he told me quite confidently that the two of you are going to—"

"I don't care what he said!" I didn't mean to raise my voice, but I couldn't help it as the frustration and bottled-up emotion poured out. "He doesn't speak for me, Asher. He never has. Yes, he's my best friend. But the things we talked about…the things *you* know about me." I sucked in a breath and looked down for a second. "Asher…he doesn't know…he doesn't know how I *feel*."

He opened his mouth and closed it again at my choice of words. I hadn't imagined it the night before. He *had* heard me.

The silence between us stretched out endlessly until, finally, he asked, "And? How do you feel, Noa?"

It was the question I'd dreaded. Not because I didn't want to tell him exactly how I was feeling, how I'd never before had such a connection with a man before and the idea of walking away and never seeing him again filled me with a pain in my chest that threatened to consume me—but because I didn't know how to put those feelings into words.

And what if I did open up and did my best to explain the unexplainable and he still looked just as closed off as he did in that moment? What if I bared my soul to him, and in return I got nothing?

Maybe it was better to walk away with what was left of my

pride and leave this time in the cabin as a special memory, which was all it was ever meant to be.

That's what I needed to remember.

I didn't want this. I didn't want him. I never had. And just because Asher happened to appear at a moment in my life when I needed a little distraction didn't mean any of that had fundamentally changed.

"I feel like…" I inhaled deeply and took my time blowing out the breath. "Maybe I should go."

ASHER

I knew it was coming. How could it not? After all, I'd been pushing her and driving us to this very moment ever since we left the lodge the day before.

Still.

Her words hit me in the gut like a punch.

Go? She couldn't go.

I wouldn't let her.

I couldn't look at her because if I did, I was afraid my face would give away everything I was thinking and feeling, and I refused to be weak in front of her. Not when she'd just willingly told me everything I needed to know about the situation.

It was a fling.

A fun distraction.

We didn't have any kind of real connection. Not like she had with her fiancé.

Ryan had warned me without even knowing what he was doing. The two of them had a connection. There was no way she wasn't going to go back to him. It had always been inevitable. She wasn't mine. And she never would be.

That was clear.

"Nothing is keeping you here." The words tasted sour on my tongue, but I couldn't stop myself from what came next. "I'll have two more to take your spot by the end of the night."

I saw the exact moment Noa realized exactly who Asher Carlson really was.

Her face crumpled—but only for a moment—before she gritted her teeth, took two steps toward me, and slapped me across the face.

"Fuck you, Asher."

I took the blow without reacting. The sting in my cheek was nothing compared to the pain slicing through my chest. But there was no way I could go back now. I'd committed to being the biggest asshole I possibly could. The only thing I could think to do was push her away and back to the life she was meant to have.

The man she was meant to marry.

"Maybe just give me some sort of timeline." I doubled down. "You know, of when you'll be gone, so I can let the ladies know when they should be here. I don't want my bed to get too cold."

There was no way I would've believed I was capable of saying such awful things to Noa if the words hadn't come from my own mouth.

For a moment, she looked like she might say something. Her pretty mouth opened and closed. Finally, she shook her head—just a little. "Go to hell."

She turned and stormed into the little bedroom.

"Fuck," I muttered under my breath, dragging my hands through my hair.

It took everything in me not to follow her, wrap her up in my arms, and beg her forgiveness for the vile things I'd said. Every cell in my body urged me to go to her, but there was a tiny part of me screaming to let her go.

It was for the best.

I'd never wanted her. Or *this*. Or any of it. I'd spent my whole life keeping love at bay. Just because a gorgeous, smart, sexy, kind woman had jumped into my truck didn't mean any of that had changed.

Yes it did.

Everything had changed.

I shook my head and tugged at the roots of my hair.

No.

Even if I did want to be with her—to try to make something out of this crazy thing we had—it would never work. She deserved more. She deserved the man who knew her inside and out and had been through everything with her. She deserved the man who would sit and wait for her even after she ran out of their wedding because he understood she might need time to sort through things before committing forever.

That's what she deserved.

What she did not deserve was a man married to his work. A man with no idea what to do with himself now that the only thing he loved had been taken away. All I had was work.

That wasn't enough for a woman like Noa.

She deserved so much more.

I turned and slammed my hands onto the tabletop, dropping my head and letting it hang while I tried to collect myself.

I hadn't woken up that morning determined to blow everything up between us. Not at all. I could still feel her skin against mine. Our heated bodies. The way we'd made love the night before.

It had been different. More intense. More—It didn't matter.

Did it?

Maybe it did. Maybe I was being a giant jackass and what we had *did* matter.

A noise caught my attention. I lifted my head and saw Noa

standing in the bedroom doorway, a small shopping bag in her hands.

"I don't really have anything to pack."

This was my chance. I straightened and cleared my throat. All I had to do was reach for her and pull her close. Whisper that I was sorry. That I didn't mean any of it. Tell her the truth.

That I was falling in love with her.

I took a step forward.

"I'll call Ryan to come get me."

Her words slammed into me. Whatever hope I'd been clinging to evaporated instantly.

"Ryan?"

"My—"

"I know who he is." The words came out sharp and ugly. I grabbed my truck keys from the counter and tossed them at her. "Don't wait for him. Just go."

"I can't—"

"Take it. Leave it at the lodge."

"But you—"

"I don't fucking care, Noa. Just get out of here." I couldn't look at her. My chest was buzzing with emotions I couldn't name. I didn't wait to see whether she took my advice—or my truck. I grabbed my boots and jacket, yanked the door open, and left.

I wasn't going to stay and watch her go.

I didn't have it in me.

Chapter Eighteen

NOA

I DIDN'T WANT to cry. I never cried. And I definitely didn't want to cry over a man I'd only known a few weeks.

A man who'd made me feel things I didn't even know were possible.

Still.

I refused to cry.

Somehow, I managed to drive the old, beat-up truck back down the mountain roads and into town. I left the keys in it outside the front door of the lodge and went straight up to the suite I was sharing with Ryan.

Thankfully, he was out when I got back. Skiing, no doubt. That had been the whole point of choosing Trickle Creek Lodge for our festivities. Ryan thought it only made sense to turn the event into a holiday everyone could enjoy, too.

Knowing Ryan, he'd likely been skiing every single day since I'd been gone, without a care in the world about whether I'd be back or not.

Not because he didn't care—but because he knew.

I groaned and threw myself onto the giant king-sized bed. He *knew* I'd be back. Was I really that predictable?

Despite doing the most unpredictable thing I possibly could by running away with a stranger, it didn't matter—because ultimately and predictably, I was back for the life that had always been waiting for me.

Even if I didn't want to face it.

I pulled the duvet up and over my head. It wasn't until I closed my eyes and saw Asher's face—the moment he told me to get out—replaying over and over in my mind that I finally let myself cry.

ASHER

It had been two days since Noa had driven away with my truck, leaving me alone. The days had been long and lonely—not that I was about to admit it.

I filled my time splitting wood and restocking the pile in the house for the fireplace and in the woodshed next to the cabin. Winter was long and cold in the mountains; I'd need a lot of wood to keep the place warm.

Especially without Noa in my bed.

The thought, like all the thoughts I'd had for the last few days, popped unwelcome into my mind. I lifted the axe and brought it down hard.

And again.

Hard, physical labor was the only way I could keep her out of my head for longer than a few seconds at a time.

If I could exhaust myself completely, maybe I'd stop thinking about where she was. What she was doing. Whether she was with her *fiancé*. Whether she was thinking about me. Whether she hated me.

Although I was pretty sure I already knew the answer to that one.

Of course she hated me. How could she not? I'd been cruel. The way I'd treated her had been inexcusable.

Yes. She definitely hated me.

I hated myself.

It was better that way. At least then she could go on with her life and not waste even one more moment of her time on me. She deserved at least that much.

It was laughable that I'd entertained—even for a second— the idea that I could be enough for a woman like Noa. I didn't have anything to offer her. Beyond a secret little, shitty house in the woods, I had nothing.

My father had seen to that.

He'd single-handedly ruined my life.

From the grave, no less.

I laughed out loud, the hollow sound echoing in the cold. "It takes a special kind of skill to fuck over your kids from beyond the grave, Dad. Then again, I probably shouldn't be too surprised."

I bent to retrieve another log from the stack and set it on the chopping block.

I lifted the axe and brought it down hard. The wood split into two pieces with a satisfying crack.

I reset the wood and lifted the heavy steel again.

"I wasn't good enough then." *Thwack.* I brought it down with a grunt.

"And you made sure I knew that." I swung the axe again. "Didn't you, Dad?"

Instead of resetting the wood, I grabbed a piece in my free hand.

"I was never good enough for you," I yelled into the crisp quiet of the day. "All I ever did was try to make you proud." I heaved the wood with all my might into the forest, where it struck a tree. "I worked my ass off for you." I picked up another piece and hurled it, too. "No one else wanted what you built. Only me." I threw another piece. "But you didn't care." And another one. "You've made that perfectly fucking clear."

I bent to pick up another piece, this one bigger than the last. "Fuck. You." With a guttural scream, I flung the log into the trees before dropping my head and folding over myself as a sob tore out of my chest.

Bent over in the cold winter day, for the first time since my father had died, I gave myself over to the grief I'd never let myself feel.

I'd been too busy trying to keep everything running in the wake of his death. There'd been no one else to do it. Without me, Carlson Corp would have struggled. Sure, my father had his assistant, Steven Larson, and his attorney, but they didn't have the experience I did. I'd been preparing to take over the company almost from the moment I was old enough to ask for a part-time job in the office.

I couldn't remember a time when I'd wanted anything else from life. I'd watched everything my father did—both in business and in the community—with pride. He gave so much of himself to the town of Trickle Creek, and many would argue that Michael Carlson was responsible for saving its livelihood. Everyone loved him.

His loss had been felt keenly.

By everyone except me.

It wasn't something I'd admitted to anyone. Not even my siblings. But the only way I'd been able to keep going—running the business, getting through the days without him—was by pretending, at least a little, that he was only on vacation.

As the sobs worked their way through my body, I finally accepted the truth in all its certainty.

My father was gone.

He wasn't coming back.

He would never again preside over our chaotic family dinners. He'd never sit in on another board meeting and offer his opinions on annual projections. And he would never—ever—have the chance to tell me that he was proud of me.

I gave myself a few more minutes before straightening up and pulling my shoulders back. I cleared my throat and wiped my face with the back of my sleeve.

My sisters were always telling me I'd feel better if I let myself cry and feel things. But it was obvious they were full of shit, because the only thing I felt was exhausted—and relieved that no one had been there to witness it.

I stacked the remaining wood and stored the axe, leaving the pieces I'd flung into the forest for another day.

The sun was sinking low when I made my way around to the front of the cabin.

A familiar truck was parked in the drive, and for a moment I considered turning around to chop more wood.

But my visitor spotted me first.

"Hey there, brother."

NOA

"We're going to need to talk about this sooner or later, Noa." Ryan sat hard on the bed, causing me to bounce a bit on the mattress.

I pulled my pillow up over my unwashed hair and ignored him, just like I'd been doing for the last few days.

After Ryan discovered me in our hotel suite, he'd known enough to give me the space I needed to process. The irony that this man knew me better than anyone else and cared enough not to push me while I processed whatever it was I'd had with a man who'd rejected me wasn't lost on me.

"Noa?"

I shook my head and grunted in response.

He chuckled a little, and a moment later the pillow was pulled from my hands. "You can't ignore this forever. We need to talk. If only to give your parents some sort of explanation. They know you're back."

"How?" My voice was muffled by the bed.

"I told them."

"You what?" I flung myself onto my back. "How could you—"

His grin stopped me, and despite myself, I smiled. "Ryan… I'm…" The smile dissolved as tears once again took over.

"Oh shit. You're crying? Dammit."

I didn't resist as Ryan reached down and gently lifted me from the tangle of sheets and blankets and pulled me into his arms. He held me and stroked my dirty, greasy hair while I sobbed like a baby. It was as if once I opened the faucet of my emotions, I had no way to turn it off again. In all the years of our friendship, I didn't think I'd ever let myself cry like this in front of Ryan. Not even when our siblings died.

The very few tears I had shed during that dark time, I'd done in the privacy of a hot shower. But this was different. In ways I couldn't even explain—not to myself, not to anyone. Least of all, Ryan.

Everything I was feeling was so, so different than anything that had ever come before.

"I've made a mess of everything." I finally pulled myself together enough to sit up and talk. "You must hate me."

"You know that's not true." He chuckled a little and sat back on the bed to give me space. "I could never hate you, Noa. You know that."

I did.

"But I've never left you at the altar for another man before."

"Ah ha." He pointed at me. "So this is about a guy."

I dropped my head into my hands and groaned. "This is weird enough talking to you about all this without details."

"Oh no. Trust me, I'm not looking for any of the dirty details. But I do have to say, Noa, I've never known you to get so broken up about a guy before. So, he must be—"

"He's an asshole."

It hurt to say it, but at the same time, it was true. Asher *was* an asshole. A cruel, heartless, cold asshole. I was falling for him. *Really* falling for him. In a way I'd never let myself fall before, and he knew it. He *had* to know it.

How could he not?

But it didn't matter, because even if he did know how I felt —or even suspected it—he'd tossed me out like yesterday's trash.

I could still see the look on his face when he told me to go. *I don't fucking care, Noa. Just go.*

A fresh sob slipped from my throat, but I quickly clamped my hand over my mouth. "Ugh. I don't want to care. He's not worth it. He's a—"

"An asshole?" Ryan supplied, but the smile was gone from his face. He grabbed my hand and squeezed. "I don't want to sound insensitive, but—"

"You should never start a sentence that way." I tried and failed to smile.

"Fair." Ryan shrugged. "But isn't this exactly what we were trying to avoid, Noa? You and I both know that romantic relationships aren't for us. They never have been. That's why you and I make so much sense. We love and care about each other more than any other couple I know."

It was probably true that Ryan didn't know a lot of happy couples, but he wasn't wrong. There was so much love between the two of us. So much that I couldn't argue.

I took a deep breath and looked up at my best friend. He

was so patient and kind. It didn't even feel real. "How are you not crazy pissed off at me right now?"

"Pissed off?" He chuckled and ran a hand through his hair. "Why? Because you left me at the altar and ran off with a virtual stranger to have all kinds of crazy sex in the middle of —well, I don't actually know where you were." He shrugged dramatically and continued, "Only to reappear without notice and spend the next few days crying as if your heart had been ripped out and stomped on? You think I should be pissed off about that?"

I couldn't help it. I laughed. At first it was the slightest giggle that bubbled up inside me, but then it gained power and turned into uncontrollable, almost hysterical laughter.

Ryan waited me out.

Truly the most patient man I knew.

And when I finally regained control of myself, I said, "Yeah. All that. Why aren't you mad?"

This time he gave me an honest answer. "I won't lie to you, Noa. It's not like I'm super thrilled. And I'm pretty sure that every single person we know back in the city is talking about us, and I'm going to have to do all kinds of damage control when we get home. But I'm not mad. Not really." He took my hands in his and tugged me a little closer. "I know this whole thing is strange, and I don't blame you for having some reservations about it all. I'd be lying if I said I didn't have some, too."

"You do?"

"Of course I do." He looked at me as if I were crazy. "You don't really think I'm that dead inside."

"I don't think you're dead inside at all, Ryan," I said honestly. "You really are the most caring, kindest man with the biggest heart."

"Aw shucks." He flushed a little but laughed it off and continued. "When we came up with this idea, it seemed like the perfect solution to make our families happy again. We're perfect together in almost all the ways." He winked, and I rolled my eyes. "But as you know, that didn't concern me either. We're going to be partners in work—why not in life? We get along so well, and I think our parents all demonstrate how important that is in a marriage."

I nodded.

"I know marriage is a big deal," he said. "But the only concern I have when it comes to this arrangement has nothing to do with me, Noa. A traditional marriage or romantic relationship isn't something I've ever wanted for myself. You know that. But..."

"But?"

"But I think you do."

I shook my head automatically. "You know I don't."

"That's what you always say." He squeezed my hands in his. "But it's not true. And I think we both know that now more than ever."

I shook my head and tried to pull out of his grasp. "What are you saying? That because I had a little... whatever it was with Asher, that all of a sudden I now know what a real relationship could be like? That just because for the first time in my life I felt alive with a man, that I—oh shit."

"Oh shit, indeed." Again, Ryan squeezed my hands, but this time he let them go. "I think we both know that just because you came back, it doesn't mean you're going to marry me. Not now."

He was right.

Of course he was.

There was a reason I'd run away in the first place, and that hadn't changed just because Asher rejected me. What *had* changed was that now, instead of knowing I didn't love Ryan in a way worthy of marriage, I did love someone else.

And even if he wanted to ignore that, I couldn't.

ASHER

"I don't know why you bothered coming, Chase."

I was being a dick, and I knew it. But the last thing I wanted was company of any kind—especially not in the form of my eldest brother.

"We're worried about you, man."

"Don't be." I pushed past him and walked into the cabin. I flung the door shut behind me, but Chase caught it easily and welcomed himself inside. I shot him a look as I kicked my boots off, but he either didn't notice or didn't care that I wanted nothing to do with him. "I'm fine."

"Obviously."

I spun around at the humor in his voice. "Is something funny? Because you don't have to be here." I tugged my coat off and dropped it on the floor instead of hanging it on the hook. "In fact, you shouldn't be here at all."

Chase slipped his own snowy shoes off before striding confidently into the room. "Oh, settle down, Asher. I'm not here to pick a fight with you."

Another retort was hot on my tongue, but I swallowed it down. Chase and I had worked hard on building our relationship since our father died. I didn't need to undo all of that just because I was in a bad mood.

"Want some coffee?" It was as close to an apology as I was going to offer.

Fortunately, Chase recognized the peace offering for what it was. "If you're making some, that sounds great."

I went through the motions of filling the kettle and measuring the grounds into the French press I'd found in the cupboard.

"Just like Dad used to make," Chase observed.

"Makes sense since this was his place." I shrugged dramatically. "Apparently."

"Yeah. That's crazy that there was a whole cabin in the woods that nobody knew anything about, don't you think?"

I gave my older brother a look. "Did you come to check it out for yourself? Feel free to take a look around." I waved my arm to encompass the small space. "This is pretty much it."

If Chase recognized the sarcasm in my voice, he didn't mention it. Instead, he began slowly moving around the cabin, investigating every corner.

I ignored him and pulled mugs from the cupboard before pressing the coffee. When I poured it and turned around, he was standing in front of the Christmas tree.

I growled under my breath. I should have taken it down days ago. I should have chopped it into firewood and fed it into the fireplace, burning all the decorations with it. Including the star that still sat proudly on the highest branches.

But I couldn't. Something stopped me every time.

"I should have taken it down by now." I crossed the room and handed Chase his coffee. He nodded a thank-you.

"I have to admit, I'm surprised to see you with a tree. I didn't really think it was your thing."

"It's not."

Chase lifted an eyebrow, and I shook my head. "It wasn't my idea."

"Oh. Noa."

"Noa."

"About Noa—"

"No."

"No what?"

"Just…no. Whatever it is you're going to say or ask me about her—don't."

In true Chase fashion, he ignored me completely. "I was just going to ask you where she was. I noticed that your—"

"She's gone."

"Gone? Like gone to the store? Or gone gone?"

"Does it matter?" I took a sip of my coffee, burned my tongue, and cursed. "She's gone," I said again. The words sounded more permanent the second time.

"It does matter, Asher. You and her...she seemed...well, it seemed—"

"It doesn't matter how it seemed," I snapped. "Because she's gone."

Gone.

I hadn't said it out loud yet, and now that I had, it hit differently. It was way too real.

Gone.

Chase didn't speak right away, and as the silence dragged on, something snapped in me.

"This is going to sound crazy," I said after a moment.

"I've heard a lot of crazy."

I took a deep breath and said something I never thought I would. "I think I have feelings for her."

Hearing the words out loud hit differently. I took a step back like I'd been slapped and turned to my brother, waiting for him to tell me exactly how crazy I sounded. But Chase didn't say anything. He just grinned and pressed his lips together.

"Didn't you hear me?"

"I did," he finally said. "I'm not sure what you want me to say."

"I want you to tell me how crazy it is." I spun and stalked into the tiny kitchen, setting my mug down with too much force. I barely noticed the coffee splashing over the edge. "I want you to tell me that I can't possibly have feelings for her because that's not how it works."

"Not how it works?" Chase shook his head. "Asher, that's exactly how it works. You spend time with a woman, you connect with her for a variety of reasons, and—" He waved his free hand. "You develop feelings."

No. I couldn't accept that.

I shook my head. "But it takes time. Weeks or months. Years even. But not days."

Chase only shrugged. "Not necessarily."

"What does that even mean?"

My blood pressure was rising, and the tiny cabin suddenly felt too hot. My breath was stuck in my chest, and I couldn't slow my thoughts long enough to make sense of them.

Chase chuckled and joined me in the kitchen. "It means there are no rules in love, Asher. There's no playbook with step-by-step instructions."

"Then how do you…" I pulled out a chair and sank heavily into it, dragging my hands through my hair and tugging at the roots. "How do you *know?*"

I felt like crying out in frustration. Or hitting something. There was a buildup of emotion inside me that was unfamiliar and deeply uncomfortable.

Chase exhaled slowly, set his coffee down, and took the seat across from me. "I don't think this is what you want to hear. But…you already know the answer to that question, brother."

Chapter Nineteen

NOA

I FINGERED the golden rose around my neck as I descended the large wooden staircase to the lobby. After my conversation with Ryan, I'd showered and changed into fresh clothes and felt like a new woman.

The ache in my chest still lingered, but the weight of the impending wedding was gone. Mostly.

I still had to face a conversation with my parents that I wasn't looking forward to. But it was long overdue. And even if it was going to be hard—which I was certain it would be—I owed it to them.

I found them in two oversized wingback chairs situated by a picture window that faced the ski hill. My mother had a book open on her lap but wasn't reading. She stared out the window at the skiers and families on the hill. My father watched my mother.

I paused a moment and took in the sight of them. I loved them more than anything in the world. It had been heartbreaking to watch them for the last few years as they worked through their grief. They deserved so much more.

I inhaled slowly. Released my grip on the rose and stepped forward.

"Mom? Dad?"

Startled, my mother almost dropped her book as she swung around to look at me. My father jumped from the chair and greeted me with a hug.

Guilt flooded me as I looked at my parents. They looked as if they'd aged decades in only a few short weeks, and I knew I was a huge part of that. My dad brought me a chair and I pulled it up close, so I faced both of them.

"Noa." My mother reached for me the moment I sat. "We've been so worried."

"I'm sorry." It was inadequate, and I knew it. But there were no other words. "Ryan said he told you I was okay. I just needed to…" I blew out a breath. "I needed some time to think." It didn't seem like the right time to tell them that I was nursing a broken heart on top of everything. One thing at a time. "I can't tell you how sorry I am," I said again, looking between them. "For everything."

"Noa," my father said. "It's fine. We're just happy you're okay."

From the moment I was born, my dad had a soft spot for me. I'd been a daddy's girl from the very start, and I'd known it. Even as a teenager, he'd never raised his voice at me, and I could do no wrong. But this was different. And I wasn't going to let myself be let off the hook so easily.

"Dad." I gave him a soft smile. "I appreciate that. But I really do owe you both an apology. A real one." I looked at my mother then. "I've been acting…well, it's been selfish. So selfish, and it wasn't okay."

"You're back now," Janice said. "We can go ahead with—"

"No, Mom." This was the part I'd been dreading. "I never

should have agreed to marry Ryan. It wasn't fair to anyone, but we didn't do this to hurt anyone. Especially not the two of you and Jeannie and Brad. I know it seems crazy," I continued. "But we did all this for the four of you."

"Did what, Noa?"

"Ryan and I aren't in love," I stated simply. "He's talking to his mom and dad right now, too."

"What do you mean?" Janice sat up straight in her chair. "You're not in love? That doesn't make sense. You two are—"

"Best friends," I finished for her. "Don't get me wrong. I love Ryan, and he loves me." I reached for the rose necklace. "But it's not a stuck-in-your-throat kind of love." I smiled a little to myself as I said it, thinking of my grandmother. "It's the type of love that goes skiing together and watches a movie. It's not the type of love that commits to marriage and a life together. Does that make sense?"

"No." My father spoke. "None of this makes sense. If you don't love Ryan that way, and he doesn't love you, why would you agree to get married? Why are we here? What is all of this, Noa?"

"Ryan and I agreed to get married to make you all smile again." The words came out in a rush of air. Once they left my mouth, I closed my eyes and took a deep breath. "We thought we could make it work together because neither of us really ever cared about getting married for real, and we all just needed a reason to be happy and celebrate again ever since Tom and Olivia died."

It wasn't until I was finished talking that I carefully and slowly opened my eyes again to see my parents watching me with expressions I couldn't read.

After a few moments of silence, I dared to speak again.

"Well? I know it sounds kind of crazy, but—"

"Crazy?" My mother shook her head and blinked hard against tears. "You think it sounds *crazy*, Noa?"

I nodded.

"It's beyond crazy." Janice released me and buried her face in her hands.

The sound of my mother's sobbing filled the space, and immediately, I wanted to recant everything I'd just said.

A little voice inside me was screaming. Yes. I'd marry Ryan. I'd put a white dress on and walk down the aisle and pledge my life to a man I wasn't in love with if it meant that my mother would smile again. Or at the very least, just. Stop. Crying.

"Mom. I'm so—"

"No." My father reached for me and pulled me away from my mother, to face him. "Give her a minute, kiddo. This was… well, to say it was unexpected would be an incredible under-statement." He dropped his eyes and shook his head for a moment before looking me in the eyes. "You really thought marrying Ryan would make us happy?"

I pressed my lips together and nodded. "You've just been so sad."

He chuckled, but there was no humor in it. "Oh, Noa. Of course we've been sad. Your brother died. That rocked our worlds in the worst way. How could it not?"

I shrugged dumbly.

"But the answer to that isn't for you to sign up for a lifetime of unhappiness."

The word stopped me.

Would I have been unhappy with Ryan? A few weeks ago, my answer would have been unequivocally no. But now, after spending time with Asher and feeling…what it felt like to be with Asher, I had a very different answer.

Maybe he wasn't my person and we weren't meant to be— no matter what my heart was telling me. But just knowing that I could feel that way changed everything.

Before I could respond, my father continued.

"Noa, it's not your job to fix everything. You know that, don't you?"

"I do know that. But—"

"No buts. We're sad because Tom and Olivia died. Nothing you can do will change that. And nobody expects you to even try."

"But you were so happy when Ryan and I—"

"Honey."

I turned to face my mother, who stared at me with a tear-streaked face.

"We weren't happy that you were marrying Ryan. We were happy because we thought you were happy. That's all we want for you. We just want you to be happy because we're your parents, and that's our job. We wouldn't care if you were marrying a jobless bum who couch-surfed from place to place as long as he made you happy."

"Well, wait a minute."

My mother and I laughed at Charles's objection.

"The point is, you're not going to make us happy by making yourself unhappy," Janice said. "That's not the way through this. The way through is just to get through it. Nothing is going to bring your brother or Olivia back, and neither of them would want you and Ryan to sacrifice your future because of their accident."

We were all crying by that point. I stood and pulled them both into a tight hug.

I should have known my parents would understand. But more than that, I should have known that they never would have wanted the wedding for the wrong reasons in the first place.

But I couldn't have known, because we'd all been in survival mode for the last few years since Tom and Olivia's accident. It was hard and awful, for sure. But we needed to move on. Somehow.

"We need something good," I said through my tears as I wiped my nose with the back of my arm. "We're so overdue for some happy. And don't worry, I'm not suggesting that I marry anyone else."

My mother shot me a look that suggested she knew more about my last week and where I'd been than she'd let on. But even if I could begin to sort out my feelings for Asher, there was no way I was going to rush into the idea of marriage again.

"I agree, Noa." My father took a step back and straightened his shoulders. Before Tom's death, it had been rare for him to show his emotion, and I knew he still wasn't entirely comfortable with it. "Do you have any suggestions?"

I let a smile cross my lips. "I have a few ideas."

"Excellent." Janice looped her arm through mine and once more pulled me close. "You can tell me all about those ideas. Right after you tell me about this mysterious man who has you twisted up in knots."

"Wha—"

I didn't even bother finishing my protest when my mom gave me a knowing wink. Besides, maybe some motherly advice at that moment was the very thing I needed.

ASHER

If someone had told me a year ago that I'd be talking to my oldest brother about love, of all things, I would have laughed in their face and probably recommended them for some kind of mental help.

But sitting in the little kitchen of the cabin, talking things out with Chase over another cup of coffee, had been oddly therapeutic. And by the time we were done with our drinks, I felt a little bit clearer.

At the very least, I no longer felt like I was going to burst out of my skin.

"Thanks, Chase." I gathered up our cups and took them to the sink.

"For what? Talking? That's what brothers do."

"It's not really what *we* do, though, is it?"

Chase pressed his lips together and nodded a little. "But we could."

I couldn't disagree with that. Our relationship had come a long way since we were kids. Our mother married Michael Carlson when Chase and Charli were young. Shortly after, I was born, followed by Craig and Kat.

We'd all been raised together, and our father had never treated Charli and Chase as if they weren't his children. But Chase had felt differently and left Trickle Creek as soon as he had a chance, only returning home intermittently. It wasn't until our father's death that he'd returned for good and we'd had a chance to rebuild a relationship properly.

For reasons that a therapist would no doubt have a good time digging into, I'd grown up with a low level of resentment for my eldest brother and had spent a lifetime trying to be enough son for both of us.

"We could," I said, and I meant it. After a moment, I dropped my head and blew out a sigh. "I bet Dad didn't think that this would happen when he stripped me of my job and banished me to the woods, did he?"

I tried to laugh it off, but I couldn't hide the frustration and anger I felt for my father, and Chase saw right through it.

"That's not what you really think, is it? That he banished you?"

"That's exactly what he did, Chase." I looked up and scratched at my beard, which had grown a little out of control over the last few days. "The only thing I've ever loved is my job. Carlson Corp has been everything to me. And he took it away." I gestured dramatically around the small room. "And then just to rub it in, he sent me here."

Chase didn't respond for a moment. Instead, he bit his bottom lip and finally nodded a little. "I can see how you might think that. What did the letter say?"

"The letter?"

"The letter Dad left you? He left them for all of us."

I'd heard my siblings talk about the letters over dinner before. Neither Chase, Craig, nor Charli had discussed specifics of what their letters contained. They were personal, after all.

But the one thing they could all agree on was that whatever was in them, it had changed everything and helped them gain clarity on why our father had done what he'd done.

I hadn't given much thought to the letter, only vaguely paying attention at all. I knew, as they all did, that my turn would come for me to carry out whatever stipulation our father had thought up for me, and I'd do it and move on. Letter or not.

I shook my head. "All I got was a key and the paperwork to this place."

"Well, that's more than most of us. But maybe check with Steven. There's probably a letter waiting for you somewhere."

I didn't know how to feel about that. Did I even want a letter from my dad? Would it explain his actions? How could it? How could he possibly explain why he'd taken away the one thing I loved?

"Don't shake your head." Chase grabbed me by the shoulder and shook gently. "I know this whole thing is…well, strange."

Strange didn't even begin to describe the way our father was handling his legacy.

"But the letter will make everything so much clearer," Chase continued. "It did for me. And the same for Charli and Craig, too. I know you're mad now, but one thing I've learned from all of this is that Dad had his reasons for everything."

I gave my brother a look, and he laughed as he gave me another little shake.

"But you'll see," he said. "There's something about reading Dad's handwriting. It's almost as if he—"

"His handwriting?"

The notebook.

Chase nodded. "He hand-wrote all the letters. You'll—"

"I saw his handwriting. He kept a notebook in the tool shed."

"A notebook?"

I moved toward the door and grabbed my boots. "I haven't made my way through it all yet, but it looked like mostly lists of projects and chores he wanted to do or had done out here." I tossed Chase his coat. "Maybe there's a note or a letter in there for me." I shrugged. "I'll be honest with you, it felt like just a to-do list he left for me to finish once he was gone." I rolled my eyes. "Just like everything else."

"Whoa." Chase stopped me. "What do you mean by that?"

"You know what I mean." I shrugged his hand off my arm. "Just like everything else, Chase. Dad left me his little secret house with a list of things to finish because he knew I'd do it. Out of all of us, he knew I'd be the one who'd follow through and get it done, because I always do."

My brother took in a deep breath and blew it out slowly as he pulled his coat on. He offered me a sad smile. "This is something you need to do on your own, brother. But check the notebook. If the letter isn't there, it'll turn up. And I really hope it's sooner rather than later."

I assessed him but didn't speak, unsure of what I could possibly say.

"I'll bring Craig back tomorrow," Chase said. "With a truck for you. That way, you don't have to be stranded out here. In case you decide to follow your—"

"Do not say heart."

Chase wiggled his eyebrows and chuckled. "Go look for the letter," he said as he walked past and slapped me on the shoulder. "I really think it'll make you feel better."

I didn't know about that.

I followed him outside and waited while he walked toward his vehicle.

Before he got in, Chase turned. "Dad thought a lot more of you than just the one who gets things done, Asher. You do know that, right?"

I dropped my head for a moment and inhaled deeply.

"I wish I did, Chase. I really wish I did."

Chapter Twenty

ASHER

IT WAS COMPLETELY dark by the time I watched Chase's taillights fade away down my drive. The air was heavy with the promise of snow, which meant it was likely to be a cold night and I'd need more wood for the fire.

I made multiple trips between the shed and the house, loaded down with enough wood to get me through the night and then some. Despite my exhaustion, I welcomed the physical exertion and the deep sleep I'd be able to fall into.

I was exhausted from thinking about Noa and then my father. It was all a little too much for one day. I'd be able to think clearly in the morning and, despite Chase's urging for me to find the letter, it felt easier not to think about it. At least not for the moment.

I made one final trip out to the shed. I flicked off the overhead light and was about to close it up for the night when, at the last minute, I reached for the notebook and tucked it under my arm.

Maybe it wouldn't hurt to read through the lists my dad

had made. After all, it was in my nature to be the doer. Without even knowing what it was, I knew I'd cross every one of those things off any list my father had made.

It was what I did.

Once the fire was stoked and I was settled on the couch with a glass of wine, my back to the Christmas tree I still couldn't bring myself to take down, I opened the book and started to read through the pages.

I went in order and soon was able to decipher some kind of pattern to the entries. There were gaps of weeks and even months between entries, and then three or four in a row. Mostly there were bullet-point items of projects he wanted to complete, or even things he'd finished.

He'd put new shingles on the roof, re-sided the cabin, built a new porch, and even the shed, in his time. But there was a lot more on the lists, too, including a wood-fired hot tub and a back deck.

"You don't ask for much, do you, Dad?" I muttered, rolling my eyes at the lists, knowing I'd figure out a way to get the projects done.

As I worked my way through the lists, ideas of my own sparked, too. After all, the cabin belonged to me now. I could change it and make it my own, and to my surprise, the idea excited me.

When I was almost at the end of the notebook and the date on the top of the page changed to eight months before the date that Michael Carlson had died, I took a break. I poured myself another glass of wine and braced myself before opening the book again.

It was in the second last entry, on the final line, that I noticed the item.

Box under the sink.

It was only four little words, but they sent a chill down my spine. I set the book down and went directly to the sink.

There were the usual bottles and cleaners. A bag of rags, and there, tucked into the back corner, was a rectangular wooden box.

Box under the sink.

I withdrew the box and put it on the kitchen counter. I lifted the lid and there it was.

The letter.

I shook my head with a quiet chuckle because dammit, Chase was right, and I hated that.

I picked up the envelope addressed to me in my father's handwriting and returned to the couch to open it.

When I slid the paper from the envelope, a small photo fell out onto my lap. It was a grainy photo of my father as a much younger man.

And me.

I couldn't have been more than four or five. I was perched on my father's shoulders. We stood in a forest, each of us wearing matching smiles.

I swallowed down the lump in my throat as I stared at the photo for a moment before picking up the letter.

Asher. My son.

If I know you at all, you're probably pretty pissed off with me right now.

I shook my head. "You know it, Dad."

And I bet you have a few questions about the cabin you're sitting in right now.

I raised my eyebrows and blew out a breath.

I know it probably all seems a bit secretive and strange that I had a little cabin in the woods that nobody knew about, but a man is entitled to a few secrets as he gets older, and this was mine. When your mother died, I was lost in a way that I wasn't sure I'd be able to come back from.

I still had all of you kids, and I knew I had to be strong for all of you, and I did my best. But ultimately, it was this place that saved me from myself.

You see, I didn't know what to do with myself when Angela died, and I threw myself into my work in a way that was entirely unhealthy. As rewarding as my work was, it wasn't enough. And it kept me from facing the truth.

That there was more to life than work.

It wasn't until I bought this little run-down shack in the woods on a whim one day that I started to feel differently.

At first, I would come out to the woods to be alone and feel closer to your mother. But it didn't take long for it to become like a type of therapy for me, son.

Working with my hands, fixing things, and breathing life back into this place healed me.

And I hope it will do the same for you. We always did share a love for the woods, even if we didn't spend as much time together out there in recent years.

I stopped reading and looked into the fire. I didn't need healing. I never had.

Don't sit there and think you don't need the healing, son.

I laughed out loud.

You do. I see it in you. You're so much like me, with your drive and your work ethic. But there's more to life, son. I didn't realize that until I met your mother. She taught me what living really was. She gave me a family and a purpose beyond myself.

She saved me from myself and healed me the first time.

My greatest wish for you would be that you find that kind of love, too. That you find a woman who loves you, accepts you, and makes you a better version of yourself and teaches you that there is so much more to life than working all the time. But since I can't give you that, I'm giving you this cabin, and the time to discover it for yourself.

Asher, I've watched you give your all to the company and your work. And I want you to know that even if I didn't tell you enough when I was alive, I am so proud of the man you've become and the work you've done. But now it's time for you to learn that there's more to this life.

Spend your six months in the cabin or with one of your siblings. Travel and see the world, or simply explore your own backyard. But I hope you take this time to discover yourself in a new way. Let people in, Asher. Not only your brothers and sisters, but everyone.

And when you find that special person, the one who makes you feel things you didn't know were possible and sees you for who you really are, hold them close, son. And never let them go because that person will be the greatest gift of your life.

Noa.

I swallowed hard, but didn't try to stop the tear that streaked down my cheek.

Make this cabin your own, Asher. And when it's time, go back to work and continue to make Carlson

Corp and the town of Trickle Creek great, if that's what you still want to do. But whatever you choose, I hope you do it for yourself. You don't need to make me proud, son. I already am. I always have been and I always will be.

    Love, Dad.

NOA

I woke up with a clear head despite the late night I'd had. After talking things out with my mom, I'd returned to our suite to find Ryan fresh off a conversation with his parents. The two of us ordered room service, and like the best friends we'd always been, stayed up until after midnight talking.

I was beyond grateful that our ill-fated engagement hadn't ruined our friendship. And maybe it wasn't a relationship most people would understand, but that didn't matter.

"I hope you don't have a headache this morning." Ryan knocked on my door with a cup of coffee in his hand. "Maybe we shouldn't have opened that second bottle of wine?"

I sat up against the pile of pillows and reached for the offered cup. "I regret nothing."

Ryan sat on the bed next to me, the mattress sinking under his weight. "Except maybe…" He used a finger to gesture between the two of us.

I threw a pillow at him. "Never. If it wasn't for this whole mess, I would never have…" I reached for the gold rose around my neck.

"Are you going to call him?"

We'd spent far too long the night before discussing Asher.

For the first time, I'd been honest with Ryan and, most importantly, myself about how I felt about my time with Asher.

I knew now it was possible to have strong feelings for someone after only a few days. A connection like that couldn't be predicted and it couldn't be ignored. When you knew, you knew.

And I knew.

But just because I knew didn't make things any different.

"I don't think there's any point," I said after a sip of the hot coffee. "He made that pretty clear when I left the other day. I don't think he feels the same way."

"Or he does, but he was too scared to do anything about it." Ryan shrugged. It was a message he'd tried to relay more than once the night before.

It wasn't that I didn't appreciate the insight, but Ryan also didn't know Asher the way I did. Or the way I thought I did.

"I'll consider it," I said after a moment. "But not today." I put the coffee cup on the nightstand and clasped my hands in front of me. "Today is going to be a great day, and it's not about me."

He looked like he was going to protest again, but ultimately, Ryan grinned. "Today is going to be pretty fantastic," he agreed. "I have to hand it to you. This was a great idea, Noa. And so much better than us getting married."

"Agreed."

We laughed together before I kicked him out of my room. It was going to be a great day—but a long one—and I needed to get moving.

An hour later, I walked into my parents' hotel suite—and utter chaos.

"This is never going to work, Noa!" My mother all but

threw herself into my arms the moment she saw me. "Look at my hair. I can't do a thing with it and Sarah is gone."

I worked hard to bite my tongue and keep from laughing. As long as I'd known her, my mother had never once been worried about her hair.

"And what am I going to wear?"

"You're going to wear the dress you bought for my wedding." I took her hand and led her to the sofa. "As for your hair…" I ran my fingers through her shoulder-length bob. "I'm sure I can—"

"You're going to do my hair?" Janice looked at me in horror, and I didn't bother biting back a laugh.

I wasn't known for my beauty skills.

"I wasn't going to suggest that," I said quickly. "What I was about to say is that I'm sure I can find someone to do your hair for you." My mind immediately went to Asher's little sister, Kat. "I met a local woman who is amazing with hair. I can give her a call, if you like?"

"Would you do that?"

"Only if you promise to calm down and enjoy today, Mom." I kissed her cheek. "Remember, today is about making new memories." I squeezed her hands and forced her to look at me. "It's time for us to smile, remember?"

She blinked back tears, but she managed a smile. "I remember."

Once it was clear that Ryan and I wouldn't be using any of the plans and preparations for our own wedding, I'd come up with the idea of turning the celebration into a vow-renewal ceremony for both sets of parents. They'd all been through so much and come out the other side of it. I couldn't think of four people who deserved to be celebrated more than my parents and Ryan's.

My dad had jumped at the idea, along with Brad and Jean-nie, but Janice had been a little more reluctant. After all, it was

New Year's Eve—and the anniversary of Tom and Olivia's accident. Which, as far as I was concerned, was the best reason of all to go ahead with it.

We were all desperately in need of some new, happier memories.

"It's going to be great, Mom. I promise." I smiled. "Let me get you a mimosa before I organize the hairstylist, okay? You just relax. Ryan said his mom will be here soon and you two can get ready together."

I slipped out into the hallway before I could get caught up in any more of her stress.

"Don't tell me you're allergic to weddings that aren't your own, too."

I looked up to see Grandma Rose smiling at me.

"Give me a hug, Noa. I've missed you."

I didn't need to be asked twice. I wrapped my arms around her and inhaled her sweet, baby-powder scent. "I've missed you, too, Grandma. So much."

"I'm glad you're back." She stepped back and studied me. "And I'm really happy to hear that you're not marrying Ryan. Nothing against him, of course."

"Of course." I winked. "Talking to you helped more than you'll ever know, Grandma. Thank you." Without even thinking about it, my fingers moved to the rose around my neck.

She followed the movement and smiled. "Does this mean there's a new young man in your life now?"

"Oh, well..." The question caught me off guard. "I..." The emotion I'd been holding back for the last twenty-four hours surged all at once. I turned away, swallowing hard, determined not to let her see how much it affected me.

When I turned back, Grandma Rose was watching me with a knowing smile.

"I see."

"What?"

"It's the stuck-in-your-throat kind of love. I had a feeling it might be." She patted my arm.

I just stared at her.

"And I'm not talking about your fiancé, my dear."

"It's crazy, though." I didn't bother denying it. She was right. Maybe it was crazy. Maybe it was too soon. Maybe it wasn't based on anything real or lasting. But none of that mattered, because that's exactly what it was. A stuck-in-my-throat kind of love. Just thinking about never seeing Asher again made it hard to swallow. Hard to breathe. "I thought it might be," I admitted. "But now I'm not so sure. It didn't…he didn't…well, it's complicated."

"It always is, sweetheart."

"I really need to focus on today." I tried to redirect the conversation. "Maybe tomorrow, I can—"

"There's no maybe about it." She winked. "I may be a little old lady, but there are a few things I know for sure. And one of them is that when that kind of love hits you, the biggest mistake you can make is turning away from it." Her expression grew serious. "I understand that today is important to the family."

I nodded.

"But don't let too much time go by, Noa. Whatever you do in life, do it with no regrets."

No regrets.

I nodded again.

"Promise an old lady," she said, smiling.

"I promise, Grandma." I laughed and kissed her cheek. "No regrets."

ASHER

Everything felt so much clearer in the light of day.

After an emotional night of reading and rereading my father's letter—and for the first time in my life, allowing myself to get really honest about what it was I wanted—I woke up knowing exactly what that was.

Or more specifically, *who* I wanted.

Noa.

There wasn't a doubt in my mind that Noa Briggs was the woman for me. From the moment she entered my life, everything changed, and in all the best ways. I never would have believed that one woman and one week could have such an impact. I'd always thought I was far too realistic and pragmatic for that.

Or so I'd believed.

Now all I knew was that there had been a reason Noa jumped into my truck that day. Maybe it was divine intervention. Maybe it was a message from my father. Or maybe it had just been a random coincidence. But more than ever, her presence in my life felt like a gift.

My father had been right—she really was the gift of a lifetime.

And I had no intention of letting her slip through my fingers.

If it wasn't already too late.

I poured myself another cup of coffee and walked to the living room window, staring out at the snow-covered drive.

A fresh layer of thick, white, sparkling snow blanketed everything in sight. As beautiful as it was, it looked deep. Very deep. Chase had already called to let me know that he and Craig were delayed bringing me the truck he'd promised. The snowplows hadn't made it out of town to the big house yet, and the mountain roads were impassable.

"It'll be a few hours yet," Chase had said. "If I can't even get down the mountain to town, there's no way we'll get out to the cabin before the plows clear things up."

Any other time, I would've been happy about the snowfall. It was good for the ski hill, and therefore good for the hotel and all the condo developments Carlson Corp was involved with— never mind the rest of the businesses in town.

Business.

That had always been my first and last concern.

But not anymore.

Now the only thing occupying my mind had nothing to do with business at all.

I paced the small room and, for what had to have been the dozenth time, tried to slow my breathing.

It was futile.

I couldn't relax. I couldn't wait. Now that I'd finally come to my senses about Noa, every minute mattered. I'd been horrible to her when I sent her away.

No.

When I sent her *back*. To Ryan. To the man she didn't want to marry.

I tugged at my hair and groaned. I was such an asshole. I could only hope she'd forgive me.

If I could get to her.

"Screw this. I can't sit around and wait."

I dumped my untouched coffee into the sink, grabbed my parka, pulled on my boots, and tugged my knit cap over my head. I could be waiting all day for a plow. Maybe longer. There had to be something I could do—even if it meant digging out the road myself.

That was exactly what I was doing twenty minutes later.

I worked up a sweat shoveling the heavy, wet snow, and when I finally turned to survey my progress, disappointment hit hard.

"At this rate, it's going to take me three days to get out of here."

I wiped my brow with the back of my arm and leaned on the shovel, assessing just how much more there was to clear.

It was a lot. A real lot.

Before I could get back to work, my phone rang from my inside pocket. I tugged off a glove and fished it out before the caller could hang up.

"Hey, Kat," I said, forcing a smile into my voice. "Don't tell me you're calling to say you've got a snowplow I—"

"Asher, I need to know what the hell is going on."

The smile vanished instantly. "What do you mean? What's going on?"

"I just got a call from Noa."

"Noa? My Noa?" The words came out automatically. It probably should've felt strange to say that—especially since I didn't even know if she'd speak to me—but it didn't. She'd always be mine on some level.

"Well, I thought she was *your* Noa," Kat said. "But that's why I'm calling. She just asked if I'd come to Trickle Creek Lodge to do some hair for a wedding."

A wedding.

The air rushed from my lungs, and pain punched me square in the gut.

She couldn't possibly be getting married to him. Not after everything...not after we... *Fuck.*

But why shouldn't she?

I'd practically shoved her back into Ryan's arms. It had been days since I'd seen her—days where he could've been convincing her that they really were meant to be together. Hadn't he told me himself how confident he was that she'd come back?

"No."

"Yes," Kat said. "So you can see why I'm confused. When

you brought her to Christmas, it seemed like the two of you were—"

"I know," I cut in. "It's…complicated."

"I think that's an understatement. Didn't she run away from her wedding and jump into your truck?"

I didn't have time to rehash everything.

"I'm not even going to ask."

"I appreciate that," I said. "Do you have her phone number?"

It had never seemed important before. She hadn't even had her phone with her while she was here, and then…well, asking for it hadn't exactly felt appropriate while I was being a first-class dick.

"I'll send it," Kat said. "And Asher? I don't really know Noa, but seeing the two of you together—it felt different."

I nodded, even though she couldn't see me.

"That's why I called."

"I appreciate it, Kat."

I disconnected, and the second her text came through, I dialed without hesitation.

I couldn't let her marry Ryan. Even if she never forgave me. Even if she never wanted to see me again. I could live with that. But I couldn't live knowing I'd let her make such a mistake.

The phone rang.

And rang.

Then went to voicemail.

Hearing her voice nearly stopped me cold. For a split second, I almost hung up just so I could call again and hear it one more time.

Instead, when the beep sounded, I spoke.

"Noa. Don't do it. Don't marry him. Please." I swallowed hard. "I'm sorry I was such an asshole. I didn't mean to… I shouldn't have… I just—"

I shook my head, muttering under my breath. It was too late to start over.

"I'm coming. Just wait. Please."

I disconnected and stared at the phone. There was no way to know if she'd get the message in time, but one thing was certain. Waiting for my brothers to bring me a truck was no longer an option.

I was running out of time.

Fast.

I fired off a quick text to Kat.

Stall her. I'm coming.

I stuffed my phone back into my pocket and lifted the shovel over my shoulder.

It was time for plan B.

Chapter Twenty-One

ASHER

EVEN GROWING up and living my whole life in the mountains, I had never shoveled as much or as fast as I did as I dug out the shed behind the cabin. My plan still wasn't fully formed, but it was better than doing nothing. I had to try.

I was exhausted by the time I'd cleared enough snow to open the door of the shed, but there wasn't any time to rest. I walked directly to the back where I'd seen a stash of snowshoes and cross-country skis.

"You couldn't have an old snowmobile, could you, Dad?" I shook my head and pulled out the stack of dusty old skis.

There were a few different pairs, and I selected the ones that looked to be in the best shape. Luckily, I had the same size feet as my father, and the old boots tucked under the work-bench fit me.

Cross-country skiing had always been my mother's thing when we were young. She'd forced us all out on our skis once or twice a season back then, but I'd never enjoyed it. As soon as

I'd been given a choice, I chose downhill skiing and never looked back.

"I suppose I probably remember a few things," I muttered to myself as I eyed the old skis. "After all, it's not like it's that hard."

It wasn't hard. Not *technically*.

But after packing myself a small backpack with a bottle of water and a snack, it only took about twenty minutes for me to remember why I hated cross-country skiing.

It was *exhausting*.

I had a few false starts where I tripped over my poles and crossed my ski tips, but after a few minutes, I fell into a rhythm of sorts and began to glide with relative ease through the deep snow.

The safest way to town was to follow the forestry service roads until I reached the highway. That way, if anything went wrong or I needed help, I wouldn't be stranded alone in the snowy forest.

Fortunately, the cabin sat high up the mountain, so I was able to use gravity and the natural slope of the roads for most of the way.

Still, even at a steady pace, it would take me a few hours to reach the lodge.

I just hoped it wouldn't be too late.

NOA

"Thank you so much." I greeted Kat Carlson at the door to my mom's suite. "I know it's super last minute. And especially after that crazy snowstorm, I can't tell you how much it means that you came."

"Of course."

When Kat smiled, I was instantly struck by how much she resembled her older brother. It took me off guard.

"Any friend of Asher's is a friend of mine."

My smile faltered a little bit. I worked hard not to let my emotions show, although I couldn't tell by Kat's reaction whether I was successful with my efforts. "My mom and Jeannie aren't quite ready yet," I said. "Can I get you something to drink?"

"Water is great."

I led us through into the living room and waved my arm in the direction of the table. "You can probably set up here."

"This is great." Kat set her bag down and started laying out her tools. "You mentioned your mom? You want me to—"

"Yes. I know it's all a little last minute and everything, but Mom was all worked up. So if you could start with her and then Jeannie. She's my mom's best friend. And then if there's time left, maybe I'll have you try to do something with this." I lifted my mane of hair off my back and dropped it again with a laugh. "But I'm not too worried about myself."

I didn't miss the strange look Kat gave me, but it was easier to ignore it than to try to explain everything that had happened.

I went to the small kitchen of the suite to get a glass of water for Kat and give myself a moment to collect myself.

I'd been trying too hard to focus on the vow renewal and my family, and not think of Asher until it was over, but now, with Kat in front of me, that was proving to be impossible. Everything about her reminded me of Asher, and I couldn't help but wonder how he was. What was he doing? Was he still out at the cabin all by himself? Was he snowed in after the storm? Did he have enough food, and if he didn't, had anyone taken him a vehicle, or was he—

"How is Asher?"

I hadn't meant to ask at all, but I couldn't have stopped the question if I'd tried.

Kat's pretty face twisted up in confusion. She tilted her head and gave me a strange look. "I thought maybe I should ask you the same question. After all, he's spent more time with you lately than with anyone else..."

I blew out a breath and turned to lead her into the living room. "I know it's all been...well...I don't know how much you know, but—"

"I don't know anything," Kat said with a laugh.

I appreciated the levity of the moment. "Your brother and I...we are...well, I guess we were...dating is the wrong word, I think. I suppose we were—"

"You don't need to explain," Kat said gently. "It's really none of my business. Just like your wedding isn't really any of my business. And don't worry, I'm not judging you or any of your decisions. I just..."

She sucked in a breath, blew it out, and continued before I could completely register that she'd just said *your wedding*.

"I hope I'm not overstepping too much," Kat continued. "But I just need to say that I've never seen my brother the way I saw him with you at Christmas. To be fair, I've never seen him like that at all."

I swallowed hard against the lump in my throat.

"The way he looked at you," Kat said. "And the way he laughed and smiled." She shook her head. "I can't remember the last time I've seen him look that...well, that happy."

I couldn't stop myself when I asked, "There must have been someone else? Another woman at some time?"

Kat pressed her lips together and shook her head. "Nope. Not one. Don't get me wrong. Asher isn't a saint, and it's probably not my place to say so, but he's definitely had the company of a lot of women."

I knew they'd discussed it. Still, hearing it from Kat stung a little, but I didn't say so.

"But Asher has never dated anyone. Not even one time."

"That's crazy." He'd told me as much during one of our many long conversations. Still, there'd been part of me that suspected Asher might have been telling me only what I wanted to hear. "Not even one girlfriend? Not in high school?"

"No." Kat shook her head. "Never. And he certainly wouldn't have brought a woman home for Christmas. That's how we knew that you were special. Even if he had only known you for a few days. There must be something pretty unique about your connection for him to bring you to the big house."

The moment the words were out of her mouth, Kat squeezed her eyes shut and waved her hands in front of her face. "I'm so sorry. I shouldn't have said any of that. It's totally inappropriate to talk about him like that on your wedding day. And it's really none of my—"

"My wedding day?" I said. So I *had* heard her right the first time. "No. I think you misunderstood. I'm not getting married today."

Kat almost spat out her water. "You're not? Oh, thank goodness."

She looked so relieved that I couldn't help but laugh. "I guess I didn't really make it clear on the phone, and given recent events, I can see how you might have…but no. I'm not getting married. Ryan and I decided it wasn't a good idea. Today is actually a vow renewal for my parents and Ryan's parents, Jeannie and Brad. We decided to use all the wedding planning for them instead."

I stopped short of telling her that there was no way I could marry another man after the time I'd spent with Asher and the feelings I'd developed that I didn't even know I'd been capable of.

Kat put her things down and threw her arms around me in a spontaneous hug that made me laugh.

"I didn't realize you had such strong feelings about it."

She stepped back and straightened her hair. "Sorry. I'm sure that was kind of weird. I don't really know you. But…"

She glanced around the room.

We were still alone, so I pulled out two chairs for us to sit at the table.

"This is going to sound strange and I'm probably completely oversharing, but I don't care." Kat reached for my hand and squeezed. "I know I hardly know you, and I don't know your story or why you decided not to get married and jumped into my brother's truck."

I opened my eyes wide. It maybe wasn't my proudest moment, but it had led me to Asher, and I'd never regret that experience.

"So I can't speak to that," Kat continued. "But what I can tell you is that it's been a rough couple of years for my family. Since my father died, we've all been learning a lot about ourselves and each other. It's not my turn yet, but I've been paying really close attention and I'm learning that there's one common thread with all of the things my dad is asking of us."

I nodded. "Asher told me about the will and the stipulations."

"Right. And they're all as different as we are," Kat continued. "But there are two things that remain true every time." She held out one finger. "The first is to be true to yourself and what you really need and want, because knowing who you are matters."

I couldn't disagree with that. It was a lesson I was learning myself.

"And the second thing, maybe the most important one, is that love, and those you love, is the only thing that's truly important in life. More than money or status or the jobs we think we need, it's love."

I swallowed hard.

"Like I said." Kat shrugged and laughed a little. "I haven't had my turn yet, but I suspect that's what it will ultimately come down to."

I stared at her for a moment before taking a deep breath. "How did you get so wise, Kat?"

She looked me straight in the eyes. "Like I said, I've been paying attention. You'd be surprised what else I've picked up on just by watching."

She winked and laughed before it was my turn to pull her into a tight squeeze.

ASHER

I was sweating and exhausted by the time I made it down the forestry roads to the highway, but there was no time to quit. Looking back at what I'd just skied through, I knew I'd made the right choice. No vehicles were getting up that road without a plow, and with so few residences tucked up into the forest, it would have been days before a snowplow would get around to going up that way.

I stopped to chug a bottle of water and check my phone. There weren't any missed calls. Not that I'd expected any, but I'd secretly been hoping that Noa would have returned my call to tell me…what, I wasn't sure. All I knew was that I needed to hear her voice. I needed to know she hadn't made a huge mistake marrying a man she didn't love.

Even if she never spoke to me again, I at least needed to know that much.

I thought about calling her again, but there wasn't much time. Instead, I dialed my eldest brother.

Chase answered on the first ring.

"Hey. I was wondering how you were doing up there in this storm. I guess you know I'm not going to get up there with a vehicle for you today?"

"That's why I'm calling," I said quickly. "I need you to meet me on the highway. I'm skiing into town, and if you can pick me—"

"Wait. What? You're skiing?"

"Cross-country. It was the only way out." I didn't have time to explain everything to him. "Just, can you get in the truck right now and meet me? I need to get to the lodge and I don't have much time. I need to stop Noa before she…well, I just need to get there."

"I'm on my way." In the background, I heard the jingle of Chase's keys, and I knew he'd be on the way soon. "Just stay to the side of the road, okay, and don't get hit."

"Hurry."

I hung up, tucked my phone away again, took another swig of water, tugged my gloves over my hands, and started moving toward town once more.

Chapter Twenty-Two

NOA

IT TURNED out that having Kat come in and pamper both of the brides had been the best choice I could have made. I decided to forgo the professional hair and makeup myself and instead slipped into an emerald-green dress. I pulled my hair up into a twist and swiped on some mascara and lip gloss.

I left Janice and Jeannie in Kat's capable hands for final touches, each of them with a mimosa in their hands, laughing and smiling in a way that made my heart sing, and slipped down to the lobby. Things were about to begin.

With all the snow, the ceremony had been moved inside, and because most of the original wedding guests had long since returned to the city, Penny, the general manager who'd been helping me with the shift in plans, suggested an intimate setup in front of the stone fireplace.

It was perfect.

They'd created a huge arch from timbers and pine boughs. White flowers and red berries had been tucked into the greenery, and not only did it look gorgeous, but the scent of pine filled the air.

There were a few chairs set out that had been filled with the few guests still in town, and among them, small tables filled with large pillar candles that gave the whole space a romantic and cozy feel.

I paused on the landing of the stairs to take it all in.

"It's something, isn't it?"

I turned to see Ryan, looking as handsome as ever in his suit, next to me on the stairs.

I looked back at the scene in front of me. Light piano music drifted through the air. "It's perfect."

"It's not too—"

"Don't say it." I held up a finger. "I swear, Ryan. I—"

"I was only teasing." He grabbed my finger in his large hand and grinned. "This was the right decision." He gave me a chaste kiss on the cheek. "For a lot of reasons."

"I'm really glad you feel that way." I gave him a genuine smile, and he offered me his arm. It was time.

I looped my arm through his, and together, we walked down the last few stairs and continued slowly down the aisle.

The guests all turned to watch us approach, and I knew they must all be wondering why they weren't there to watch the two of us get married as planned. But it didn't bother me, the way it might have a few weeks ago.

My family was fine with our decision and, more importantly, I was.

That's all that really mattered.

New memories were about to be made, and there was nothing that could make me happier than that.

The music changed a little, and our fathers appeared at the front of the room beside the fireplace, looking extremely handsome, and a little nervous in their suits.

"Dad. You look so good." I reached for my father and gave

him a kiss. "And Brad…" I kissed the other man on the cheek as well. "You both look so handsome."

"Noa." Brad took my hands in his. "I know this hasn't been an easy time."

I blinked hard and refused to cry, even when I saw the emotion in the older man's eyes.

"I want you to know how much we love you. Jeannie and I both. You are like a daughter to us. No matter what."

I squeezed his hands. "I know, Brad. And I love you both, too." I elbowed Ryan, who stood close. "And this one, too. Like a brother," I added quickly. "We're all going to be okay."

"We are." Ryan slipped his arm around my waist and pulled me from his father's grasp and back toward his. "And before all this starts, I just wanted to say—"

"No!"

A voice boomed through the room. The music stopped abruptly, and as if in slow motion, everyone turned to look at the source of the interruption.

ASHER

If I had been thinking straight, I might not have charged into the wedding the way I did, covered in snow and soaked with sweat from the effort of skiing down from the cabin, no doubt looking like a deranged mountain man. But I hadn't been thinking straight.

How could I be?

All I could think about since that phone call with Kat was that Noa was about to make a horrible mistake, and I needed to stop her. No matter what.

Over the last few hours, with nothing but time to think, I'd come up with a dozen scenarios of what I would say when I saw her, and what I'd tell her about how I felt about her.

In my head, I was smooth and confident and everything made perfect sense.

In reality, the moment I walked through the front door of the lodge and saw her, all of my carefully planned speeches flew out of my head. And then when I saw *him* touching her, and the way they stood together at the altar, under that arch… I saw red.

I stumbled my way across the slate floor, toward them.

My gaze moved from the other man's arm around her, to Noa's eyes.

"Don't do it, Noa." My words came out in a garbled gasp. I dropped my head and sucked in a breath in an effort to calm my breathing before I once more straightened up and looked into her beautiful brown eyes.

"Asher, I—"

"I don't know what this is with us." I interrupted her, afraid if I didn't say what was on my heart, I'd never again get the chance. "I never could have expected to feel this way about a woman I've only known for such a short time. But then again, I never could have imagined you. You are not just any woman. Not even close." I tugged my knit cap off and ran a hand through my wild hair before I continued. "Noa, the day you jumped into my truck, you changed my whole world. But it was the moment I saw you in your toilet paper dress that I knew you were different." I laughed a little at the memory, but Noa's face didn't change. I couldn't read her expression, but she hadn't turned away. And that was something.

"Together, *we* are different, Noa. With you, I'm softer. I smile. I feel. And…I care. About everything. Not just you, but I care about you, too, Noa. So much."

I knew I wasn't making any sense, but I couldn't seem to stop myself.

"I never should have said those things the other day. I never should have pushed you away." I swallowed hard and dared to take a step closer. "I was scared," I confessed. "I was so scared about the way you made me feel because I've never felt that way about anybody. Not even close. And here I was, falling in love with you when the entire thing seemed so improbable that you couldn't possibly feel the same way."

"I do."

"I know now that it's okay if you don't feel the—what?" I blinked hard and shook my head. "What did you say?"

Finally, the corner of Noa's lips quirked up and a small, tentative smile slid across her face. "I do," she repeated as she moved away from the other man and stepped toward me. "I do feel the same way."

"You do?" More than anything, I wanted to believe her. "Then, why…" For the first time, I looked at Ryan, who was watching the scene with an amused expression on his face. I looked back at Noa. "Why are you getting married?"

Noa's mouth fell open in surprise seconds before she laughed. "I'm not getting married, Asher." She pointed over my shoulder and slowly I turned to see two older women standing at the base of the steps with small bouquets in their hands. My little sister Kat stood above them on the landing, with a hand over her face. "They are," Noa finished. "Our parents decided to renew their vows today."

I spun and looked at her and Ryan again. For the first time, I noticed the two older gentlemen standing behind them. Their fathers. "So, you're not…"

"Nope," Ryan said. "She turned me down." He lifted his arms in a dramatic shrug. "She said something about this guy in a cabin in the—"

"Enough." Noa smacked him in the arm.

Ryan chuckled and stepped back, leaving the two of us alone, still standing in the middle of the aisle, all eyes on us.

"Do you really think I could marry him after…well, after everything?" Noa stepped forward and took my hands in hers.

The touch of her skin on mine sent a shot of energy through me that gave me strength. "I was such an asshole."

"You were."

"I'm so sorry." I'd never meant an apology more. "Will you ever be able to forgive me? After all the things I said…I don't blame you if you—"

"I already have, Asher." She squeezed my hands and pulled me toward her. "I was scared, too." Her words were little more than a whisper, but I heard them loud and clear. "The way I feel about you…" She dropped her gaze for a moment. "I've never felt like that about anyone else. Ever. I didn't think it could be real. How could I possibly feel so strongly about someone after such a short amount of time, right?"

I nodded.

"But when I'm with you, I feel like the very best version of myself. And these last few days without you, they're so…"

I stepped forward and cupped her cheek with my hand when the words escaped her. "Hard?" I finished for her. She nodded. "Empty?" This time, she smiled a little when she nodded. "Lonely?"

"Oh, God yes. All of that."

I couldn't resist her a moment longer. My lips crushed hers in a hungry kiss. My arms came up around her, and I held her tight as we kissed like no one was watching. We made up for the days we'd been apart, for the angry words we'd spoken to each other, for all the things we should have said. Everything was in that kiss.

"I love you, Noa." The words flowed easily, no longer stuck in my throat because I'd never meant anything more. "I don't care about anyone else's timelines, but our own. And right now, that means telling you that, without a doubt, I love you."

"I love you, too."

We kissed again.

"I'm not going to do anything crazy like ask you to marry me, but—"

"Marry?" Noa pulled back from my arms, and her hand flew to her mouth as she looked around at the crowd who were all still watching our reunion. "The ceremony," she said. "I'm sorry. I totally forgot."

"This is my fault." I was reluctant to leave Noa, but I had to do the right thing. "I'm so sorry I interrupted your special day." I spoke first to the men before turning to Noa and Ryan's mothers. "I know today is a difficult day for you all, and Noa told me how important it is to make new memories. I will just—"

"That's exactly what just happened, my dear." An elderly woman stepped forward and took my hand. "My name is Rose, young man."

"Grandma Rose," Noa added.

"I've heard a lot about you," she said to me with a little wink. "I know you didn't intend for this to happen quite like this," she continued. "But today is all about making new memories and that's exactly what we've just done. I don't think anyone is going to forget about this anytime soon."

"You make a very good point," I said. "But there's room in today for plenty more new memories. Maybe if it's not too late, you could start the ceremony over again?"

Rose put my hand into Noa's and patted it. "It's never too late for love, my dear."

Chapter Twenty-Three

NOA

"WHERE DID YOU LEARN TO DANCE?" Asher moved me around the dance floor with perfectly timed steps. "Don't tell me you're secretly a professional ballroom dancer?"

He laughed at my question as he spun me out and pulled me back into his chest. "Hardly a professional." He kissed me gently. "My mother taught me. She insisted that we should all know the basics of dance. Just in case."

"In case of…"

"In case I were to ever find myself on the dance floor with the woman I love," he finished smoothly.

"Your mother sounds like she was a very smart woman. I'm sorry I didn't get a chance to meet her."

"She would have loved you, Noa."

"You think so?"

"I know so." He winked. "Because I know she'd say that any woman who can put up with me, and hang in there while I worked through some of my insecurities, is a keeper for sure."

"Some of your insecurities?" I looked up and gave him the side eye, but Asher only laughed.

"Oh, sweetheart, I can't promise that a lifetime of doubt and uncertainty about relationships was resolved in only a few days. But what I can promise you is that I will always work my hardest to be the best version of myself for you."

His feet stopped moving and right there in the middle of the dance floor of the New Year's Eve party that had followed the vow renewal, he held my face between his hands. "I won't lose you again, Noa." He was completely serious as he stared into my eyes. "The last few days without you were the worst days of my life. I didn't know how much I needed you until I had you, and then lost you. Say what you will—I might be stubborn and hard-headed, but I know how to learn my lessons. And I've learned this one, sweetheart. I swear to you, right here and right now, I will work hard every day to be the man you deserve."

I lifted myself on my tiptoes and kissed him softly. "You already are."

With a whirl, he spun me out dramatically and I laughed, before we once more resumed our dance around the floor.

I was ready for a break when my father appeared. He tapped Asher on the shoulder. "May I cut in?"

"Absolutely, Mr. Briggs."

"Charles."

Asher's smile was genuine. "Charles." He nodded and stepped back with a wave of his hand. "By all means."

My father stepped forward but hesitated before taking my hand. It wasn't like him to get emotional, but I could see the emotion shining in his eyes. He swallowed hard and spoke to Asher.

"I can't remember the last time I've seen my daughter smile the way she's smiling tonight." He shook Asher's hand. "Everything about this situation is unusual to say the least, but I want you to know, Asher, her mother and I...well, all we've ever wanted for our children is for them to be happy. You only get one shot at this thing called life. It's important to be as happy as you can. And you make our little girl happy."

"Not nearly as happy as she makes me, Charles." Asher was serious. "And I'll spend the rest of my life working to bridge that gap."

My dad pressed his lips together and nodded before exhaling and turning to me. "Shall we?"

It had been a long time since I'd danced with my father. The last time would have been a cousin's wedding, years earlier, but the moment we started moving in time to the music, we fell into an easy rhythm.

"It was a beautiful ceremony, Dad. I don't think there was a dry eye in the house when you all read your vows."

He smiled. "We've been through a lot, your mother and I. We're some of the lucky ones," he continued. "Our trials have only made us stronger."

Their strength, as well as their love for each other, had been evident in the vows they'd recited for each other earlier that evening.

After the false start when Asher had burst through the doors and stopped the first ceremony, they'd taken an hour to reset and give him a chance to shower and change so he could join us before starting over.

I'd been a little bit concerned that my parents' first impression of Asher might not have been the most positive—after all, he'd looked like a madman in his sodden winter clothing and wild hair. When I'd heard about the way he'd cross-country skied for hours to get to the lodge and stop the wedding, I couldn't help but swoon a little bit. And I was far from the swooning type.

My parents both agreed that although his entrance could use a little work, the message Asher had delivered was perfect.

And all they'd needed to hear to know that, despite their apprehensions of their only daughter falling for a man so quickly, he was obviously just as taken with me.

And as my father had just told us both, life was short. It was important to be happy.

And I was.

I really was.

"I wanted to ask you, Noa." My dad spun me gently and guided me to the edge of the dance floor, where we stopped moving. "What's next for you?"

"Next?" I hadn't given any thought to what was next. "I guess…I don't…"

"You don't have to answer now." He released me so we stood face-to-face. "But I always wondered about you working in the firm."

"Wondered? How?"

His smile was kind. "I never really thought it suited you, Noa. Corporate law, I mean. I have to admit that I was surprised when you and Ryan both told us you wanted to come work with Brad and me. Not Ryan so much…he's always had a mind for corporate, but you…"

"Me what?"

He tilted his head and looked at me in a way that only a father could look at his daughter. "I always thought maybe you were meant for something different. I know you'd be amazing in the firm, and you know I'd love to have you. But remember when I just told you to be happy because life was too short?"

I nodded.

"Will corporate law make you happy?"

I squeezed my eyes shut and sucked in a breath. "No."

When I opened my eyes again, my dad was watching me.

"Be happy, kiddo." He reached into his breast pocket and handed me an envelope.

"What's this?"

He waited while I slid my finger under the flap and pulled out the piece of paper. It was an itinerary for the round-the-world flights that had been meant to be my and Ryan's wedding gift. "But this is—"

"We all agreed." He stopped me. "Brad and Jeannie, your mother and me. And Ryan. That's what he was going to tell you before Asher…well, before he stopped him." My dad chuckled a little. "We want you to have them, Noa. Travel and take some time off. Figure out what you want. And now, well, it looks like you might have a travel companion, too."

I turned, and my eyes immediately locked on Asher on the far side of the room talking with his siblings. As if he sensed me watching him, he turned and caught my gaze. He winked, and I laughed.

"Thank you, Dad." I threw my arms around his neck and squeezed. "For everything."

ASHER

"You two are so freakin' cute." Charli followed my gaze across the ballroom and giggled. "I'm so glad you both finally came to your senses."

"What does that mean?" Reluctantly, I looked away from Noa and her father and focused on my siblings once again. The moment I'd been free, they'd cornered me, wanting to hear all the details.

"Only that we could all see it from the moment you walked into the big house on Christmas Eve, brother." Craig shook his head. "Even Meri asked me if you two were going to get married."

"She did not!"

"She did."

I ran a hand through my hair and chuckled. Only a few short weeks ago, the mention of that word in any reference to me would have had me running back to the snowed-in cabin. Now, much to my surprise, I simply shrugged. "Let's take it one step at a time, okay?"

"I think that's a great idea," Chase said with a sly grin.

I knew how happy my oldest brother was for me, and I'd always be grateful for the way he'd hopped into the truck without hesitation to fetch me from the side of the road and take me to Noa.

"And it looks like it happened again," Craig said. "Just as predicted, the will stipulation had you falling in love, just like the rest of us."

I stared at my brother, then finally shook my head and looked away because I couldn't deny it.

Next to me, Kat groaned. "Can it be my turn now?"

"Well...speaking of cute..." Charli nudged our littlest sister. "It looks like Ryan might be looking for a dance partner tonight."

"He is cute," Kat agreed. "But I don't think big city lawyer is really my type."

Charli looked like she was about to protest, but Kat smoothly changed the subject. "Asher, did you get a letter from Dad? I know it's only been a few weeks since...well, but I'm dying to know."

She looked so hopeful that I almost felt sorry for her. We all knew how much Kat missed our father and how badly she wished it were her turn to see what his will had in store for her —just so she'd get a letter from him.

"I did find a letter," I said to Chase. "It was in the back of a notebook Dad kept in the shed."

"It was in there!"

"Well, there was a mention of a box that had the letter." I

nodded. "And you were all right." I looked at my siblings in turn. "Dad didn't do any of this to punish me."

"I'm glad you finally figured that out, brother." Chase clasped my shoulder and squeezed. "And you know what, I think Mom and Dad would be pretty happy, too."

There was a small catch in my throat as I swallowed. "I think you're right," I told him. "Dad had no way to know about Noa. But it's almost like…" I was not the type to believe in the *woo-woo*. But with everything that happened over the last few weeks, it was pretty hard not believe a little bit. "It's almost like he knew."

"Isn't that the truth?" Craig shook his head and blew a kiss toward the dance floor where his fiancée Lucy was dancing with Annie.

"No fair." Kat pretended to stamp her feet. "Why can't we skip ahead to my turn? Asher learned his lesson fast."

"You know that's not how this works, Kat." Charli wrapped an arm around her shoulders and squeezed as Symon and the baby joined us.

"Wasn't it you who told me there was a method to all this?" Craig asked Kat before chuckling. "Patience."

"Yeah, right." Chase joined in the good-natured ribbing before turning back to me. "I think the real question now is, since you came to your realization so quickly, what are you going to do with the rest of your six months before you can get back to work? Assuming you want to get back to work," he added quickly.

"Oh, I do." I scanned the ballroom. The familiar itch to find Penny and talk logistics hit me hard the moment I stepped into the party. Standing back was difficult. Very difficult. "I don't know what I'm going to do to fill the time," I admitted. "All I know for sure is that it's going to have something to do with this amazing woman right here."

I extended my arm just as Noa approached.

I kissed her on the cheek and wrapped my arm around her waist as each of my siblings offered their own versions of a welcome to the family.

I was about to whisk her back to the dance floor when someone by the bar caught my attention.

"Excuse me for a minute," I whispered into her ear before pressing a kiss to the sensitive skin of her neck. "I'll be back."

It took me a few minutes to navigate through the crowd to the bar. Fortunately, Ryan was still there.

"Whiskey please, Brian." I nodded my thanks and turned to Ryan.

"Cheers." He lifted his glass, and we clinked before drinking.

I wasn't sure what to say to the man who'd very recently been engaged to the woman I loved. I would have expected anger. What man wouldn't be? But Ryan only looked amused.

I took another sip of whiskey and lowered my glass. "I wanted to thank you, Ryan."

"Thank me?" He gave me a wry grin. "For being cool with you stealing my woman?"

I almost choked on my drink, but Ryan only laughed. "I'm kidding, man. Calm down."

"Holy shit," I said, wiping my lips. "I thought maybe you wanted to kick my ass."

"If I wanted to kick your ass, you'd know it." He chuckled. "But I don't. You're good. For now."

"For now?"

His humor vanished as he met my gaze. "If you hurt her, there's no doubt about it—I will kick your ass. She's a very special woman."

"Don't I know it." I held his gaze. "I'll never hurt Noa, Ryan. I love her."

He nodded slowly. "I know. I can see it. And she loves you, too." He smiled. "I never thought I'd be able to say that.

Honestly, I didn't think either of us were capable of it," he admitted. "Noa and I...we're just built a little different than our brother and sister were. Or maybe I just am." He shrugged and the smile returned to his face. "But I see it in you both, Asher. I think the two of you are going to be good for each other. And don't worry...you and me..." He used his glass to gesture between us. "We're good."

That was when Noa joined us. She slipped an arm around my waist and rested her head against my shoulder.

"Who's good?" she asked.

"We are," I said.

"You are," Ryan said at the same time.

She raised an eyebrow at us.

"You're good," Ryan clarified. "Together. You're both great. I'm happy for you, Noa. And you were right."

"I was right?"

"About all of this." He waved an arm around the room. "There are definitely some new memories being made tonight. So many smiles we haven't seen in way too long. And that's all because of you."

"No." She hugged him. "You know we wouldn't be here without you, too." She kissed his cheek and returned to my arms—right where she belonged.

"Never say never, Ryan. It could be your turn next."

He laughed. "I'll leave all this mushy stuff to the two of you."

"Your loss," Noa said. "But I do need to steal Asher away for a minute, if you don't mind."

"Not even a little."

Ryan waved us off, and before I could ask where she was taking me, Noa took my hand and led me out the door behind the bar and into the corridor.

NOA

"Do you remember the last time we were here?"

"In the hallway?" Asher looked around, confusion lining his handsome face. "Umm…"

"You were rescuing me," I said. "And now, it's my turn to rescue you." With his hand still in mine, I started to walk down the hall toward the door I'd arranged and then double-checked earlier.

"Rescuing you from—oh!" He laughed the moment he remembered. "From the wedding party and that toilet paper dress."

I turned. "I knew you'd remember."

"I did like that dress." Asher wiggled his eyebrows. "But not as much as this one." He reached for me and let his hand trail down my side, sending all sorts of sparks directly to my core.

I had to force myself to pull away, intent on my mission.

With a groan of frustration I could relate to, Asher followed me. "Did I look like I needed rescuing from Ryan?"

"Maybe a little," I said over my shoulder, before opening the door I'd left ajar earlier.

"What are we…that door is supposed to be locked. I'm going to have to—"

I spun and pressed a finger to his lips. "You're not going to have to do anything, because you're on a sabbatical, remember?" I winked. "Besides, I organized it with Penny and Gwen. Come on."

Before he could protest further, I dragged Asher into the kitchen. "Remember when you were trying to convince me that weddings weren't so bad?"

"That was before I knew we were talking about your wedding. I think I would have had a very different approach had I known that."

"Even then?"

I slipped my hands to his waist.

"Even then," he said without hesitation. "I don't think I knew exactly what it was, or what it would turn into, but I knew you were special."

He kissed me, long and slow, and I melted into his embrace. Exactly where I wanted to be in that moment.

"Is that what I think it is?" Asher looked over my shoulder when he finally dragged his lips away from mine.

"Of course." I turned and picked up the plate with the piece of cake on it. "After all, you did say it was the best part of weddings." I used the fork to feed him a piece. "Or in this case, vow renewals."

He took the fork from me and fed me a piece, before setting the plate behind us on the counter. "I think I was wrong," he said after a moment.

"You were wrong?"

Asher nodded. "The best part of weddings isn't the cake."

I tilted my head. "It's not?"

"Nope." He pulled me close so our bodies were pressed together and stroked one finger down my cheek. "The best part of weddings is the feeling they give you."

I had all kinds of feelings in that moment. All of them very, very good. "What feeling is that exactly?"

"Oh. Where do I even begin?" His voice was light, teasing. "First, there's obviously the feeling of love." He kissed me chastely.

"Of course."

"But then there's the feeling of happiness." Another feather-light kiss.

"Are you happy?"

"So happy," he said. "But don't forget about the best feeling of all."

"And what's that?" I couldn't have wiped the smile off my face if I'd tried—and I certainly didn't want to try.

"Easy," Asher said, full of confidence. "It's hope." He gave me another G-rated kiss.

"Hope?" I didn't bother trying to hide my confusion.

"Hope." Asher smiled and nodded. "Hope for the future. That maybe one day we'll be like your parents, renewing our vows and talking about all the things we've been through together, just to come out on the other side stronger for it all."

I let his words settle deep inside me. "I don't think the man I met not that long ago would have said that."

He winked. "That man didn't realize what the love of a good woman would feel like."

"Now you do?"

"You know I do."

I bit my bottom lip. "I kind of like this mushy version of you, Asher."

"I can't help it. I'm full of all the feelings, sweetheart."

"Oh, you're definitely full of something, Asher." I laughed. "But I love it."

"And I love you."

He kissed me again, and this time there was nothing G-rated about it.

Epilogue

NOA

TWO BACKPACKS SAT by the front door of the cabin. I checked my crossbody travel purse one more time for my passport. "Are we crazy?"

"I think we've already established the answer to that, sweetheart." Asher came up behind me and wrapped his arms around me as he nuzzled the back of my neck. "We are completely, totally, and without question...crazy."

He spun me in his arms and kissed me thoroughly.

"I didn't mean in general." I laughed.

"Oh good, because I didn't want to try to explain to you again how crazy I am about you and how I know you're just as crazy about me. And how together, we're crazy in love and how we are extra crazy for taking a chance on that love after such a short time." He tried, and failed, to look serious. "I mean, I'll explain it if I have—"

"Enough." I smacked him lightly on the arm and walked toward our ready-to-go backpacks. "You know what I meant." I turned to look at him. "Are we insane for doing this? For taking this trip around the world instead of figuring out jobs, or what we're—"

"No, Noa." He silenced me with a gentle finger to my lips. "Nothing about this is insane. This is perfect and exactly what we should be doing right now. And your parents and Ryan and his parents were incredibly generous to offer this to us."

After New Year's, when we'd had a chance to recover from the chaos of everything and how fast it had all changed, I told Asher about the offer for the plane tickets, and he'd immediately thought it was an excellent idea.

In fact, although I'd had a bit of hesitancy, Asher had never wavered from his certainty that the very best thing we could do at this point in our lives was travel. With Asher's forced sabbatical until spring, and me unsure about what I did want to do now that I'd admitted that I didn't want to work in the family firm, there wouldn't be a better time to take such a big trip.

It hadn't taken him long to convince me that figuring out the future could wait a few more months, and soon we were packing our bags. But now that the day had come to get on the plane, I had a few last-minute doubts.

"Hey." Asher grabbed my hand and led me to the couch. "You're not worried about us, are you?"

"Us?" Of all the worries that had popped into my head, not once had I worried about me and Asher. Not even for one second.

"Are you worried we might not travel well together?"

I couldn't help but laugh. "Not even a little bit." It was the truth. "I might be worried about sleeping in dingy hotels or eating food that I'm not totally certain about. I might even be worried about travel complications, or getting motion sickness on a train in some country I haven't even heard of yet. But the one thing I am completely certain about is us."

I crawled up and over him on the couch so I straddled his lap. I held his face between my hands and kissed him.

"Um…" His hands came up to my hips and held me in place. "I like that."

"Me too." I kissed him again, feeling the heat between us rise.

We were so wrapped up in each other, we didn't hear the knock on the door, or the creak of the hinges as it opened.

"Knock knock, team. It's time to— Oh come on! Are you two always making out?"

ASHER

Not even my little sister's voice could deter me from kissing the woman I loved, and I would have happily made out with her all day right there in the living room if Noa hadn't pulled away with a laugh. And if we didn't have a flight to catch.

"Kat. You're—"

"Right on time."

I looked over in time to see Kat roll her eyes.

"Do you think the two of you can keep your hands off each other long enough for me to drive you to the city and put you on an airplane?"

With my expression as serious as I could make it, I pretended to consider the request before shaking my head. "No promises."

"Ugh." Kat threw up her hands and turned away while Noa laughed.

"We're ready to go," Noa said. "We just need to lock up."

"Thanks for agreeing to help out with the cabin while we're gone." I reluctantly got up from the couch. There'd be plenty of time to make out with Noa on our trip. "Now that we actually know about it, I don't like the idea of leaving it empty and unattended the entire time we're gone."

"No problem." Kat walked slowly into the kitchen, running one hand over the surfaces. "I think I'll be able to put this place to good use."

I groaned and put my hands over my ears. "Don't tell me—"

"Okay, I won't." She spun around and winked at me. "But I was talking about a quiet retreat with a girlfriend or two." She tossed a kitchen towel at me. "I can't believe your mind went there."

Not that my mind wanted to go anywhere near there when it came to my sister. But Kat was an attractive woman, and everyone was continually surprised when she failed to bring someone special home. Or even mentioned dating at all.

"I have to admit," Noa said as she picked up the towel and returned it to the kitchen, "I kind of thought there might be something between you and Ryan after the New Year's party."

It was true that even after Kat had insisted that a big city lawyer wasn't her type, she had spent most of the rest of the night dancing with him, and rumor had it that the two of them even shared a kiss at midnight.

"He's nice." Kat shrugged. "And very cute."

Noa nodded, and I pretended not to notice as I headed into the back bedroom to do one more sweep of anything we might have left behind. I wasn't jealous. She could have married him if she wanted to, but she hadn't. Noa had chosen me. And I was completely confident in that.

"But…if I'm being totally honest." Kat lowered her voice, which made my ears perk up from the other room. "Can I tell you something?"

I shouldn't have been eavesdropping, but I justified it with the fact that Kat knew I was right there. If whatever she was about to share was any kind of serious secret, she wouldn't be saying anything while I was in the next room.

"I'm kind of sort of seeing someone," I heard Kat say. "But we're not…well…we can't really be together."

Now I *really* paid attention.

"I'm not going to get into it," Noa said. "Because I don't think it's the right time. But…wasn't it you who told me that love was the most important thing?"

I moved to the bedroom door and didn't even try to pretend I wasn't listening to the exchange.

Kat's gaze flicked toward me, and then back to Noa. "I told you love was one of the most important things."

"Right." Noa nodded. "So, maybe…"

"Why not take a chance?" I offered as I stepped all the way into the room. "I'm not going to pry, Kat, and I'm not going to pretend I know everything about it, but I do know a thing or two about taking a chance on love."

I wrapped my arm around Noa's waist and pulled her close.

Kat blew out a sigh and shook her head. "Here's the thing, you guys. Advice is for giving. Not for taking." She blew us a kiss and spun on her heel, causing us all to laugh. "Now, get your things. You have a plane to catch."

Go along with Asher and Noa on their trip around the world and peek in on a very special moment you won't want to miss with an exclusive bonus scene. Click here to grab that scene!

Next up is Kat's Story in Keep On Loving You!

And if you want even more romance…click HERE for an exclusive FREE novella that isn't available anywhere else!

Bonus Scene

THREE MONTHS LATER...

NOA

When I opened my eyes, it took me a moment to remember where I was, just as it had almost every morning for the last few months. Not that I would trade in a familiar bed for the adventures Asher and I had experienced since embarking on our trip. Not for anything.

I'd always heard that the best way to get to know someone was to travel with them, and I had to wholeheartedly agree.

With a stretch and a yawn, I rolled over and dropped an arm over Asher's still-sleeping form. He responded at once with a sigh of pleasure, just the way I knew he would.

The way he had every morning since we'd been together.

Together.

It was still hard to believe that the man who'd unwittingly rescued me from what would have been my biggest mistake was now my partner. My boyfriend. The word felt so juvenile in so many ways, but at the same time, I loved the way it sounded.

I'd never had a boyfriend. Not a real one. Not one like Asher. Not even close.

His back was warm as I snuggled up against the length of him and left a trail of kisses across his shoulders, before turning away and rolling out of bed in search of the bathroom.

"Where are you going?" Asher reached behind him. "Stay."

"I'd love to. But I'm in desperate need of the toilet. And probably a shower, too."

He turned to his back and wrinkled his nose in jest.

I tossed a pillow at his head and spun away. "If I'm stinky after that long flight, you are too, buddy."

"Buddy?" Asher sat up against the pillows. "Is that what you're calling me now?"

Before I could get out of the way, he lunged for me, wrapped his arms around my waist, and hauled me back onto the bed on top of him.

I squealed, but his strong arms had me in a tight grasp. With an easy flip, I was on my back and he hovered over me. For a moment, my breath caught in my throat at the sight of him, the way it always did when I saw his chiseled naked chest.

He pinned my arms over my head and held me down, a sexy-as-hell grin on his lips. "I think what you meant to say was *love of my life.*"

"Oh yeah?"

He nodded.

"Okay." A grin of my own slid over my lips. "Let me try again." I pretended to think about my words and finally said, "If I'm stinky after that long flight," I made an elaborate show of turning my head to one side, pretending to sniff myself before looking at him again, eyes wide, "then you are, too, love of my life." I emphasized each word, bursting into a fit of giggles when I was finished and Asher dropped down on me, covering me in kisses.

"I like you stinky."

"You're a weirdo."

"Maybe so." He held himself up by one arm. "But I'm *your* weirdo."

"Good." I kissed him quickly and then slid out from under him until I stood next to the bed. "I love that you're my weirdo. But I still need to shower. Besides, it's early enough that I think we'll be able to catch the sunrise from the roof."

Asher pretended to be disappointed as he rolled to his side and grabbed his phone to check the time. "Go shower then. I'll make some coffee."

"I knew there was a reason I kept you around." I blew him a kiss and headed up the steep stone stairs to the next floor of the tower, which held the bathroom and a perfect little library where we'd enjoyed a glass of wine the night before.

Our trip around the world had been nothing short of amazing, and we still had a few months left on our itinerary. After visiting Australia and New Zealand, we'd gone to Fiji and Vietnam and were now scheduled to spend a month in Europe before heading to South America.

We'd slept in huts on the beach, a camper van that had been home for most of New Zealand, expensive hotels, and tiny out-of-the-way hostels. But Drummond Tower was our first castle. Tall and skinny, the kitchen was on the main floor, and up a tight, tiny staircase was the bedroom; more stairs led to the bathroom and library, and at the very top was a beautiful open-air deck where we gazed at the stars when we'd arrived.

It was cute, historic, and romantic, and the perfect way to start the European leg of our trip. But for the moment, the only thing I was interested in was a hot shower.

I was just rinsing the shampoo from my hair when Asher popped his head into the bathroom. The strong aroma of coffee hit my senses, even through the shower door.

"When you're finished in there," Asher's voice came

through the glass, "I have a fresh pot of coffee waiting for you on the roof. Hurry if you want to catch the sunrise, sweetheart."

ASHER

The sun was just starting to come over the horizon. I sipped at my cup of coffee and looked out over the expanse of green, gently rolling fields all around the tower, divided only by rock wall fences squaring off the pastures into neat parcels. It was serene and absolutely gorgeous as the sun slowly started to rise.

Perfect.

I'd poured a cup of coffee for Noa, letting it cool a little before she arrived so it would be drinkable right away. Not even two minutes later, she appeared, fresh-faced, wearing only a tank top and shorts. Her hair was still wet from the shower, hanging over her shoulders and leaving two little damp spots on her shirt.

She'd never looked more beautiful.

"You made it." I extended a hand to Noa and helped her over the little ledge at the top of the steps. "Just in time." I guided her toward the edge of the tower wall so she could face the sunrise. "It's gorgeous." I let my hand rest on the small of her back. "But not as beautiful as you."

She turned over her shoulder and gave me a look. "Asher. Seriously. I look like a drowned rat. I rushed so I didn't miss the sunrise."

"You're gorgeous." I leaned in and kissed her cheek. "And I'm sure the coffee was part of the draw as well." I turned, grabbed the coffee cup I'd prepared, and handed it to her.

She inhaled deeply and took a big gulp. "You're the best."

"Don't you forget it." I winked and blew her a kiss.

Noa moved in to kiss me, but I dodged it smoothly, taking the cup of coffee from her and setting it on the table behind me. "Turn," I urged her. "Look at this."

With a quick, easy move, I spun her around so she could see the sun coming up over the green pastures. "It's incredible."

She leaned back against my chest, and I took a moment to inhale the sweet scent of the woman I loved and feel the weight of her against me.

"Look at the fields." She pointed. "And the sheep." Her voice lifted with excitement. "Do you think those are babies?"

I didn't answer. Instead, I swallowed hard and stepped back from her, putting space between us.

"I just can't believe how green everything is."

I watched as she slowly scanned the countryside.

"It's truly like every single shade of green that I've ever seen." She shook her head and giggled. "I guess that's why they call it the Emerald Isle, right?"

When I didn't answer, she looked over her shoulder. "Asher?"

I was already on one knee when she turned around. It took her a moment to realize what was happening—maybe it wasn't until I pulled out the ring box I'd been hiding in my carry-on for the last few weeks.

"Asher? What...what are you...are you..."

"Noa. My life hasn't been the same from the moment you jumped into my truck. It has changed in all the best ways." I swallowed hard, trying to remember everything I wanted to say. I'd thought about this moment so many times, had written these words in my head over and over, and now that it was here, I was terrified I'd mess it up.

"The last few months, traveling with you to some of the most incredible places in the world, have been without a doubt the best of my life. And it has nothing to do with the amazing things we've seen or the places we've been. There's no question in my mind that it has everything to do with you."

"Oh, Asher, I—"

"Sweetheart, please." My hand shook a little. I couldn't remember a time I'd ever been this nervous. "Let me finish, because I want to make sure I say everything I need to."

She pressed her lips together and nodded.

I couldn't tell if she was trying not to smile or trying not to cry.

"Every day since you came into my life has been an adventure I never want to end. In such a short time, you've become my best friend, my travel partner, my confidant, and honestly, my very favorite person. Because you love me, I've learned so much about myself and what I want out of life. I want you, Noa. And I think you want me, too. I love you so much, and I know this is crazy and fast and—"

"Yes." She couldn't hold herself back any longer. "Yes. I will."

"I haven't asked you anything yet."

The smile slipped from her face, replaced by a serious expression. "Asher Carlson, if you don't ask me to marry you after all—"

"Marry me." I opened the ring box, and a dazzling princess-cut diamond surrounded by tiny rubies—Noa's birthstone—sparkled up at us. "I never want this to end. Marry me."

She nodded, suddenly speechless.

"That's a yes?"

"It's a million times a yes." She finally found her voice as I slipped the ring onto her finger. It fit perfectly. "You knew it would."

I stood and pulled her into my arms. "I never know what you're going to do, sweetheart. That's why I love you so much."

I held her close and kissed my fiancée on top of our castle in the Irish countryside, while our coffees grew cold.

———

I hope you enjoyed Asher and Noa's story. Last, but not least is little sister Kat's story. She's waited long enough for her letter from her dad *and* her love story.

Keep On Loving You is next!

About the Author

Elena Aitken is a USA Today Bestselling Author of more than fifty romance and women's fiction novels. The mother of 'grown up' twins, Elena now lives with her very own mountain man in the heart of the very mountains she writes about. She can often be found with her toes in the lake and a glass of wine in her hand, dreaming up her next book and working on her own happily ever after.

To learn more about Elena:
www.elenaaitken.com
elena@elenaaitken.com